No Were To Run

SHIFT HAPPENS SERIES, BOOK TWO

BY

ROBYN PETERMAN

Dedication

For everyone's inner Dragon—the one who lets you fly
and be free.

Acknowledgements

Writing books is the best job I've ever had. Sitting in my sweatpants, t-shirt, sparkly Uggs and no make-up totally works for me! However, as solitary as the writing process may be, putting a book out is a group effort. There are many important and wonderful people involved and I am blessed to have such a brilliant support system.

Rebecca Poole, your covers are perfect and your imagination delights me. Thank you.

Meg Weglarz, you save me from myself constantly with your amazing and insightful editing. Thank you.

Donna McDonald, you are my partner in crime, one of my dearest friends and one hell of an author. I'd be in deep doodoo without you. Thank you.

Donna McDonald and JM Madden, you are the best and most honest critique partners a gal could have. I don't know what I would do without your eagle eyes and good taste. Thank you.

My beta readers; Wanda, Melissa, Susan and Karen, you rock so hard. Thank you.

Wanda, your organization skills keep me from going off the deep end. Thank you.

And my family…thank you for believing in me, understanding deadlines and putting up with my need to discuss fictional characters as if they were real people. None of this would be any fun without your love and support.

And my readers…I do this for you.

Prologue

Her lips moved frantically, but I couldn't make out what she was saying. I tried, but the ringing in my ears wouldn't go away. As I moved toward her, her face distorted in anger and desperation. What had I done wrong? She always smiled at me—she never shouted.

Everything was red. It shouldn't be red.

Shaking my head, I blocked out the screaming and groans of my brothers and glanced wildly around the room. It would take so long to clean up the mess, but I could do it. I was a good girl. I would make her smile—I would make them all smile. Everything would be okay.

I would pick up the pieces and put them back together like a puzzle. My brothers would be proud. They teased me because I was such a little girl, but I would show them.

"Dima," my mother shouted. "Go. Go now."

I shook my head no and moved towards her. She'd gotten tangled in ropes and chains. That was a silly game. I didn't ever want to play that game.

"Listen to me," she hissed as her eyes grew wide with terror. "You must leave, child. He's coming back."

I heard them gasping for air behind me, but I couldn't look at that anymore. It was not the way it was supposed to be. My brothers were big and strong—not red and broken. This was a terrible game and I wanted them to stop.

"Mommy," I cried. "I'm scared."

Her eyes fluttered shut for a moment, then flew open blazing a brilliant green. "Use your gift. Use the gift I taught you and go. Go far away from here, Dima and never come back."

"Come with me," I begged as panic filled me. "I'm too small to go away. I want you to come—and Sean and Timothy and Matthew."

"Your father will be back any moment," she wailed. "You will do as I say. Now. Find your power and leave this place forever."

"But I love you, mommy," I choked out through the tears that had started and wouldn't end for hundreds of years.

"If you love me, you will go," she growled harshly.

I backed away and put my hands over my mouth so I wouldn't beg anymore.

"I love you, my beautiful Dima. My precious daughter," she whispered. "Please go."

I nodded my head and she smiled. I would do anything to make her smile. I loved her.

So I did as she said.

I left.

But the horror of that day would follow me.

Always.

Chapter 1

Four hundred and ninety years later.

"I was thinking maybe we could *do* something fun," I suggested trying my best not to sound pushy or desperate.

I accidently on purpose let the strap of my very fitted dress fall off my shoulder, revealing a little side boob and a tremendous amount of cleavage. This tactic usually worked like a dream, but apparently not today.

"That sounds wonderful, Dima. What did you have in mind?" Seth asked kindly as he expertly cleaned the daggers we'd used for target practice while totally oblivious to the blatant display of my knockers.

He was perfect—kind of. Not only was the man panty-melting gorgeous, more importantly, he was good through and through. I'd never met a Dragon like him. Most male Dragons I'd come across in my very long life were possessive, perverted and violent. Seth was patient and kind and was perfectly fine with the fact I was a single mother to an active four year old. Any other scaled jackass would have wanted nothing to do a child that wasn't his. The thought of a female Dragon having been intimate with another was too much to handle for the pea brained fire breathers even though we were a very sexual race. Not to mention, my lineage didn't send him running for the hills.

Seth was different—hence my frustration and my need to seduce.

Why in the blazes wasn't he trying to jump my bones? Had I lost my touch? Was he gay? I'd never come across a gay Dragon in my 499 years on earth, but...

"I was thinking we could have a picnic in a deserted park. Naked," I added for good measure to see if he was listening.

"That sounds lovely, Dima. Why don't we bring Daniel? I can work with him on his flying," Seth chimed in agreeably.

He wasn't listening.

"Actually," I said, heaving a frustrated sigh, "I'm taking him to Hung Island, Georgia. He'll be safe there."

"That's an outstanding idea," Seth replied with a genuine smile and a gentle nod of his head. "I'll meet you there in two days. How does that sound?"

"Great," I said with forced enthusiasm. "I'll see you then."

***

"Is there something wrong with me?" I asked as I took critical stock of myself in the mirror.

I looked like I always did. I'd done nothing to earn my looks except be born—wild red hair, emerald green eyes, slim figure, tall and nice tatas—all inherited from my mother. Most Dragons were appealing. It helped us attract prey, not that many of us lived that way anymore. Since melding in with the humans for the last several hundred years most of us had reined in our barbaric tendencies of old. Plus we ate food just like the humans, grocery stores and restaurants were plentiful. Was I missing something that made me undesirable?

"Is that a trick question?" Essie, my new Werewolf friend asked with a smirk as she looked up from the coloring book she was sharing with my son Daniel. "You breathe fire. When you shift you're roughly the size of a freakin' tour bus with a tail that spans half a football field and the wingspan of a couple SUV's parked back to back. You're going to have to be more specific with the question."

"You're an ass, Werewolf," I said with a grin.

"Tell me something I don't know, Dragon," she shot back with a laugh and resumed coloring.

Essie's parents, permanently stuck in their shifted Wolf form, lay under the table lightly snoring while her best friend, the filter-free and fabulous gay Vampyre Dwayne, pored over wedding invitation catalogues.

Essie was getting married to Hank and Dwayne was her Man of Honor. From what I understood Dwayne was planning to wear a dress for the nuptials. I decided not to touch that one. It was Essie's big day and if she was cool with an undead Man of Honor wearing a gown, who was I to judge? The simple fact that they'd accepted Daniel and me as friends was mind blowing to me. Dragons were not popular with any other magical species. My father had made sure of that. But being here in Hung, Georgia under the protection of Essie and Hank's Wolf Pack was as safe and homey as Daniel and I had experienced in his four years on earth. For that I was thankful. However, I had a date with death staring me in the face in a few months if I didn't find a mate or kill my father.

"You're gorge," Dwayne announced as he pulled out fabric swatches and laid them next to the invitations and pictures of wedding cakes he'd torn from magazines. "Both you and Essie are so hawt, if I liked vaginas I'd be on you like white on rice."

"What's a bagina?" Daniel asked, pointing a chubby finger at the now paler than usual Vamp.

"Ohhhh, um…well, a bagina is a dance done by extinct tribes of Pygmy Goat Shifters," Dwayne stuttered as I reluctantly gave him a chance to crawl out of the body part hole. "If we say *bagina* too many times the goats will magically appear and eat all the cookies that Granny made—not to mention they smell like rotting fish—so we really don't want to use that term." He finished on a high note and gave me a mortified shrug along with an apologetic grin.

Dwayne should not be allowed to crawl out of holes. Ever.

"A vagina is a body part of a woman," I said as I sat down next to Daniel and picked up a crayon. "You know how you have a penis?"

"Yessssss," he replied with a giggle and went to pull down his pants to show us.

Quickly sitting him on my lap to end the strip show, I continued. "A boy has a penis and a girl has a vagina. No big deal."

"Can a gurl spway peepee on the wall with her bagina?" he asked seriously as Essie shoved the page she was coloring into her mouth to keep from laughing.

"Well, I did know a..." Dwayne started.

"Nope," I cut the Vampyre off as the wolves under the table growled at him in warning. "Girls can't do that," I explained to my son as I gave Dwayne the mom eyeball or momball as I liked to refer to it.

"Dat is vewy sad." Daniel shook his little head as his blond curls bounced.

"Tell me about it," Essie agreed with a disgusted grunt. "When I was little I had to bring toilet paper when I ran away to the woods for the day. None of the boys had to do that."

"Why didn't you use a leaf?" Dwayne inquired, wedding planning forgotten.

"Because once you wipe with poison ivy, you bring toilet paper," she hissed.

I stifled a giggle and hoisted my little man over my shoulder. "He needs a nap," I told my newly found friends. "Which room should I use?"

10

"Upstairs, second door on the right," Essie's grandma, Bobbie Sue said as she came out of the kitchen covered in flour. "Stay out of my sewing room. I'm working on Dwayne's Dolly Parton costume. Room's covered in thousands of sequins and I might have left the hot glue gun on. Wouldn't want our little man getting burned."

"Thanks," I said as I bit back my grin. Granny and Dwayne were famous on the Shifter drag show circuit from what I'd picked up. "Daniel and I are impervious to burns, but the sequins could be a problem if he ate them."

"Oh God," Dwayne announced dramatically. "One time I ingested a bag of sequins by accident and got excited that my poop would sparkle, but then I remembered I don't poop. Vampyres can't poop."

That statement received total silence from everyone except for Daniel who unfortunately thought it was hilarious.

"I'm not even going to ask how a blood drinker eats sequins by accident," Essie muttered as she stood and stretched. "I'm going to have to go home to Hank in a few. Will you and Daniel be okay at here at Granny's?"

"We're actually going to move over to the Hung Bed and Breakfast," I told Essie as I snuggled my sleepy boy in my arms. "Seth's coming tomorrow night and reserved a suite."

"Mr. Snuffleupagus?" Essie inquired with a grunt of laughter.

"I'm sorry?" I asked, confused.

"Big Bird's invisible friend on Sesame Street," Dwayne supplied as if that would erase my confusion.

None of my new friends had met Seth yet and apparently were doubtful of his existence.

"He's real," I said with a sigh. "Seth is a fine man. He's wonderful with Daniel and he's extremely kind and good—and um, kind."

11

"He's ugly isn't he?" Dwayne asked as he critically eyed the pictures of the cakes next to the picture of what I assumed was Essie's dress. "Or he has a small man package."

"Why would you say that?" I demanded.

"*Because* no one describes the man they're doing the horizontal mambo with as *nice* unless he's lacking in certain departments," Dwayne explained.

Sadly he made some sense—not about the small package. I wouldn't know the answer to that one as I'd never seen him naked, but the rest...

"Tell you what," Granny chimed in as she took a very sleepy Daniel from my arms and gave Dwayne a look that made even me shudder. "I'm gonna put this little bugger down for a nap before the blood sucker says something that's going to scar the child for eternity or makes you burn him to a crisp. And if you're gonna do that, take it outside. I like my knick-knacks."

Granny left the room with the two wolves close on her heels. They'd taken a real liking to Daniel and rarely left his side.

"Seth's not even remotely ugly and I have no clue what his package looks like," I snapped as I plopped down on the couch and let my head fall into my hands. "Maybe he's gay."

"I have a fabu gay-dar. I can check him out tomorrow and tell you if he plays on my team in three seconds flat," Dwayne offered as he sat down next to me.

"Have you made it clear you're interested?" Essie asked as she flanked me on the other side.

"Yep. I've all but jumped him. He's perfect in every other way. Maybe he doesn't want me."

"Impossible," Dwayne snorted and Essie nodded in agreement. "He'd have to be a blind castrati to not want you. I want you and I don't like girls," Dwayne added rather unhelpfully.

"I thought you wanted *me*," Essie said with a laugh and an eye roll.

"I want to *be* you," Dwayne assured her, which caused an even bigger eye roll from Essie.

Who wouldn't want to be Essie?

She had a fabulous mate who adored her. She had a grandma and friends who would die for her. She had her parents—even though they were stuck in their Wolf form—who adored her as well.

Deadly-as-all-get-out should be her middle name and she could shoot better than anyone I'd ever come across. Essie was beautiful, but what she had in love and loyalty far outweighed her looks.

I wasn't such a great deal—I had looks and very little else to offer. Sure I was just as deadly as Essie, but that didn't make me any friends.

"I have too much baggage," I said, revealing my biggest fear to my new friends. "Why in the world would anyone want me? My father is the reviled Dragon King. I have no family to speak of because he killed them all and I'm a single mom. Oh my God, saying it out loud is so freakin' depressing."

"It is kind of off-putting when you lay it out like that," Dwayne agreed as Essie slapped his bald head.

"Dima, you're amazing and if this Seth doucheballhole can't see that he doesn't deserve you," Essie argued as she aimed for Dwayne's head again. "Do you think he's your true mate?"

Did I? No. I didn't, but Dragons rarely ever got to be with their true mate.

"No. And Daniel's father wasn't either," I said softly.

"Should I get you guys some Twinkies and wine?" Dwayne asked as he hopped off the couch to avoid Essie's left hook.

"Why would you get us Twinkies and wine?" Essie asked as she closed her eyes and let her head fall back on her shoulders.

"Because this is getting good and I know how you gals like to eat and gossip," he offered reasonably.

"Do you have ice cream?" I asked as a little grin pulled at my lips.

"Coming right up," Dwayne said as he raced from the room to get our fattening girl-talk food.

"So, Daniel's father?" Essie prompted me.

"Do I have to tell you without ice cream?"

"No, but Dwayne has a big mouth so anything you want to stay in confidence should be said now," she replied as she tossed me a throw pillow to hang onto for courage.

"Dwayne's a talker?" I asked surprised.

"Nope. He just gets excited and runs his mouth. He'd die for any of us. He'll also pilfer your clothes, so don't let him near your suitcases."

"I can hear you," Dwayne called out from the kitchen. "Supersonic Vampyre hearing."

"No one is going to die for me," I promised with a small grin. "And I think he's already been in my suitcase."

Essie laughed and then grew quiet. It was crazy, but I trusted this Werewolf more than I trusted my own people. I'd only known her a short while, but she'd stood up for me in ways no one had—as had her mate, Hank and her Granny and Dwayne.

If I was going to tell my sordid tale to anyone it may as well be Essie. Besides, I had an enormous request to ask of her.

I'd been waiting for the right time…no time was the right time for this question.

14

"If I die, would you hide and raise Daniel?" I asked on one breath as I stared at her hard and accidentally tore the pillow in half.

"Wow. Wasn't expecting that one," she said as her eyes grew wide with surprise. "Wanna give me a few more details?"

"Yes. Long story short…Daniels father was a lovely man that I barely knew. He wasn't my true mate, but he was a good man and I was attracted to him. The pregnancy wasn't planned and he was killed by my father before he even knew about it. Any Dragon I've ever shown an interest in has been murdered by my father," I said as I picked at the torn pillow feathers that floated in the air around me.

"Dude, that is some screwed up shit," Essie said as she stood up and began to pace. "So other than being a gaping murderous assmonkey, why does you sperm donor kill all your potential mates?"

"So the line ends," I replied.

"Not following," Essie said as she took the destroyed pillow from my hands and replaced it with a cast iron doorstop shaped like a duck.

"I'm the next in line and he doesn't want me to rule."

"But if he were to have a son doesn't that trump your right to the throne?" Essie asked the appropriate question.

"I think so," I said slowly wondering how much I should spill. Since I'd asked her to take her life into her own hands by raising my son upon the very real possibility of my demise, she deserved to know it all. "That would be true if my father was of the Royal House of Dragons, but he's not. My mother was."

"And that means you and Daniel are the rightful heirs. Actually the only heirs," Essie finished the story.

The damn duck doorstop was indestructible. I needed to destroy something or set it on fire to keep talking.

Realizing my need, Essie handed me a pile of Granny's gossip magazines. I began to tear them to shreds.

"It gets even worse," I admitted as I tore the glossy paper head off of Brad Pitt and several other movie stars I couldn't place. "If I don't mate before I turn 500, I die anyway. The Royal Dragon line comes with some screwed up perks. I have to kill my father before my birthday so Daniel is safe."

"Holy Faye Dunaway with a truck load of wire hangers," Dwayne gasped as he reentered the room with several gallons of ice cream and two bottles of wine. "We've got some problems here."

"No," I said as I wadded up the pages I'd torn apart and shook my head. "I have some problems. Not you. The only thing I ask is that if I die and my father still lives, you would keep my son safe. He's the only thing in the world that means anything to me."

I wasn't used to asking for things. It was difficult and my pride was taking a beating, but my son was far more precious than my ego.

"Done," Dwayne said without missing a beat. "I'm clearly outnumbered with eight daughters and I've always wanted a son. Being gay and dead it's highly unlikely I'll get an heir in the usual fashion. I have more homes than I even know about. I can keep him hidden for eternity and the Cows will spoil his little fire-ass rotten."

Tears filled my eyes and I tried not to laugh at the thought of my son being raised by a gay Vampyre with eight adopted violent, yet sweet, Were Cow daughters but a small smile made its way to my trembling lips.

"I believe she asked me," Essie corrected her BFF.

"Please," Dwayne huffed. "You and Hank travel too much and if you become Council members it would be awfully hard to hide a Dragon."

"You think you're up to raising a preschool fire-breather, *Bagina Man*?" Essie inquired with a smirk.

"Yes, I do *I Wipe My HooHoo with Poison Ivy*," he shot back.

"Thank you," I said quietly, not quite believing my good fortune at finding this crazy crew.

"However," Dwayne continued as he shoved a tub of ice cream into my hands and stabbed a spoon into it. "I say you're not going to bite it. Are you into your gay boyfriend?"

"Um…" I started.

"We don't know he's gay," Essie reminded him as she dug into her mint chocolate chip.

"This is true," Dwayne agreed as he floated to the ceiling in excitement. "I will teach you how to seduce him. You'll be mated by the end of the week. We can then go en masse to kill your bastardass father and be back in time for me to finish planning my wedding. It's simple."

"First of all it's *my* wedding, you undead dork. And Dima needs no help in seducing anyone. She's hotter than hell in a heat wave. Have you tried flashing some boob?" Essie asked as she pulled Dwayne off the chandelier.

"Yep," I replied as they both gasped in shock.

"The boob failed?" Dwayne asked, dismayed.

"Yep."

"He's got to be gay," Dwayne fretted. "Do you have anyone else in mind?"

"No," I replied on a long sigh. "It's kind of hard to find a Dragon when most of them know my father will try to kill them."

"I can see how that might cause a few problems," Essie said as she resumed her pacing. "You don't need to mate with anyone to kill your dad. We just have to work fast. If he's dead it will be far easier to find a freakin' mate before you bite the big one. There are many ways to skin a cat or more accurately, kill a Dragon."

"He has a rather large army of insane Dragons that would do anything for him," I supplied as I pressed the bridge of my nose to alleviate the ice cream headache I'd just given myself or maybe it was Essie's way with words.

"True, but we have Junior!" Essie clapped her hands and did a little dance around the still floating Dwayne.

"Your alpha?" I asked doubtfully.

Junior seemed like a great guy, but he was also clumsy and kind of a hot mess. His obsession with a gal named Sandy who wouldn't give him the time of day was all he thought about. To me, he appeared to be a handsome good ole boy who ran a pack of Wolves.

"I know," Essie cut me off before I could say anything else. "He's all kinds of spectacularly unorganized, but the dude is MENSA."

"Shut the front door," I said with a surprised laugh. "No way."

"Yes way, and he can hack into *anything*," she added with an evil little smirk.

"Outstanding!" Dwayne shouted. "We can metaphorically slice your father's financial balls into confetti with Junior's help, and then I'll mind meld the stinky butt jammer when his army turns on him. And then of course, we can confetti his testes for real."

"Okay, those visuals are a little much, but the general idea is fairly brilliant," I said as I put down my tub of frozen sugar and started pacing next to Essie. "Money is paramount to my father's operation and I'm more than sure most of it's illegal. Destroy a Dragon's hoard— destroy a Dragon. If we can fracture his army, I have a real chance of taking him out. Is Junior really that good?"

"Junior is better than that good," Essie promised. "Tomorrow morning is the beginning of the end of Daddy Dearest."

"I think I love you," I said as I tackled Essie and Dwayne in a hug.

18

"Just don't tell Hank," Dwayne advised with wide eyes and a barely disguised smirk. "He's a little possessive of me."

"Oh my hell, Dwayne, you are going to drive me to drink," Essie griped as she giggled and punched him in the arm.

"Got ya covered," he said as he handed each of us a full bottle of very fine wine.

It was the best damn bottle of wine I'd drunk in 499 years.

Chapter 2

"It's been about a month and a half and I'm pretty sure my balls are gonna explode," Junior lamented as he moved around the Sheriff's office like a bull in a china shop.

My doubts about his ability to lead much less hack into an empire and bring it to its knees came roaring to the forefront. Junior was a hot mess on a sharp stick.

"Junior, I'm gonna need you to focus here and get your brains out of your crotch for a few hours. Can you do that?" Hank asked as he ran his hands through his hair in frustration.

"Of course I can focus," Junior huffed. "I just wanted you to know the state of my purple nuts. Not to mention Sandy's wearing a goddang miniskirt today."

Junior and Hank were brothers—gorgeous and powerful Wolf Shifters. Hank had been the Alpha of the Georgia Pack until very recently when he and Essie went to work for their Council. Now Junior was in charge. I wondered at the wisdom of having a horny and destructive Wolf as Alpha, but again, I was not here to judge.

"Being as I'm not the only one standing in the office, the state of your testicles is not appropriate conversation," Hank replied wearily.

Clearly Junior kept his brother apprised of his explosive man parts. As amusing as it all was, I didn't have time for this. Essie, Dwayne, Hank and I had come to talk to Junior and it wasn't proceeding like I'd hoped.

"I'm sorry," Junior apologized to the room. "It's just that I'm a recovering manwhore and it's been hard."

"Pun intended?" Dwayne inquired seriously.

"What?" Junior asked, perplexed.

Shit. It was going to take a lot to convince me he was MENSA.

"Ignore the Vampyre," Essie said as she physically sat Dwayne down in a chair and then did the same to Junior who was almost twice her size. "Sandy is into you, you just have to keep your thingie in your pants for a few more weeks and then she'll go out with you."

"Are you sure?" Junior asked. "I catch her looking so I've been flexing a lot, but she won't really talk to me about anything other than work."

"Um," Essie said as she tried not to laugh. "Don't flex, just act normal around her."

"That *is* normal for Junior," Hank informed his mate with a headshake and a chuckle.

"Alrighty then." Essie bit back a giggle. "Just keep doing what you're doing. If your banana sack blows you'll grow another one back. Probably bigger," she added for good measure.

"Sweet Jesus on a rollercoaster, that is the best news I've heard all week. Would it be offensive if I told Sandy the good news about my man tool?"

"Um, yes—extremely offensive," Essie told him with a snort. "Do not share with Sandy. It will not help your cause."

"Good to know. So what can I do for you good people?" Junior inquired.

I was kind of done with the niceties and the discussion about Junior's reproductive organs. I needed to get down to business or make a new plan. Seth would be here in a few hours and he was my plan B. I had no intention of letting Dwayne help me seduce Seth into becoming my mate, but I wasn't above getting a few pointers.

"Can you hack into bank accounts and drain them completely leaving no trail?" I asked Junior bluntly.

"Just US bank accounts?" Junior sat up straight. His expression went from dopey to intelligently curious.

"No, there would be stock portfolios and offshore accounts as well," I replied.

"What about land holdings? Other investments?" he queried as he went behind his desk and fired up his laptop.

"Investments, yes. What can you do with land?" I asked, confused.

"Well, if I drain the accounts and hack into the property deeds I can put them up for sale. We then buy them with some of the funds we drain. And the kicker would be we turn around and resell everything, unless you wanna keep the land," he explained logically, as if anything he was saying was even remotely logical.

Logical? No. Brilliant? Yes, yes, and *yes*.

"You can do all that?" I was shocked. I hadn't even considered the land—and there was an enormous amount.

"I have a few friends that enjoy acquiring properties. Do you care if they get a very good deal?" Junior questioned as his fingers flew over the keyboard faster than I'd ever seen anyone type.

"No, as long as they're your friends, undervalue the shit out of it and sell," I told him as I pulled a chair over to the desk and sat next to him.

"Do you mind me asking who exactly we're doing this to?" Junior gave me a goofy grin and waited.

"My father, the Dragon King."

"Holy shee-ot," Junior yelled gleefully. "This is gonna be fun. That mother humper has so much blood on his hands it ain't right. What are we doin' with the money? You want me to lock it up in an untraceable trust for you and Daniel? I can do it offshore and I'll lock that sucker up so tight no one will ever find it."

"No. I don't want any of it," I said with a shudder. It was filthy money and I wanted nothing from my father. Ever.

"I thought Dragons like to have huge hoards," Dwayne chimed in. "You could have a massive hoard with all that money."

"A Dragon's hoard consists of what is most important to him or her. I have money. I made it legally and I've invested it well over the years. It's not important to me other than for the fact I can take care of my son. The only thing of importance in my life is Daniel. He's my hoard," I said simply. No riches could replace my child.

"Damn to hell in a hand basket, I think I'm crying," Junior said as he wiped a tear from his eye. "My momma feels the same way about Hank and me. Your boy is lucky, Dima."

"Thanks Junior," I replied and handed him a tissue.

"So what exactly am I gonna do with the tens of millions I'm about to *procure*?" he asked as he dabbed delicately at his eyes and then blew his nose like trumpet.

"It's hundreds of billions," I corrected him as his smile grew wider with delight. "And I want every last cent of it to go to charity. Can you donate anonymously? I want no trace back to my father or any of us."

"Can do. Will do. Junior can hack apart a small country. This'll be a breeze. It'll take a week or two' cause I'm gonna have to have a little help here and there. And if you have any passwords or account numbers, I'd be much obliged," he said as he rubbed his hands together in excitement.

"Do you always talk about yourself in third person?" I asked as I squinted my eyes at him and grinned.

"Yes, I do. Goddangit, do you think that might be part of my problem with Sandy?" Junior asked very seriously.

He had it really bad for this Sandy.

"Well, it might be better to lose that habit," I offered diplomatically. "Why don't you ask her questions about herself? That might get her talking."

"I don't need to," he replied with a self-satisfied smirk.

"And that would be because...?" Essie cut in with a grimace on her lovely face.

"I got her under surveillance," Junior replied with pride. "I know every move my darlin' gal makes."

"That's creepy," Dwayne said with a shudder. "Please tell me you didn't hide cameras in her bathroom."

"Only one," Junior admitted. "It's aimed at the shower. I'm not a total jackhole."

At this point, that was debatable as far as I was concerned.

"Junior, that doesn't fly and if she finds out, you'll lose her for good." Hank's grunt of disgust was echoed around the room.

"What in the dang hell are you talkin' about?" Junior demanded, starting to freak out that he'd screwed up. "You stalked Essie in Chicago for a full year. I was takin' my cue from you, bro-bro."

"Stalking someone and filming them are two totally different things," Hank argued. "I didn't watch her eat her cereal in the morning."

"Excuse me? I call bullshit on that one," Dwayne reminded Hank with raised brows and pursed lips.

"Fine," Hank groused. "It was only once or twice and I was hiding in the tree outside the kitchen window."

Oh my God, Werewolves were more insane than Dragons.

"I think that's kind of hot," Essie admitted with a shrug and a wink at Hank. "So here's the deal Junior, you can spy on Sandy in person, but you have to get the damn cameras out of her house."

"What about her car, the yoga studio, the grocery store, the library where she heads up the book club, the park where she runs, the hair salon and her dad's church?"

We were all stunned to silence—even Dwayne.

"Get rid of all that shit," Hank growled. "You've lost your damn mind, man."

"I love her," Junior whispered and scrubbed his hand over his face. "I don't want anything to happen to her. Sandy won't let me protect her, so I figured out a way to watch over her and keep her safe."

It *was* creepy, but it was also very clear that the poor sap was head over heels in love with her. He just had an unusual way of showing it.

"Can I re-suggest simply asking her questions about herself or maybe you should take up yoga or possibly running. Find out when she does her activities and make sure you do yours at the same time," I said, praying to end this conversation in Sandy's favor.

"Dima, you might be onto something there. How'bout I hack the shit out of your father's holdings and you help me work on Sandy?" Junior bargained.

"I can do that," I agreed with a laugh. "But you have to remove all the cameras immediately. I'd burn a dude to a crisp if I found out he was watching my every move."

"Done," Junior said as he crossed his heart. "So about the passwords, you got any?"

"As a matter of fact, I do. I was able to procure some of them them a few years back," I told him as I pulled his laptop toward me and typed in some information that I'd memorized.

"You mean steal?" Essie asked with a grin.

"Semantics." I laughed and shrugged.

Junior examined the screen as the information came up and whistled in appreciation. "Well slap my ass and call me Sally, this is gonna be even easier than I'd first thought as long as he hasn't changed anything."

"My father is a creature of habit," I promised. "He isn't capable of change."

"Then y'all skedaddle. I got me some Dragon accounts to take down," Junior mumbled. He became immediately engrossed in his computer screen as if we'd already left.

"Come on," Hank whispered as Junior typed away. "He doesn't even realize we're here anymore."

"Can we eat?" Essie asked. "I'm starving."

"You got it, babe," Hank said as he took her hand in his.

I watched them with a mix of envy and happiness. I wanted love like they had, but I knew it wasn't in the cards for me. If I could make Daniel's life safe that would be the best gift I could receive in this life. Real love had eluded me for 499 years. It certainly wasn't going to find me now.

"Do you guys mind if I call Granny and have her bring Daniel to meet us?" I asked as I followed them out into the bright Georgia sunshine.

"Already done," Hank said over his shoulder with a smile. "They're meeting us at the diner."

God, I liked these Wolves. I knew I couldn't stay here forever. It would be too dangerous for them if I did. My father was always searching for me and Daniel. However, I was going to treasure every single moment that I had in Hung, Georgia. Real friendship was new to me and it was getting addictive.

**

26

"I'd like to do a little show at the wedding reception," Granny told Essie as she cut Daniel's chicken fingers up so small I almost laughed.

We were all crammed into a booth at the Hung Diner. The place was packed and hummed with happy people eating fried food. I hadn't felt so relaxed in a long time. Letting down my guard was dangerous, but I was in the company of two deadly Werewolves, a Vampyre and a half-Vampyre half-Wolf.

Essie's granny had almost died in a fight with Dragons and feral Werewolves. Dwayne had taken a chance—and with Essie's permission, had turned Granny. Other than the people at this table and Junior, no one knew of Granny's new bizarre DNA. It was the only reason I'd told them about Daniel. Essie needed to know my most precious secret because I'd inadvertently learned hers. Very few people knew about Daniel and I wanted it that way. His life was in constant danger with my father alive.

"What kind of show?" Hank asked warily as Essie's eyes narrowed at her grandmother.

"I want it to be a surprise," Granny hedged as she put an obscene amount of ketchup on my son's plate.

"Does it involve exposing your breasts?" Essie's lips pursed as she questioned her grandmother and Hank's eyes closed in pain.

It was a fair question. Granny was apparently notorious for stripping in her younger years. She had to be in her eighties now, but didn't look a day over forty. She was a looker and then some.

"Um…no," Granny mumbled.

Dwayne grinned and watched the drama unfold.

"Nipples?" Essie demanded.

"I wear pasties—so, no. Mostly my bottom will be exposed as I'll be wearing ass-less leather chaps," Granny explained. "White ones because it's your wedding."

"What?" Essie choked out as Hank paled and tried not to gag.

"I only face the back when I do my leaps across the stage, so my tushy will be displayed minimally. Plus there are quite a few feathers near my butt," she promised. "Now, normally I wear the nipple-less sequined bra for this number, but since it's your special day I'm just fine with wearing white jeweled pasties. Dwayne's gonna rap while I dance. He'll be dressed as Nicki Minaj. His wig is fabulous."

Hank's guttural groan and Essie's squeal of terror were eclipsed by Dwayne and Granny's peals of laughter. Daniel, who was now covered in ketchup and looked like he needed hospitalization, joined in even though he had no clue what he was cackling at. These people were nuts and I so wished they were mine.

"Got ya!" Granny yelled with delight. "Shoulda seen your face. Hank near passed out!"

Essie's sigh of relief was so audible I started to laugh.

"You realize you will pay for this prank when you least expect it," Essie warned Granny and Dwayne with an enormous grin on her face.

"I'll be ready, sweetheart," Granny vowed as she kept laughing.

"I think it would have been fabulous," Dwayne said as he attempted to wipe all the ketchup off of Daniel.

"You should never think," Hank snapped as he shuddered.

"Excuse me," a huge muscled man interrupted.

The man rocked back and forth on his feet, clearly uncomfortable. He was a Shifter, but I'd never seen him before.

"Howdy Jimbo," Hank said evenly as he sat up straighter and put on his game face. "What can we do for you?"

"You're sittin' with Dragons," he stated the obvious as his eyes squinted at Daniel and me.

"Yes. And?" Essie replied with a dangerous edge to her voice.

"We don't want no Dragons' round here," he shot back and crossed his arms over his massive chest.

My inner Dragon wanted to fry him like all the food offered in the diner, but I refrained and pulled Daniel closer. However, one false move on his part and he was dead. I could take him out in a heartbeat, but I'd only be proving why he didn't want me here in the first place.

"She has every right to be here," Dwayne said in a voice that made the hair on my neck stand up.

Either Dwayne's tone didn't faze Jimbo or he was stupid enough to tangle with a Vampyre that could blow people up. With a name like Jimbo I didn't know why I expected brilliance.

"We don't like Vampyres much either," Jimbo informed the table bluntly. "Didn't have no problems like this till recently. We ain't gonna stand for it much longer."

"How bout this?" Hank offered as he leaned back and got comfortable. "You can move your prejudiced ass right on out of Hung. The Sheriff and the Pack are fine with this. These particular Dragons pose us no threat and are under our protection. And the Vampyre saved the town's ass if I'm remembering correctly."

"You are," Dwayne added as he too sat back.

Relaxed Shifters and Vampyres were not a good thing in my vast experience.

"Or we can go out back and I can kick your ass to hell," Essie offered with a smile that didn't reach her eyes.

"Awwww, come on Essie, I wanna have a go at Jimbo. He's always kinda bugged me," Granny complained and cracked all her knuckles, readying herself for a fight.

Jimbo blanched and backed away.

"We just don't want no trouble here," he said stiffly. "Dragons ain't nothin' but trash."

"You know, *Jimbo*," Hank said as he picked at Daniel's fries and popped one into his mouth. He chewed slowly and stared hard at the now very uncomfortable Jimbo before he spoke again. "Never really liked you much and your intimidation tactics don't work on me. In fact, they make me want to run you and your hate mongering family out of town, but I'll just leave that to Junior since he's the Alpha. He has a craw up his ass for species intolerance and he's been itching for a fight for a while now."

"Since he's giving up being a manwhore, he has a hell of a lot of unused aggression," Essie added with a shrug. "Pretty sure he killed the last guy who pissed him off."

"Nah," Hank corrected her. "He just permanently maimed him. Never gonna walk again. And if I'm recalling correctly, the guy's a soprano now."

Jimbo continued to back up.

"This ain't the end of this," he hissed as he turned and practically ran from the diner.

I knew it wasn't. Dragons were not welcome in civilized places. I needed to leave this town sooner rather than later. I would not be the reason for discourse or death in Hung, Georgia. I let my head fall for a brief second and wondered if I'd ever find a safe place for Daniel. Even if my father was eliminated, our welcome wasn't guaranteed anywhere in this world.

"Dat's a bad man," Daniel said quietly as he patted my face with his chubby ketchup covered hands. "Me will take care of you, Mommy."

My heart grew bigger as I stared at my beautiful child. He was everything that was good and I was hell bent on making sure he grew up safely.

"No, my precious man, Mommy will take care of you," I promised. "You get to be a little boy for a few more years."

"And Dwayne will kill the shit out of anything that wants to harm you," Dwayne promised as he leaned over and gently kissed Daniel's forehead.

I didn't give Dwayne any crap about cursing in front of my son. Daniel would hear much worse in his life and at least this swearing was meant with love. Furthermore, if Dwayne was going to raise Daniel, I was certain the salty language would come with it.

Daniel raised his arms to the Vampyre and cuddled up in his lap as Granny absently played with his curls. These people meant too much to me to put them in harm's way. I'd wait for Seth and then find another place to hide while I planned my father's demise.

"He's just the tip of the iceberg," I said wearily. "We won't stay much longer. It's not safe for you or for us. I can defend myself, but Daniel is just a child."

"We're going back to the Sheriff's office," Hank said as he stood and tossed some money on the table.

"Why?" Essie asked as she too stood and then reached for Daniel.

"Dima and Daniel need to be chipped," he said.

"Perfect," Dwayne said as he took Granny's hand in his and put his other on my back. "I'll feel much better if we can always find them."

I wasn't quite sure what they were talking about, but I was willing to do almost anything to keep Daniel alive.

I had to trust someone and these people were it.

Chapter 3

"Um...Sandy, I'm gonna need your help in here," Junior called out as he spastically winked at all of us, nodding like a dummy with a plan.

Dear God, what was he up to now? His waggling eyebrows and snickering clued me in. I was clear on what chipping meant now and I suspected Junior had found another way to keep Sandy under surveillance without cameras.

Again, his reported MENSA status boggled me.

"What do you need, Sheriff? I'm in the middle of balancing the town budget and deconstructing the encryptions on the passwords you gave me," Sandy said, avoiding eye contact with the besotted Junior.

She was just as lovely as all the other Werewolf shifters I'd met—wild long blonde curls framed her heart shaped face and her eyes were a beautiful shade of cornflower blue. However, far more impressive than her looks was her brain.

"I'm gonna chip Dima and her son Daniel. Since you're working for the city government now, you're gonna get chipped today too," he answered briskly as he pulled a sharp knife from his desk and some miniscule pieces of metal.

Sandy rolled her eyes and shook her head as Essie tried not to laugh.

"And who monitors these chips, *Sheriff*?" she asked as she folded her arms across her chest and narrowed her eyes at Junior.

"Um…I do, but only if someone goes missing," Junior told her as he busied himself sharpening the knife that I realized he was going to use on me and Daniel to insert the chips under our skin.

Not really my idea of a good time since I didn't want any of the people I cared about coming to my rescue. No one was going to die for me. However, Daniel was a different matter altogether.

With a grunt of disbelief aimed at Junior, Sandy turned to me and smiled.

"Hi, I'm Sandy," she said warmly, extending her hand to me. "It's lovely to meet you. I've heard such wonderful things about you and Daniel from Essie."

"Likewise," I said as I took her hand in mine.

Her grip was strong and she met my eyes—not an easy thing to do with a Dragon. She was not one to screw with and I liked her. I liked her even more when she squatted down and offered her hand to Daniel. She didn't even flinch as he covered her in ketchup when he avoided the shake and went right in for a hug.

"You're a handsome little man," she said, ruffling his hair and then scooping him up in her arms. "I have a nephew about your age. Maybe you can come over and play."

Daniel's eyes grew wide and he began to tremble. He'd never played with anyone his age and guilt washed over me yet again at how sheltered his life had been.

"Ohhhhhh Mommy, can I pway with Sandy's neffu?" he asked.

"I think we might be able to work something out," I said carefully, wondering if it would be safe. If others in the town held the same opinion of Dragons that Jimbo did, I wasn't so sure about Daniel being out of my sight.

"I'll go with him," Dwayne offered as he either read my mind or expression.

"Me too," Granny added quickly. "I haven't seen Sandy's momma in ages. I'm due for some town gossip."

Being around people I trusted was seductive. I'd never had it except as a child. My mother would have died for us…and in the end she did. She basically ran interference so my three brothers and I could escape my father's deadly wrath. My brothers didn't make it and neither did my mother. I did and I'd lived with the guilt of being the only survivor for hundreds of years. Until Daniel came along I lived my life in my mother's and brothers' honor. Avenging them was my only mission. Having Daniel only increased my need to end my father before it was too late.

"Sandy?" my son asked in a shy tone as he gently patted her hair inadvertently smearing it with red, crusty ketchup. "Will you mate wif me?"

Her laugh sounded like bells and I giggled at the audacity of my four-year old Romeo.

"Daniel, I think I might be a *little* bit old for you, but you have made my year in a big way," she told him and hugged him tight.

"She's gonna mate with *me*," Junior informed the room as he grinned and winked at Sandy.

"We'll see about that," she muttered as she put Daniel down and took the knife from Junior's hand.

"Sumbitch!" Junior crowed joyously as he picked a shocked Sandy up and swung her around the room. "You people heard it here. Sandy is mine and she agreed to it."

"I wouldn't go quite that far," Essie said with a laugh. "But I will say you're making progress."

"Sandy is right here," the gal in question grumbled as she eased her way out of Junior's arms a little slower than someone who hated the person would. "I've agreed to nothing, but I'm slightly impressed with your restraint in the lady department."

"There are no other women," Junior promised as he crossed his heart and gave her lopsided grin that even melted my heart a little bit. "You're it for me. The sooner you come to your senses, the sooner I'll take you out in my truck and make you see Jesus and all the angels and saints."

"Um, Junior, you probably should have stopped after the 'you're it for me' part," Hank said with a grimace.

I couldn't have agreed more. I half expected Sandy to slug him.

"Dream on, Big Boy," Sandy snapped at Junior as she extended her arm. "Chip me and then you can remove all the cameras you have trained on me all over town."

"You know about that?" Junior was flabbergasted and began to pace the room in distress.

"What do I look like to you? An idiot? I completely disabled the one you put in my *bathroom*. Which by the way, makes you a total jackhole," Sandy informed him as she took a seat behind his desk and watched him wreak havoc in his office.

"I thought it was a little weird that you never took a shower," Junior mumbled as he jogged the perimeter of the room knocking everything off of the walls and every surface he passed.

Essie pulled me and Daniel up on the couch so we didn't get stepped on. Books and papers flew everywhere. Granny and Dwayne levitated and watched with glee. Hank was the only one brave enough to stay put.

"I swear to Jesus in a jockstrap I was gonna take those down," Junior bellowed in a panic as he dropped to his knees in front of her. "I can't stand the thought of anyone hurting you, so I um…figured out a way to keep you safe. I know it was a jackhole move. I'm no longer a manwhore, but I might be a jackhole for the rest of my days. Please Sandy," he shouted causing everyone in the room to slap their hands over their ears—including Sandy. "Just give me a dang chance. Tell me that you can find it in your heart to love a jackhole."

The room was quiet as we watched Sandy mull over the jackhole proposition. It was a doozy.

"Three dates," she told him calmly as we all let out a collective sigh of relief.

"How about three weeks of dates every night?" Junior countered.

"Why three weeks?" Sandy asked, perplexed.

"Well, Essie said I had to date you three weeks before I could get into your pants," he explained innocently, as if he wasn't bargaining to get laid.

"I said a month," Essie volunteered.

"I figured three weeks was close enough," Junior said.

Sandy closed her eyes and breathed in slowly through her nose and then let it out even more slowly through her mouth. She had a hell of a lot of restraint...or she liked him a whole lot more than she was letting on.

"You get three dates. If you behave like a gentleman, you *might* get another. However, you're on trial, Jacob. And you will not be getting into my pants any time soon. Are we clear?"

"Totally," Junior, aka Jacob said in an outdoor voice, but thankfully not quite loud enough to damage eardrums. "She is so into me," he told the room.

"We done here?" Hank asked with a smirk.

"We are," Sandy replied as she stood and left Junior on the floor behind her. "Dima, are you all right with getting chipped?"

"I'm all right with Daniel being chipped," I admitted. "But I don't want any of you in danger because of me."

"I live for danger," Dwayne announced as he floated back to the floor. "And I'll sleep far better if I know where you are."

"Heavens to Murgatroyd, you should see him when he sleeps. He looks dead," Granny said as she too floated back down.

"He is dead. He's a Vampyre," Essie stated the obvious as she gathered the chips and swabbed Daniel's arm with alcohol. "Dima, I want you chipped and I don't want to have to kick your ass to accomplish it."

"She's right," Hank agreed as he carefully slit my son's skin and inserted the chip. "Whether you like it or not, we consider you part of our mismatched pack. We take care of our own."

Daniel barely flinched when Hank cut him. My boy was brave. Hank grabbed him and planted a big kiss on his cheek as Daniel giggled with pride.

I lowered my eyes so no one saw the tears gathering there. Luck didn't play into my life, so I had to believe this was fate. I'd found these people because I was supposed to. Hopefully I'd be able to return some of the gifts they were giving me.

I extended my arm to a still smiling Hank and let him chip me. Having my back covered was new and it felt dangerously good.

Sandy let Junior chip her with a large eye roll and enough attitude and back talk to keep him on his toes. He was going to have a hell of a time truly winning her over, but I suspected he eventually would. Not because he would lose the jackhole part of him overnight—or ever, but because Sandy wanted him just as much as he wanted her.

"So you wanna bring *Seth* over for dinner?" Essie asked with a grin as she put a super hero bandage on Daniel and a Sponge Bob one on me.

"Yes," I replied. "I think you all will like him. He's a lovely Dragon."

"I still say he's gotta be ugly," Dwayne announced to the general population as we all made our way out of the office. "You just don't describe someone who is *do-it* worthy as a lovely person."

"Dwayne," Essie said mildly.

"Yes?" he inquired politely.

"Shut your cakehole or I'll shut it for you."

"Fine point. Well made," my opinionated Vampyre friend said as he hoisted Daniel up on his shoulders.

"Cakehole," Daniel shouted as he played Dwayne's bald head like it was a drum.

Never in my years did I ever think I would see a Dragon sitting on a Vampyre's shoulders using him for percussion that didn't end in a bloody death. Lately, my life never ceased to amaze me.

"Damn it, Dwayne, don't cuss around the child," Granny groused as she too took a swipe at Dwayne's head. "We're gonna take this little man on a play date and meet you and your friend at Essie's for dinner. Sound good?"

My hesitation was brief as I observed Daniel's excitement at getting to play with someone his own age. I knew he'd be safe with both Granny and Dwayne, but it still worried me.

"Yes," I said slowly, putting a smile on my face for Daniel's benefit. "Just make sure he doesn't burn their house down or shift. Might be a little awkward."

"Got it," Dwayne said as he gave my arm a quick squeeze. "You go enjoy your really, really nice Dragon. And you know...he might be an ass man since the boob flopped."

"I have some booty shorts in my purse if you wanna borrow them," Granny offered as she began to dig for them.

"No. No, I'm good," I insisted. I didn't know whether to laugh or scream. While the sentiment was um...lovely, the reality was wrong on too many levels to even explain. However, I did briefly consider that fact that Seth might be an ass man.

"Six thirty," Essie said as she grabbed Hank's hand and pulled him down Main Street. "Be there and bring your appetite. And don't worry. I'm ordering out so it will be edible!"

"Thank God for small favors," Granny whispered as she, Dwayne, Sandy and Daniel piled into her car.

"Heard that, you old bat," Essie called over her shoulder as Hank laughed. "Just for that I'll be making your plate."

The laughter was real and the love was evident. This was as good as it got.

It was just too bad it couldn't last.

Chapter 4

"I won't be able to stay," Seth said as he took my hand and led me to the lovely couch in our three-bedroom suite. The Hung Bed and Breakfast was cozy and homey. I was hoping to get cozy with Seth, but clearly we weren't of the same mind.

I was thrown by the fact that he'd reserved three bedrooms, not two. I stared at Seth and again tried to determine if he was gay. Male Dragons were perpetually horny. Seth was an anomaly. Maybe he was asexual. I'd never come across this phenomenon, but I also never thought I would be welcomed in a pack consisting of Werewolves and Vampyres. Unusually strange was my new normal and I decided to embrace it.

Hell, I was 499 years old, sex was just sex. I'd had plenty of sex in my lifetime and sadly it often ended in the death of my partner, thanks to my psychotic father. Seth would probably live longer if we didn't have an intimate relationship. And to be honest, even sex had gotten old in my long lifetime.

I realized in that moment that there were far more important things than the physical. A good male role model for Daniel beat my need for sexual release by a mile. Seth's kindness and loyalty to me and my son was something beautiful in a very violent world. My needs would always come second to my son's. There was no way

I could do better than Seth. If he was willing to mate with me, I would love and accept him exactly as he was.

"When do you have to go?" I asked, holding tightly to his large warm hands.

"I leave tonight. The Resistance has called a gathering. I want you to be there."

"Um…not sure that's a great plan," I said as I stood and began to pace. "I'm the daughter of the person the Resistance wants eliminated. That sounds a little like I'd be walking into a shitshow ending in my fiery death."

Seth's gentle laugh at my unladylike language made me smile. Everything the man did made me smile. My determination to please him only increased. I sat back down and prepared myself to listen before I came to a conclusion about going—not my normal MO, but I was turning over a new leaf.

"The Resistance needs you, Dima and you need the help of the Resistance. Neither one of us has been able to defeat your father alone. It's far past time for us to join forces," he said as he tucked a few curly strands of my hair behind my ears.

I laid my cheek in the palm of his hand and felt safe and content. "They won't want me there."

"Some will be averse at first, but the truth remains unyielding. Success is unattainable without trying something new. Your father could never imagine that you would go to these extremes to take him out."

I got lost in Seth's beautiful eyes for a moment and couldn't find my train of thought. I really could love this man. I was certain I already loved him and I felt his love in return. It wasn't the kind of love that consisted of fireworks and raw need—it was more mature and lasting. Something I'd never experienced before. It was real and I was going to fight for it. If Seth thought I should go. I would go.

"The leader, Nicolai," I said haltingly. "He won't stand for it. I can guarantee that."

41

"Nicolai is a good man—deadly, but good," Seth said with a chuckle. "He can be difficult, but he's far from stupid. He will see reason. You, my dear, are the missing puzzle piece he has been looking for. Nicolai may not realize this yet, but I'm quite sure of it."

For a moment I wondered if all Seth wanted from me was my help with the Resistance, but pushed it aside immediately. He was a pure hearted man. I could tell. I hadn't lived as long as I had without being able to judge true character.

"You really think this would work?" I asked.

I resumed my pacing as it helped me think. I'd known of Nicolai and the Resistance for several hundred years. I'd actually considered joining them once or twice in the last few decades, but after Daniel's arrival I'd dismissed the thought. It was too dangerous to have all my cards on the table.

"I know it will work."

"They cannot under any circumstances know about Daniel," I stated firmly.

My life was expendable. My son's was not.

"As you wish." Seth nodded and pulled me into his strong arms.

I relaxed and let his steady warmth sink into me. However, something held me back from telling him about emptying my father's coffers. As much as I trusted Seth, if the Resistance didn't accept me, I still needed a plan. Seth was part of the Resistance. If they denied me, I would not ask him to choose. Daniel was my first priority and no matter how wonderful Seth was, he would always come second.

"Can you come to dinner with me at Essie's? All my friends will be there and Daniel will too. He'll be so disappointed if he doesn't see you."

"Wouldn't miss it for the world. I need to meet these Wolves and Vampyres that accept Dragons," Seth said, squeezing me tight. "I'll leave after dinner and you'll meet me at midnight tonight."

"Where am I meeting you?" I asked, silently beginning to second-guess my quick acquiescence.

"Chicago."

Thank God, I knew Chicago well. If I needed to make a quick escape, it would be far easier in a city I was familiar with. Seth might be correct. I hadn't been successful on my own. Even if I drained my father's assets, he would still have a small group of loyal followers. It could be strategically outstanding if I had an army of my own. His death would be more assured and I could die on my 500th birthday knowing Daniel would be safe.

But if Seth would mate with me, I might get a happily ever after…

"You ready to meet my ragtag pack?" I asked as I pushed my hopeful thoughts away and focused on the man in front of me.

"Am I?" he questioned with a lopsided grin.

"Probably not, but I can promise you'll have fun."

With one last sweet hug he let me go and extended his hand. "Let's do it. No one is going to believe me if I regale them with this story, but I've been waiting a long time to break bread with a species other than Dragon."

I giggled at his proper speech and took his hand. I knew I was older by at least a hundred years, but Seth was an old fashioned Dragon all the way. A gentleman was a new thing for me—and I liked it.

Steadfast and kind were good. Fireworks exploded. I needed no more painful infernos in my life. Seth was the man for me.

***

"My gay-dar says Seth's as straight as an arrow and my eyes say he's hotter than Satan's underpants on fire," Dwayne whispered, fanning himself dramatically as we plated the hors d'oeuvres Essie had ordered in from the one fancy restaurant in Hung.

I popped a shrimp into my mouth and grinned at Dwayne.

"Dude," Essie gushed as she emptied containers of steak, potatoes and braised veggies onto platters. "He's amazing—funny, hot and so good with Daniel. If I was into cross species dating, I would have jumped his bones so fast."

"Excuse me," Hank growled. "Your mate is standing in the kitchen."

"You're the only one for me, Sexy Pants," Essie reassured him with a laugh and a quick grab of her jealous Wolf's ass. "I'm just doing a compare and contrast for Dima."

"Will I ever understand women?" Hank muttered as he wandered back to the den with beers for the guys.

"Nope, not unless you start playing for my team," Dwayne called out as Junior and Sandy rushed into the kitchen.

"Dangit, there's been a break in at the hardware store. I'm gonna have to skedaddle," Junior said as he grabbed a steak and basically swallowed it whole.

"Humans or Weres?" Essie asked, slapping his hand before he could pilfer another steak.

"Humans," Sandy said as she quickly ate a few sausage stuffed mushroom caps. "Oh my God, these are so good. Sorry we're going to miss dinner."

"You're going too?" I asked trying to hide my grin.

"Um...well," she stuttered as a blush began to rise on her pretty face.

"Yep, tonight is mine and Sandy's first date. We're just gonna apprehend the dumbasses, throw them in the overnight lock up and then go make out for a few hours," Junior confirmed with a thumbs up.

"That's not exactly how it's going to go," Sandy warned him with her eyes flashing. "You *might* get a goodnight kiss if you behave, but that's it, buster."

"She is so into me," Junior said with a shit-eating grin.

Her eye roll beat all the eye rolls I'd ever seen. My bark of laughter was echoed by both Essie and Dwayne.

"Let me tell ya something," Junior said to me as he handed me a squirt gun and a large bottle of solution. "That sumbitch in there is a good man. I like him. Not really crazy'bout you going to Chicago, but if Seth says you'll be okay, I'm apt to believe him. But you're gonna take this Dragon shit with you. I like Seth, but I've never met the rest of the flying bastards. And if you have time, go get yourself a hotdog from that stand behind Wrigley Field. I dream about those wieners."

Junior's way with words would never cease to render me silent.

The solution Junior referred to was something he'd developed to prohibit a Dragon's shift. Every time I doubted his brilliance, I just needed to remember this fact. When I'd first met Essie and Hank, they'd made me drink the solution. It worked. The vile liquid left me defenseless. While I didn't blame them, I hated them for it. However, Essie had risked her life to save me when I was unable to defend myself. It showed her true character and she'd gained my fickle trust.

Hence the beginning of our unlikely friendship.

"I've also got some poison tipped daggers I want you to strap to your inner thighs," Essie added. "I'd make you take a gun, but they're worthless on Dragons."

"I'm hoping I won't have to use any of those items, but I'll take them gladly," I said as I grabbed another piece of shrimp and then thought better of it.

"And I'm going to dress you," Dwayne announced. "Seth said it's a formal affair and what I'm going to put you in will defend you as much as any weapon."

"Thanks," I said as the reality began to hit.

My appetite had disappeared. The thought of what I was about to do weighed heavily. My life was expendable if it kept Daniel alive.

Junior and Sandy left after a round of hugs and I idly wondered if I would ever see them again.

"Essie, Dwayne, I have no plans of dying tonight, but," I started only to be cut off.

"Daniel will always be safe as long as we both are alive," Essie promised.

"I'll move him immediately if you're not back by morning," Dwayne said in a more serious tone than I'd ever heard from him. "The Cows already know about Daniel and are so excited they scooped all the poop out of the yard so he can run freely. You *are* going to come back. I'll accept nothing less, but Daniel still has to visit. My girls will be devastated if they don't get to babysit."

"It's a deal," I said, forcing a smile to my lips. If tonight was successful, my father's end was in sight. I needed to focus on that. "Let's go back in. I want to be with Daniel."

"Good idea," Essie said as she handed me the platter of vegetables and then grabbed the steaks and potatoes herself. "We need to save Seth from Granny. She's flirting up a storm. I'm a little concerned she might feel the need to do a show."

"Sweet Kathie Lee and Hoda on wine drinking Tuesdays, that would be mortifyingly fabu," Dwayne squealed as he hightailed out of the kitchen.

"Thank you, Essie," I said as I met her eyes and tried to tell her more than any mere words could express.

"You're welcome, Dragon," she replied with a smile and a very serious look in her eyes. "I will love and kill for your son. You *will* come back, but if you don't, Daniel will always be protected. You have my word."

"I'm not sure you know how much that means to me," I told her. "One day when you have children, you'll understand the magnitude of the gift you've given me. Hopefully I can repay you, but I can't imagine how."

"Live," she said simply. "That's the gift I want. I want you to stay in my life."

"I'll do my best."

"Works for me," she said lightening the heavy vibe. "Oh hell no, I hear music. Granny's gonna dance. Move your ass or everyone is gonna see her no-nos."

Granny was dancing, but thankfully she was totally clothed. She was teaching Daniel hip-hop and Dwayne was filming with his phone diligently. The laughter was loud and my eyes got misty. Hank and Seth were in deep discussion and the mutual admiration was obvious.

I wanted to stop time and savor this moment forever. In my mind I imagined having a little house down the road from Essie and Hank. It would have a big yard for Daniel and a swing set. Seth and I would figure out some kind of business that would be socially acceptable. Essie and Hank would have children and Daniel would play with them. Dwayne and Granny would be the surrogate grandparents for my son and the Cows—as crazy as they were—would be his aunts. Life would be perfect.

But it was a silly dream. Perfect had never existed for me—plus I was probably a little too violent for that scenario.

Life for Dragons never worked out easily. I knew this, but I knew I could eliminate the biggest danger in my son's and all other Dragons' lives. Partnering with the Resistance was either going to be the most brilliant move I'd ever made or my last.

I was going to go with most brilliant. I was a Dragon who didn't lose. I hadn't beaten my father yet, but the new war was just beginning.

Seth's smile warmed my heart as he patted the empty seat next to him. Cuddling up with him on the couch was homey and nice. Granny and Essie handed out food and the conversation flowed with ease.

"Here's the invitation. The address is on it," Seth said as the meal ended, handing me an expensive embossed card.

He pressed his lips to my forehead and then scooped Daniel up in his arms.

"See you at midnight," I said hoping he would kiss me for real.

He didn't, but that was okay. The way Daniel looked at him was enough for me. It had to be.

"It was astonishingly lovely to meet all of you," Seth said as he hugged the women and shook hands with the men. "I am honored to have been asked and I am forever in your debt for your protection of Dima and Daniel. After we defeat the King, we need to have serious talks amongst our species."

"I'm in," Hank said. "It's time to end the war."

"God, it's so *hot* when alpha guys get all serious. If I had pores I'd be sweating up a storm," Dwayne announced as fanned himself with a wedding magazine.

"Dima, I'll see you shortly," Seth said as he walked toward the door. "It will be fine. I promise. It's the way it's supposed to be."

"I'll be there," I said.

"And she'll be looking fabulous," Dwayne added with a wink at Seth.

"Till we meet again," Seth told the room and then he left.

There was a brief silence and then Daniel started dancing again. I picked him up and kissed him all over his chubby face until he squealed and squirmed away. He had no clue it might be the last time we would be together, but I did.

"Daniel," I said as I squatted down to his level. "Mommy loves you more than anything else in the whole world. I want you always to remember that. Can you do that for me?"

"Yes! Daniel woves Mommy too," he shouted and then did a move that made me giggle.

My child was my world and I was determined to make it a better place for him. I just prayed I would live to be part of it.

"Come on, Lady Dragon, it's time to get you gussied up," Dwayne said as he pulled me toward Essie's bedroom.

He was right. I needed the armor of designer duds to face the Dragons and Dwayne had plenty of armor. His taste was a little iffy, but I'd been out of the formal world for so long I was going to trust him.

Maybe I'd be able to attract Seth with something a little sexy...

Chapter 5

"God, keep me alive and on my feet tonight and I'll owe you a big one," I whispered to the vast starry sky.

I'd dressed with extreme care, down to the delicate diamond-encrusted choker, earrings and sky-high strappy stilettos, but suddenly I felt naked and exposed. Designer clothes were not armor. Fabric wouldn't protect me from fire or death, no matter how expensive the material. Hell, the dress I was wearing barely covered my body. I was terrified I'd flash boob any moment, but when in Rome...

The huge warehouse on the outskirts of Chicago appeared run down and shoddy. I'd almost tripped twice on the crumbling asphalt that led to the rusted out door. In contrast the parking lot was full of expensive cars and limos. The single streetlamp that had illuminated the area at one time was riddled with bullet holes and only the evening sky lit my way. Even the golden glow of the full moon did little to disguise the poor condition of the building.

However, I'd learned early in life that exteriors could be wildly deceiving.

"Son of a bitch," I mumbled as my stupidly insubstantial heel got caught in a loose pile of gravel. "Stilettos suck ass."

"Swearing isn't very lady-like," a deep voice whispered from behind as a strong hand closed around my throat stopping the little bit of forward progress I was making—not to mention my breath.

My body was trapped against something enormous, strong and not even remotely human. This was not how I had planned on spending my last moments on earth. How in the hell had anything snuck up on me? I was trained, deadly and not one little bit human either. No one had ever taken me from behind in my ridiculously long life.

I knew what he was. I'd just never come across one quite so powerful—or that smelled as good as he did.

What the fu…? I did *not* need to be enjoying the scent of the beast that was going to tear my head from my shoulders in the next minute or two. I needed to figure out how to remove his head. Shifting would work, but it would attract the attention of the Dragons in the warehouse. Since I had no clue how many were inside, shifting was out.

To add insult to injury, the guard was a pervert. I deduced this when the hand that wasn't busy choking the life out of me brazenly grazed my somewhat exposed breast. This bastard was messing with the wrong chick.

"You're gonna to cop a feel before you kill me, *jackass*?" I choked out as I tried to shore up my footing. If I could get my balance I could kick back and hopefully connect with his family jewels. All I needed was a second and he was a dead man.

"My hand slipped." He chuckled as his warm breath tickled my neck.

My instinct was to lean back and get closer. Clearly my instincts had gone to hell on the express train. What was wrong with me?

"What are you doing here, pretty Dragon girl?" he inquired casually as if he didn't have me in a damn death grip.

"I was invited," I tried to snap, but it came out more like a squeak.

"Interesting," the deadliest asshole I'd ever come across said as he loosened his hold, but still kept me firmly pressed to him.

"Is this how you greet all your guests?"

I reached over my head and tried to gouge out his eyes. He was too tall—had to be well over six foot four. My fingers ended up in his mouth. At least I drew a little blood.

"Only ones I'm unfamiliar with," he replied as he bit down on my fingers. Hard.

Tit for tat…he drew a little blood as well.

Why I thought his behavior was hot was a fine reason for me to seek therapy. Being choked and getting bitten was *not* healthy foreplay. This was absurd, but at least I was fairly sure I wasn't in imminent danger of dying. The goon clearly had no clue who I was and that was a very good thing at the moment.

"You're meeting someone here?" he asked as he pressed his nose to my hair.

"Yes," I said as I futilely tried to disengage myself from him before I rubbed up against him like a cat in heat. "I'm meeting my mate."

It was a lie, but it flew out smoothly. I needed to get the deadly sexy Dragon dude off of me. I was here for a reason. It was beginning to seem like an insane reason, but I'd come and I was going to see it through. There was no time at all to be attracted to a lowly, muscled, horny guard dog in a deserted parking lot. I had things to do and a father to kill.

"You're mated?" he asked, surprised as his grip on me tightened.

"Yes," I ground out. "And my mate will destroy you when he learns of how I've been treated by the help."

His laugh went all through me. It set my lower girlie region into overdrive and made me want to tear his head off at the same time. This Dragon was bad news. The sooner I got away from him the better. I had Seth—kind of. I didn't need any complications—not that killer guy would even want me for more than a roll in the hay. Dragons were over-sexed perverts. The mind-bogglingly large bulge in his pants that he had pressed up against my back was proof that they all wanted one thing.

"You're not mated," he stated firmly. "I'd be able to tell."

Damn it, he was correct. If I were mated, I'd have the scent of my mate on me. Hell, I hadn't even slept with my *mate* yet. I knew that Seth wasn't my true mate even though I wanted him to be. However, the bastard that wouldn't let go had no claim on me.

Dragons technically had one true mate, but rarely did we have happily ever afters. Violence followed us everywhere and more often than not, a Dragon's true mate was killed before they ever met. Or the female's true mate was killed by a stronger Dragon that desired her…exactly what happened to my mother.

"I'm not mated *yet*," I snarled as I broke his hold and turned on him. "I will be very soon. And if you lay your hands on me again, I'll fry your ass to a crisp."

The look of shock on his face at my escape was priceless. However, I wished I'd kept my back to him. He was hotter than hell on fire. Wouldn't it figure? If I'd met him under different circumstances, I'd have jumped him in a heartbeat—a meaningless one night stand. But I didn't meet him in a normal situation…whatever normal meant for Dragons who lived hundreds of years. And I wasn't looking for a meaningless lay—at all. Ever. I was a single mother with a boyfriend who wouldn't sleep with me. I was perfectly fine.

It didn't help that the Dragon bouncer was devastatingly beautiful. His eyes were a golden green and his shoulder length hair was jet black. Cheekbones that could cut glass and a body that belonged on the set of a Hollywood action adventure where the men wore no shirts.

Crappity crap crap.

I wondered if his Dragon form was as beautiful as his human form. Hopefully I would never see his Dragon. If his human was this deadly, his Dragon would be a freakin' nightmare.

But damn, it would be fun to shift and have a bloody fight with someone—even a gorgeous jerk. I'd been on the lam and hiding my true nature for so long my own Dragon was angry with me.

"By all means, go in and find you *mate,*" he replied with a smirk on his stupidly full and kissable lips. "Do you have a name, feisty girl?"

"Nope, I don't," I replied as I turned on my flimsy heel and prayed it didn't snap. "And if I did, I wouldn't give it to you."

"Oh, I'll get your name. That's a promise," he purred as he slipped back into the darkness preparing to scare the life out of the next unsuspecting guest.

"Don't make promises you can't keep, big boy," I said as I marched away, refusing to look back.

"I don't," he said quietly. "Never have. Never will."

I whipped around to level him with an insult and a zap of fire that would make him hurt, but he was gone. I couldn't scent him or see him. What the hell kind of Dragons did they have here in Chicago? This night couldn't get any worse.

Who was I kidding? It could always get worse.

With one last scan of the parking lot, I shrugged and approached the warehouse. The guard was very good. I hoped that wasn't telling of the power and skill inside—or maybe I did. If I were to ally myself with these Dragons it would be outstanding if they were all as crazy and powerful as the idiot standing guard.

Only one way to find out.

I pushed at the heavy metal door and it was quickly opened from the other side. My stomach lurched with a queasiness I hadn't felt in ages—first the sexy killer in the parking lot and now this. The opulence of the interior blatantly belied its outer shell. It reminded me of my youth and not in a warm and fuzzy way. Could these people be as evil and materialistic as the ones I'd been running from for years?

"May I take your wrap, Miss?" a formal, tuxedo attired attendant inquired in a monotone. He had as much emotion as the ornate marble covered floor. Handing him my invitation, I shook my head no as I stood at the mouth of Hell and knew I'd made an enormous mistake.

Every instinct I had was to run. Trust was earned. I trusted no one here and as soon as my identity was revealed, I was certain no one would trust me either. What the hell had I been thinking when I told Seth, *my kind-of sort-of boyfriend*, I would join him? These people didn't want my help and I didn't want theirs. And where in God's name was Seth?

"Are you here alone?" the doorman asked as I stood frozen in my spot.

"No. I'm looking for my escort," I replied as I scanned the room trying my best not to let my distress show.

That was impossible. My distress was very clear to the personality-free Dragon who'd requested my wrap. It was going to be obvious to every Dragon in the room—and there had to be at least two hundred of them present.

Again. What the hell was I thinking? I was still breathing because I'd avoided my people for years and now I willingly entered a lair? Stupid, stupid, stupid.

"Perhaps I can be of assistance," boring coat-taker dude suggested as he valiantly tried not to stare at my chest.

Dwayne was a dead man. No wait, he was already *dead*. I had no one to blame but myself. I'd let the Vamp choose the scraps of material that somewhat covered my body. He'd insisted that all eyes would be on my chest and if I needed to make a quick get away my boobs would be an outstanding distraction. An hour ago it had made sense. Now…not so much.

Note to self—never take fashion from a Vampyre who moonlights as a drag queen.

Seth was nowhere to be found. This was not at all like him. I inhaled slowly through my nose and exhaled quietly through my mouth tamping down my anxiety. Pink and gold smoke wafted in thin delicate tendrils from my nose, but there was little I could do about it.

Why was I so nervous? I was a freaking killing machine. I could shift in a heartbeat and probably take out half of the room before they knew what hit them. Poison laced daggers were strapped to my inner thighs. In my clutch I had a squirt gun filled with solution that could prohibit a Dragon shift and according to Dwayne, my boobs were freakin' weapons.

However, boobs were not going to save me tonight.

This was a grave error on every level. I could feel it in my bones. I didn't need these Dragons to remove my father from power. I was certain their correctly placed hatred of my father would transfer directly to me. I didn't have time to die at the moment. I had to kill him before death caught up with me.

Seth was wrong about me coming here. He was convinced that the leader of the Dragon resistance would welcome me. I now heartily disagreed. The leader, Nicolai was a notoriously egotistical, womanizing, hard-ass. Surprisingly, I'd never met him, but I'd heard stories about him for the last several hundred years.

I'd already met one handsome deadly idiot in the crumbling parking lot. I wasn't sure how polite I could be if I met another.

"You must be new," a delicate and lovely female Dragon said with a giggle as she took my hand in hers and led me into the room. "My my, you are just gorgeous! The men are going to want to eat you up! No worries, I'll protect you."

WTH? I followed because I was certain I'd cause more of a scene by resisting the nutty chatterbox.

"Um, okay," I muttered as she pulled me along behind her.

Dragons in human form wearing their finest eveningwear parted for her and nodded with respect. Some glanced at me curiously while others ignored me completely. Who was she? The woman didn't seem very powerful, but older Dragons could mask that. I certainly did. It was never wise to show your hand. Dragons loved a challenge almost as much as sex. I hated having to kill those who wanted to see if they could best me.

Was she the consort or mate of Nicolai the leader? I could tell she was mated by her scent, but it was faded—as if her partner might be dead. Her beauty was absurd, but I guessed she was a very old Dragon by the way she was treated. I said a quick thanks to the man upstairs that she'd been the one to grab me first. Without Seth, I was a lone female Dragon in a lair that wasn't mine. This silly woman was a lifesaver. I was beginning to think she was far older than I'd assumed.

We stopped aging in our mid thirties, but it was always obvious who our elders were.

"You can sit at my table," she went on as she greeted Dragons left and right.

"I'm actually meeting someone here," I told her as I was shoved unceremoniously into a seat at a large beautifully appointed table.

"Oh really?" she asked with raised brows and a kind smile. "Who?"

"Seth. Do you know him?" I asked cautiously. Dragons were quite unpredictable. The wrong name or expression could set off a three-alarm fire. I adored Seth, but maybe he was out of favor. I was certain he would become unpopular after his weyr found out who I was.

My crazy new friend clapped with glee and then placed her slim, well-manicured hands on either side of my face. "You're in luck! He's at this exact table. What a wonderful coincidence."

Her smile was contagious and she almost made me comfortable. Again I reminded myself, looks were deceiving. Trusting strangers made you sloppy. I had no time to be careless—there was too much at stake. This silly woman might seem kind, but in reality it could be a façade.

"I don't believe in coincidences," I said as I gently removed her hands and moved to a seat with my back against the wall.

"Neither do I," she admitted as she joined me and scooted close. "What do you think of some of the dresses here tonight?"

Her nose was scrunched, but her eyes twinkled with naughty delight.

"Well, um…I just got here and…" I started, not sure how to respond. My dress was scandalous. Where were we going with this?

"This is a party," she huffed. "Half of the women here looked like they walked out of a Victorian painting. I mean I loved living in the Victorian era, but come on that was centuries ago."

I was correct about her age.

"Well," I said as diplomatically as I could. "Some of the gals could have checked the calendar year as a style guide."

"Agreed." My benefactor nodded curtly and then turned her focus on me. "It's wonderful to see a new face. I don't believe we've met. I'm Elaina. Welcome to the Resistance."

"Thank you and, um…I'm a friend of Seth's," I replied with a wince of embarrassment at my lack of manners. Telling her my name could end the evening quickly. I needed Seth here for back up and to vouch for my character. Shit. Where was he?

The beautiful creature stared at me with shrewd eyes for a brief moment and then smiled. "Well, *Seth's friend*, it's nice to meet you. He should be along shortly. Tell me what you think of the gala."

I let out an inaudible sigh of relief that she didn't press for more information and didn't call security on me. These Dragons had the same goal as I did and I didn't want to have to kill them to save my own hide. As unsettling as it was I felt happy being amongst my own people again.

"I find it curious you're having a party at all," I told her truthfully. "It would seem that this would make you sitting ducks for my…for the monarchy."

"Oh my dear," she said kindly as she took my hands in hers. "When you don't know if there will be a tomorrow, you must live today to the fullest. And we have outstanding protection here."

She winked and gave me a thumbs up. I found myself grinning at her. She was a lot smarter than I had originally thought and she reminded me a bit of my mother. If the security was anything like what was in the parking lot, she was correct. No one had ever come up behind me before and lived to tell about it.

"Speaking of protection, you have a very um…overzealous guard outside," I said carefully, not wanting to insult anyone and end up a pile of ash on the floor.

"Yes," she laughed and nodded. "He's quite a character that one. However, there were far more out there than just the one you met."

"How do you know which one I met?" I asked, confused.

"Darling, you're a beautiful woman. He wouldn't have let any of the others near you. He's quite territorial that way," she confided with a smirk that seemed vaguely familiar.

Did I know her? I didn't think so, but when you live for almost 500 years you meet a lot of Dragons. And when you're the daughter of the most evil Dragon King alive, you meet more than your share. I couldn't place her. Odd.

"So the over-sexed jerk in the parking lot was an anomaly?" I asked with raised brows and a smirk of my own.

Elaina's giggle turned my smirk into a full-blown grin.

"Ohhhhh, he *is* one of a kind. I'd love to hear you call him that to his face!"

"I did call him a jackass," I offered up hoping to hear her giggle again.

She didn't disappoint.

"And you're still alive. Amazing," she said as she stared at me with open curiosity. "He doesn't take well to backtalk, but I'm quite sure he deserved it. His manners are somewhat boorish even though his parentage is impeccable."

"He doesn't have any manners at all as far as I could tell," I replied enjoying the gossip. Clearly she didn't think too highly of Parking Lot Rambo either. "He was quite powerful though."

"That's an understatement, child. There is no other like him anywhere in the world."

"Your leader, Nicolai must be happy to have the guard pig in the weyr—even as uncouth as he is," I said with a shrug as I remembered how good the big oaf's hands felt on me.

"An uncouth jackass and a guard pig," Elaina repeated with delight. "I don't believe I've ever heard anyone brave enough to call him that."

"You've been hanging out with the wrong people," I told her, liking her more and more.

"Perhaps you're right! Although you should probably know..." she started, but the rest of her sentence was drowned out by loud cheering.

"Who's here?" I shouted over the din.

"It's Seth," she yelled back as she pointed to the door. "Nicolai will be along in just a moment. This is protocol."

What the hell was she talking about? Was Seth part of the government of the Resistance? He never mentioned that little fact. In my experience the first in was the Seer. Was Seth the freakin' Seer? Oh my God, no wonder we hadn't had sex. Seers were celibate. Had he been playing me?

Kill me now.

I'd told the guard dog that I was mated to a damn Seer. Wait…I hadn't said Seth's name. Thank God for that. And I'd only told Elaina I was his guest.

I had to get the hell out of here. Immediately.

Of course there was one way in and one way out. Dragons were not stupid, but apparently I was. How had I trusted Seth? He'd seemed so wonderful and kind. We wanted the same thing—to end my father's reign of terror. I thought he was my boyfriend or at the very least, my friend.

I'd lost my edge where my people were concerned. We were not nice. We couldn't be trusted. We were foolish if we trusted others. I was all kinds of a fool, but I wasn't going to be a dead fool. I had a child and a limited amount of time left on this earth. I needed to accomplish my goal so my son could live in relative safety and not have to be on the run as I'd been for most of my life.

It was becoming abundantly clear to me that Seth had tricked me—lured me here to use me for leverage against my father. Little did he know, that wouldn't work. My father wanted me dead just as much as I wanted him dead.

Maybe these Dragons planned to hand me over to him in exchange for I don't even know what.

I was so out of here. Getting killed was something I could do all by myself. I didn't need any help in that department.

With my head down, I quickly edged my way along the wall toward the exit. Seth was moving into the room and I was certain their leader Nicolai was close behind. The excited chaos was to my advantage. I'd just get near the exit and slip out after the arrogant man in charge made his entrance.

Not my best plan, but it would have to do. Sadly my boobs were not working in my favor as every male I passed ogled them. I was going to kick Dwayne's undead ass if I made it out of here alive.

Nicolai was clearly a dawdler because the guard pig from hell was the next in. Time was not on my side. Seth was scanning the crowd for me. Getting out was my only goal. I had a trick up my sleeve that I would only use in the most dire circumstances. It was a gift from my mother. It hadn't saved her life, but it might save mine.

As Seth's eyes landed on me a huge gentle smile pulled at his lips. My God, his acting skills were impeccable. If I wasn't onto his plan for my demise, I'd think he was genuinely happy to see me. Note to self...have the words *gullible idiot* tattooed to my forehead. Never again would I trust a male Dragon. They were all bad.

Screw Nicolai, I didn't have the luxury of his entrance as a distraction to aid in my escape. Getting past Rambo presented a challenge, but as long as he wasn't behind me I could take him if I had to.

The midnight oil was burning and I only had seconds before Seth reached me. No time like the present to make the party more exciting.

"Move it, you uncouth, jackass guard pig," I hissed as I shoved hard at the enormous sexy Dragon and tried to get away.

The expression of shock on his face would have made me laugh if I didn't have to run like hell. Clearly no one had ever spoken to him as I'd just done. Asshole Dragons like him needed to be taken down a peg or two. It would be very satisfying to continue but I had death coming toward me at a rapid rate and no time to have fun.

Wait. What was happening?

The cheering had stopped abruptly and I could feel every eye in the room glued to me. The silence was deafening. This was not part of my escape plan. This was a clusterfuck. Who exactly had I just insulted?

A sick feeling rolled through my gut. I was pretty sure Rambo *wasn't* just a guard.

A stupidly sexy, evil smile lit his face and his attention was focused solely on me. For the briefest moment I wished that his smile was real and that he was truly happy to see me in the way a lover would be. His lust was unmistakable. Unfortunately mine was as well. Dragons had a distinct scent when aroused—a clean scent that could be best described as the ocean after a storm. Part of me wanted to run him over and get the hell out of Dodge and the other part wanted to run to him and wrap his strong arms around me.

However, there was my life to think about.

"Dima, my dear, I see you've met Nicolai," Seth said warmly as he took in the standoff in the entryway with interest.

"*This* is Dima?" Nicolai demanded as the smile left his face and his eyes narrowed to slits.

"Yes," Seth said as he stepped between me and his leader. "We spoke about this. You knew I was bringing her."

"The guard dog is Nicolai?" I asked with unhappy shock.

"Well, I suppose you could call him that," Seth said as he tried unsuccessfully to hide his grin.

"Seth is who you were meeting here?" Nicolai snapped as he pushed Seth aside and pinned me against the wall. "Our Seer is your *mate*?" he sneered in a whisper.

"Get off of me," I growled as I fought my death-wish of a need to press closer to him.

"Nicolai," Elaina admonished as she grabbed the deadly Dragon leader by the ear and pulled him back. "That is no way to treat a guest of your brother."

Nicolai and Seth were brothers?

"Mother," Nicolai snapped. "Leave this to me. There is much you don't understand here."

Oh. Hell. No. Elaina was their mother? I'd told her that her son was an uncouth jackass, guard pig. Was the sky going to fall next?

"I *understand* that your behavior is appalling," she hissed as she once again yanked him by the ear, throwing him off balance. "This will stop now."

"I was just leaving," I said stiffly and edged closer to the door.

All of the Dragons in the room were riveted to the scene. Tendrils of smoky aggression wafted around the room menacingly. My chances of survival were getting slimmer by the second.

"You're not going anywhere, *Princess*," Nicolai growled as his took my arm in a vise-like grip.

The hisses started low but gained volume as the crowd correctly pieced my identity together.

"Nicolai, unhand her now," Seth said in an authoritative voice I hadn't heard before. "This is the way it's destined to be. I've seen it. We can't succeed without Dima."

Ripping my arm away from a surprised Nicolai, I turned on Seth. "You," I hissed. "You are a liar and you betrayed me."

"Dima, you don't understand," Seth said gently as he approached.

"No, I understand too well," I ground out through clenched teeth as I realized the bastard Nicolai was blocking the doorway along with about ten other mean looking Dragons. "You're scum and I'm stupid. Good luck with your fight. I will have no part of this."

Seth continued to move closer along with his mother, Elaina. Gasps of outrage filled the room and several small fires broke out. God, I was a fool. Dragons were bad, myself included, but I was trying to make so many wrongs right. Letting these people stop me by using me as a pawn was not an option.

"Dima, calm down and let me explain," Seth pled.

He looked hurt by my accusations and a humorless laugh left my lips.

"You're really good," I said flatly. "And you're an arrogant ass from hell," I tossed over my shoulder to Nicolai. "But I'm better. I'd say see you later, but if I ever see any of you again, I'll kill you."

With that fabulously threatening last line I used my gift—the one I should have kept secret from all Dragons. Although when life or death was on the line, secrets meant absolutely nothing.

I waved my hands and in a fiery blast of shimmering golden smoke and fire, I disappeared. I knew they'd come after me, but they'd have to put out the massive explosive fire I'd created first. I had about an hour head start. I'd worked with less and succeeded.

I could work with this.

I had no choice.

I didn't need these Dragons to destroy my father. I'd been on my own for years. Keeping it that way was going to be the wisest move I could make.

My father was mine alone and I would succeed.

I had to.

Chapter 6

"Where's Daniel," I shouted frantically. "I have to get him out of here. *Now.*"

In a blast of fiery smoke, I arrived back at Essie's house in a panic. Essie, Hank, Dwayne and Granny flew into the living room coughing due to the thick smoke my arrival created. With wide eyes and shocked expressions they stared at me as if I was an alien.

"Sweet Baby Jane without mascara, did you just poof here from Chicago?" Dwayne asked as he swiped at the air to tamp down the glittery golden smoke.

"Yes," I said tersely. "Seth's a liar. They want to kill me and I don't have much time to get Daniel out of here and find a safe place to hide."

"Come with me. I'll take you to the Cows. I really do have homes all over the world," Dwayne said. His eyes began to glow and he levitated toward the ceiling.

"I'll get Daniel ready," Granny said, hustling out of the room on a mission.

Thankfully they'd all decided to stay at Essie and Hank's since I was going to meet Seth in Chicago. A one-stop shop was a very good thing right now.

"I want you to take Daniel away. They'll be coming after me first. It'll be safer for him if he's not with me," I ground out as I paced off the effects of transporting. I was dizzy and slightly nauseous. I'd only transported once in my life, at my mother's insistence and that was several hundred years ago.

"Are you all right?" Essie asked as she stomped out a few small fires on her living room floor.

"No. And I'm so sorry I've destroyed your house."

"No worries, I didn't like the carpet anyway," she replied as she led me to a chair and squatted in front of me. "Tell us what's going on."

Hank was right behind her. His fangs had dropped and he was dialing his cell. I assumed he was alerting Junior of the potential shitshow that was impending.

"Junior, it's Hank. Dima's back from Chicago. They tried to kill her. I'm putting you on speaker. Guessing we have some Dragons on the way to Hung."

"Well, sumbitch," Junior shouted. "I'll get re-enforcements and pull out the vat of solution. Any chance we could get the Cows down here?"

"No time," I said tersely. "I figure we have about an hour. I blew up the warehouse and they'll have to deal with that first. All of you will just be back up. Do you understand me?"

"Well, I can hear you, but I'm definitely not on the same page," Hank replied, snapping his fangs and clenching his fists. "We fight with you and that's an order. Period."

"Hank," I said evenly as I stood and tested my balance. "That's not the way it's going to go down. I want Daniel gone and then I'll meet the bastards on the beach. I plan to shift and fly like Satan himself is on my heels. I'll lead them away from Hung. You people are the best thing that's happened to me in hundreds of years. There is no way in hell I plan to watch you burn."

Hank's growl was low, but his displeasure was obvious.

"Should we fly Daniel to the Cows?" Granny asked as she ran back into the room with a sleepy and confused Daniel in her arms. As Vampyres, both Granny and Dwayne could fly.

My heart was in my throat as I stared at the beautiful child I'd created with a man I barely knew. Daniel was the reason I would fight to the death.

"No. I want you to drive. We can't take a chance that you'd come across the Dragons in the air," I said as I took my son in my arms and held him tight.

"What's wong, Mommy?" he asked, touching my face and snuggling close.

"Daniel, there are some bad Dragons that want to hurt us," I told him. Sadly my four year old needed the ugly truth. "Dwayne and Granny are going to take you far away from here and Mommy is going to make the bad guys leave us alone."

"Are you going to die, Mommy?" Daniel asked with a serious expression that didn't belong on the face of a child.

"I don't know," I said haltingly. "I promise with all I am that I'll do everything I can to come back to you, but you must always remember how much I love you. You mean more to me than anything in the world."

"Me can fight with you, Mommy. I will save you," he said as fat tears rolled down his chubby pink cheeks.

Words failed me as I held clung to my baby and memorized every part of him.

"Your Mommy is going to kick some major bastard Dragon ass and then we're going to party at my chateau in Paris," Dwayne said, gently taking Daniel from my shaking arms. "Give her a kiss for luck and we're going take you to meet some very wonderful—albeit somewhat odiferous Cows."

Daniel gave me a wet kiss and touched my face one more time. "You will win, Mommy. I know you will."

"Take him," I instructed. "Drive fast but stay safe. Junior, I want you to track them through the chip. Can you do that?"

"Yes ma'am," he said through the phone. "I'll know where they are every goddang minute. Hank, there are about six non-traceable burner phones in the junk drawer. Make sure Dwayne and Granny take a few and give the rest to Dima."

"On it." Hank sprinted to the kitchen.

"How many Dragons will come?" Essie asked as she filled squirt guns with the Dragon-shift prohibiting solution.

"There were about two hundred there, but I would guess they would send no more than three. It would be too difficult to hide that kind of attack and I'm not sure how valuable I am to them," I replied as I put several of the filled plastic guns into a bag for Granny and Dwayne.

I knew Dwayne could mind meld and blow up the Dragons, but I wanted them to have every conceivable weapon against my people.

"Not to mention a full on attack would be noticed by the Council and your father. They won't want that," Hank said, putting the burner phones in the bag and moving Granny, Dwayne and Daniel to the front door. "Take my truck, it's less conspicuous than the Hummer."

"Will do," Granny said. She squeezed my still shaking hands and looked me in the eye. "We're gonna get my daughter and son-in-law as well. They'll be extra protection for Daniel."

I nodded as my voice wasn't working. My throat was clogged with tears and a scream that I wouldn't let out with Daniel present. Essie's parents were stuck in their Wolf form, but they were deadly and they loved my son.

"Junior," I choked out. "How close are you to ruining my father financially?"

"Close, but not there yet," he said through the phone.

"You will keep several million out of what you get and use it for research to reverse the curse on Essie's parents. If you need more than that, you will take it. Are we clear?"

The room went silent and all eyes were on me.

"What?" I asked as I tore off the eveningwear and put on some fatigues that Granny had pulled for me.

"You've paid me back," Essie said quietly. "You owe me nothing for the rest of time."

"I can never pay you back, but if the money helps you find a cure you can have all of it."

Granny touched my face, her eyes swimming with tears. "You don't worry about Daniel. He'll be protected and happy always. You focus on comin' back to him."

I nodded curtly and armed myself as my world walked out the front door and left. A chill ran through my blood and the upset, shaky woman I was only moments ago was disappeared. My Dragon was very close to the surface and I embraced her. I was now the heartless killing machine that my kind was known for.

"I can't believe Seth pulled one over on all of us," Essie muttered in disgust.

"He's a *Seer*," I hissed as I pictured his lying horrible face. "And the best actor I've ever seen."

"A Seer?" Hank asked in surprise. "Seers are celibate."

"Hence the boobs not working," Essie grumbled. "I'd like to tear his head off."

"Get in line," I snarled. "I'm going to the beach to shift and wait for them. I have a fireproof bag at the bed and breakfast. Can you guys get it and load it with the phones and solution? You can put it around my neck after I shift."

"Um…guys?" Junior's voice crackled through the phone. "We've got incoming. I've got cameras along the shore and I'm seeing four flying fuckers landing on the beach."

71

"Only four?" I shouted as I sprinted for the door. I couldn't shift inside the house. It would tear it off its foundation. I needed to be outside.

"Yep, and they don't look happy."

"I call one," Essie said as she armed herself and took off ahead of me.

"No, I can take four," I muttered as I tore off the clothes I'd just put on. "Four will be a breeze."

Famous last words…

Chapter 7

Much to my extreme shock, the Dragons had shifted back to human form. I quickly did the same and gratefully accepted the loose dress Essie tossed me when I noticed Nicolai eyeing my naked body hungrily. He was a disgusting pig. He represented everything I hated about my kind—sex and death.

Thankfully, Junior was as good as his word. The beach was filled with Shifters of every kind and the air literally vibrated with hostility. I briefly wondered if Jimbob was here, but I had far more dangerous things to worry about—and all four were staring at me.

Nicolai, Seth, their mother Elaina and Boring Coat Taker Dude stood together at the shore- line and took in the scene warily. My stomach clenched as I remembered Elaina saying there was no one as powerful as Nicolai in the world. My only solace was that she'd never seen me fight. I had more to lose than they did and I would die for my cause.

"I told you the next time I saw you, I would kill you," I said calmly as I stepped forward leaving the packs of Shifters behind me. "So unless you plan on dying in the next five minutes, I'd suggest you leave."

"Dima, you've misunderstood what's happened," Seth said taking a tentative step forward.

"No, I didn't *Seer*," I growled as my Dragon demanded release. Holding her back was difficult, but I learned patience in my many years on earth. "You're very good, but I'm far better. Blackmailing my father for my release is futile. My father hates me as much as I despise him. Killing me is just stupid and shortsighted. You Dragons have hellacious intel if that's your pathetic plan. It's no wonder you've failed for hundreds of years."

Nicolai's growl of fury and the fire that sparked around him almost made me back up, but I held my ground. He was wildly overwhelming and ungodly beautiful. I despised him for igniting desire in me. He was evil and I needed to be smacked for being attracted to someone who would happily see me dead. Showing fear would be my downfall and I was not going to die.

However, I was terrified some of the Shifters on the beach might. I needed to take this battle elsewhere. The power emanating from behind me was enormous and I knew the Shifters would fight, but Dragons were not something to play with.

"Dima, we have no plans to trade or kill you," Elaina said as she, too stepped forward. "I knew you as a child and your mother was my friend."

She was no longer muting her power and she was tremendously strong. My gut felt sucker punched with her revelation and I now realized why I thought I recognized her only hours ago in Chicago. I vaguely remembered a group of women that had attended to my mother and Elaina's face was among them.

"You knew who I was the whole time?" I demanded angrily.

Were they all in on this?

"I did," she replied with a nod and a sweet smile. "Seth has seen this and we need you as much as you need us. The violence will not end unless we come together."

"I call bullshit," I snapped.

"It's true, you ungrateful *woman*. I don't want you anymore than you want us, but I trust my brother's vision more than I despise you," Nicolai ground out as he took his place next to his family.

"Back at you asshole," I growled.

It was all Nicolai could do to hang on to his temper and not go for my throat. I watched the struggle and enjoyed it thoroughly. His mother had hold of his arm and Seth stepped in front of him. Coat Guy just stood back and watched. Was he Elaina's mate? I didn't think so, but anything was possible.

"My mother tells the truth," Seth said in the same kind voice he always used. "I have seen many things and success will only be ours if we join forces."

"What else have you seen?" Essie demanded as she, Hank, and Junior moved to me and flanked my sides.

"Unbelievable," Elaina muttered as she marveled at the picture of Werewolves and Dragons united together. "She really is the link."

"I'm not a link," I corrected her rudely. "I'm a person with a mission and I have no time for incompetent Dragons to slow me down."

"This is ridiculous," Nicolai roared in fury as he paced behind his family. "We don't need her. Your vision is wrong."

"My vision is *not* wrong. And you know it," Seth told his brother. "Dima, what can we do to convince you we mean no harm?"

"Make the pissed off one apologize," Essie whispered in my ear as I barked out a laugh.

Her idea was ludicrous, but brilliant at the same time. If their powerful leader got down on his knees before me, it would set the right tone. However, I was certain it wouldn't happen in this lifetime. Male Dragons did not subjugate themselves to females—ever.

Time to see if hell would freeze over…

"I want Nicolai's apology and his word that this will be a two leader mission. I won't be treated as a subordinate if I decide to go with you." I crossed my arms over my chest to calm my erratic breathing and waited for the explosion.

Nicolai did not disappoint.

"Absolutely not," he roared as small fires lit the beach around him. "She is of the evil one's blood and I will not bow down to royalty as long as I breathe. She's worthless to us."

"Stop it," Elaina hissed at her son as she too lit up in flames of anger. "Get past your anger and your ego. This is not about you. It's far bigger than old vendettas. Our people's lives are at stake. Swallow your misplaced pride and do as she says. *Now*."

I held my breath and waited to see what the vicious Dragon would do. I was ready to shift in a second and part of me wanted him to shift as well. I was itching for a fight and I knew he would be an outstanding adversary.

"I will live to regret this," Nicolai muttered as he stalked toward me, giving his mother a glare of displeasure.

Damn, he was huge. Maybe this was a horrible idea. His ire rolled off of him and I still wasn't sure if he would burn me to a crisp. I kept my Dragon on call and met him halfway. It was the least I could do if we were going to be an antagonistic team.

He recognized my gesture and eyed me cautiously.

"Does her Highness want me on my knees?" he asked suggestively, thoroughly enjoying the sexual double entendre. He looked me up and down with undisguised lust and I wanted to slap his smug face.

"Yes, she does," I answered coldly as my insides danced dangerously with desire, imagining everything he could do to me in that position.

He was every kind of bad and all kinds of sexy. My hatred for him increased as he slowly and deliberately went to his knees in front of me.

"Next time I'm in this position I will not be begging for forgiveness. You will be begging for release," he whispered for my ears only.

My first instinct was to knee him in the throat, but that would be rather counter-productive. It would feel great in the moment, but wouldn't accomplish my goal of making him grovel.

I could feel his heat, desire and hatred all mixed together. It was heady to have him on his knees and it would be a cold day in hell before I let him go on his knees in front of me for any other reason than the one he'd chosen now.

"I can't hear you," I sang and gave him a smile that didn't come close to reaching my eyes. I was playing with fire and we both knew it.

Elaina wrung her hands and I heard Essie's gasp behind me. Nicolai's eyes narrowed to slits, but I kept the smile on my face and didn't back up even one centimeter. The Dragon had never met anyone like me—and never would again.

I'd been beaten down my whole life. I'd lived on the run for hundreds of years. I'd watched my family murdered in cold blood by my father. This man had a brother and a mother who clearly loved his insane ass. I had nothing but my son and I would move mountains to keep him safe. Nicolai was but a small rock on the mountain to me. He was nothing.

I just wished my rioting female insides would get on the same page as my vengeful brain. Lust was inconsequential. Sex was just an act to meet a need. He was beautiful—so what?

"My apologies, Princess," Nicolai said in a voice that could be heard by all on the beach. "I have always trusted my brother's visions and I shall trust this one as well. My regard for your despicable character is not of importance if we can accomplish our shared goal. I've worked with the enemy before and I can do it again. However, if you turn on us, I will kill you with my bare hands—and enjoy it."

"That was a shitty apology," Essie chimed in from behind me. "I'd make him do it again."

"I'd have to agree with you," Elaina said to Essie as she walked up behind her son and whacked him in the head. "You can do better than that. You certainly don't tell someone you're going to kill them while trying to convince them to come with us."

"Dear God," Nicolai bellowed. "What do you want me to do here? I've never apologized to anyone in my life. I'm doing the best I can."

"It's fine," I said as I bit back a laugh that I was sure would send him into a rage. "My apology would have been similar. He's an ass. I expected no less."

"I'm not sure your approval is helping me," Nicolai muttered as he stood and offered his hand. "I will work with you, not against you. I don't like you and I'm sure the feeling is mutual. As long as our goal stays the same, we will fight together."

"Well, you're correct about me not liking you, but I will concede that I've not been successful alone. I accept your crappy apology and I'll work with you until my father is dead and then I never want to lay eyes on you again."

"Likewise," he snapped.

I took his hand in mine and a zing of something unfamiliar shot up my arm. My eyes grew wide and I glanced up from our locked hands. His expression matched my own and he squeezed harder to see if it would happen again.

It did.

What the hell?

Feigning indifference, I pulled my hand back and met his gaze steadily. Whatever magic voodoo the son of a bitch had going on, I wanted no part of it. He wanted my father dead. I wanted my father dead. He would not get into my pants or my life. He was simply a tool for me to use to ensure my son's safety. That was all he was and all he ever would be.

"A truce has been reached," Hank called out to the Shifters as he approached Seth and they began to talk in earnest.

The Shifters on the beach slowly left and the horrible bloodbath everyone had been expecting was thankfully avoided. I'd made a deal with the devil, but at this point I saw no other way.

"Crazy rude dude is *hot* and he's got it bad for you," Essie whispered as she loaded me down with the solution and the burner phones. "I say do him."

"Nope, not going to happen. Dragons like him are nothing but trouble," I whispered back.

"But look at his ass," she insisted as Nicolai approached his brother and Hank. "That is a *fine* ass."

"It's fine all right, but he's an *ass* with a nice ass. I have no time for that."

"Make time, dude," Essie advised. "Tomorrow may never come. Live your life and own it. Make no apologies and have a least one massive big O before you bite it."

"I'll take it under consideration," I told her so she'd lay off.

Essie didn't understand my kind at all. If I had sex with the animal, all of my power would be negated. I needed to stay two steps ahead of the Dragons I was allying myself with. I still didn't trust any of them, but they could have come here and burnt Hung to the ground. I was alive and so were my friends. All four Dragons had taken their human forms, which was the most non-confrontational thing they could have done. They knew it and I knew it.

So unless they had another nefarious plan up their collective sleeve that involved my demise, I was going to have to trust them to a point. However, I would never trust them fully, just as I was certain they would never really trust me either—normal protocol for Dragons.

I envied the Wolves with their tight knit community and the way they had each other's backs. I'd never known that kind of life and I never would. I could only hope that after my father was gone I could meld back into Hung, Georgia with Daniel. I only had a few more months on this earth and I'd love to live them in peace. I wanted Daniel to have what was never possible for me.

"Dima, it's time to go," Elaina said kindly as she put her hand on my shoulder.

"Where are we going?" I asked as I watched the sun begin to rise.

"We have compounds all over the world, but we're going to the one in Upstate New York. It puts us close enough to the King yet far away enough to make our plans," she explained as she extended her hand to Essie in greeting.

"It's strangely nice to meet you," Essie said as she took Elaina's hand.

"You're the Wolf who can slay a Dragon, aren't you?" she asked Essie with fascinated interest.

"Yes, I am. I'd prefer not to do it again anytime soon, so please take good care of my friend Dima. You seem very nice, but I wouldn't hesitate to remove your head if I had to."

"Your loyalty is noted," Elaina said with a warm smile. "Dima's mother would be very happy indeed to know she has friends like you."

Her mention of my mother again, made my gut clench in pain. I wondered how much she knew of my mother's death. I kept my smile plastered on my face and hugged my friends good bye.

"I'll keep you posted on our *project*," Junior said cryptically as he lifted me into a bear hug and almost broke my ribs.

"We'll let you know how Dwayne's *vacation* is going as well," Essie added with a wink as she kissed my cheek.

With a sharp glance to Seth, I wondered if he'd broken his promise and revealed Daniel's existence to his family. I'd find out soon enough. At least I knew my baby was safe for the moment.

"You will call us or we will come after you," Hank said loud enough for the Dragons to hear.

"She's not our prisoner," Nicolai said flippantly. "She's free to do as she pleases. If it pleases her Highness to call her unlikely friends, she will not be stopped."

"Thanks, jackass," I said much to Nicolai's displeasure.

If he was going to refer to me as a royal, I would refer to him with all sorts of names in combo with the word ass. Two could play his game…and I would win.

"Are we going to fly in the daylight?" I asked wondering if I'd be stuck in a car with Mr. Asshead for twenty hours.

"No," Boring Coat Taker Guy said as he spoke for the first time since he'd arrived. "I can put a shield around us that will render us invisible."

"What in the hell are you?" Junior asked wildly impressed.

Coat Guy shrugged and smiled. "A Dragon Warlock—everyone's worst nightmare."

I swallowed hard and really looked at him. I'd not paid much attention the first time we'd met. He was the stuff of myths. As a child I'd heard stories about the rare Dragon Warlocks, but I never believed them to be true. He was handsome in a very non-descript way. He would easily blend in with a crowd and not be noticed at all. However, a Dragon like him was a dangerous adversary. I wondered how they'd found him. I'd always heard my father kept one prisoner, but I'd pushed that fairy tale aside. Now I wondered…

"Do you have a name, Dragon Warlock?" I asked, still staring at the myth come to life.

"I go by Lenny," he replied easily.

"That's not what I asked," I shot back equally as smooth.

"This is true," he agreed. "But at the moment it's all you will get. Possibly in the future you will receive more, but for now you haven't earned it."

"Whatever," I said dismissively. "In the future I won't even want it."

"Don't be hasty, child. No one knows what the future will bring and what we will want or need to know."

Lenny turned his back on me and walked to the edge of the ocean. If I didn't know he was real, I would have thought he'd turned into a statue.

Nicolai, Elaina and Seth watched the exchange with open-mouthed wonder.

"Dear God, I've never heard him string so many words together in my life," Seth said as he stared at me strangely.

Elaina nodded and laughed. "He must like you."

"He's an idiot," Nicolai muttered rudely.

"At least he's not an assbucket," I said sweetly.

"Enough," Elaina said to us as if we were children, not centuries old killing machines. "We must leave at once."

With one last smile at my friends, I shifted into my Dragon. The flow was seamless and my weak human form became my beautiful, powerful, sparkling golden Dragon. The gasps of everyone, including Nicolai filled my ears, but I ignored them.

I was free to be myself. With no clue how long my freedom would last I launched myself into the air and turned somersaults of happiness. The only thing that would make this moment perfect was if my child was flying with me. But everything I was about to do would make that precious moment possible.

Essie stood on the beach with Hank and Junior, laughing and waving. Elaina, Seth and Lenny shifted and joined me. Their Dragon forms were beautiful, but no one was as gorgeous and fierce as the man who hated me.

Nicolai's Dragon was huge, sleek and jet-black with glittering silver markings. His wing- span was twice mine, but I knew my smaller form would make me faster and more agile in the air—or at least I hoped it would.

Lenny huffed and blew an enormous cloud of purple smoke that rendered us invisible to my friends on the beach below. I was amazed at his skill and wondered how he did it. I'm sure they were all curious how I'd transported out of Chicago, but no one had mentioned it yet. I was sure an interrogation was coming, but they would learn nothing. My gift was mine and I wouldn't share its origin or its giver. Some secrets were meant to be kept.

With one last glance back, I joined my new comrades in flight. I'd never flown with my kind in a group and a small part of me was giddy with joy. I hid it well, but it felt so good.

I was off on a new adventure.

I just prayed it ended well.

It had to.

Chapter 8

"We have to break apart the inner circle," Nicolai said in frustration as he ran his hands through his dark hair. He paced the floor of the Command Room with wide strides as his top advisors watched him intently. "Direct attack hasn't worked and bribing the bastards to get on the inside has simply ended in the loss of millions of dollars. We've tried to take them in every conceivable way and always come up short."

"There have to be weaknesses in the inner circle we haven't found," Cade, the fierce looking Dragon lieutenant said pouring over maps and other stats of the enemy.

"Your work has been outstanding and your ingenuity humbling. We're getting closer. I can feel it," Nicolai told Cade as he spared me a brief glance.

The loyalty of his people was impressive. Over the last week I'd observed Nicolai be fair and collaborative. This was not the way I'd ever known Dragons to interact. We were an untrusting and violent race—or at least my father's regime was, and that was all I'd ever experienced of Dragon society. Furthermore, I'd lived among humans for several hundred years while hiding from my father. I was so out of practice with my own kind it was unnerving.

Of course Nicolai's disdain for me was unwavering and I returned the sentiment out of self-preservation. Even though I was now living amongst several hundred Dragons, an empty loneliness filled my hours, but that was nothing new. I missed the Werewolves and Vampyres desperately. Daniel filled most of my waking thoughts. I knew he was safe, but I missed him.

Stupidly, I longed for the same approval from Nicolai that he gave his people. It was silly and I dismissed it quickly. I'd been on my own for so long my need for acceptance was skewed. I didn't need his kindness or approval. I needed his army and his cooperation—nothing more.

Nicolai refused any title other than General but they treated him like a God. And from everything I had seen, the asshole deserved it.

"Sir, our intel has been spotty over the last few years and our only infiltrator was…" Cade said haltingly.

I was impressed they'd gotten anyone in at all. My father was quite particular when it came to whom he surrounded himself with.

"Was what?" I asked.

"Beheaded," Cade said quietly, staring at his hands. For a tough guy he seemed shaken by the loss of a comrade. They were bizarre to me. I was envious of this different kind of Dragon weyr.

"She was skinned alive then beheaded," Nicolai ground out, correcting his lieutenant and shooting me a withering look.

I stared back unflinchingly even though I wanted to heave. Of course the only way into my father's circle would have been through sex—hence a woman. I was sickened that they had even sent a woman.

I had nothing to do with my father's despicable ways and the sooner the bastard let go of that the sooner I would be trusted by his damn people. I was beginning to think coming here was a grave mistake on my part. I had a limited amount time and a lot to accomplish.

"Is there a reason you feel the need to punish me for my father's sins? I'm not the one who sent a woman to his weyr. However, *you did.*" My voice was as cold as ice and everyone in the room sat up straighter and became visibly uncomfortable. The hostility was thick.

"It was not my choice," Nicolai shouted and slammed his fists on the table in front of me sending paper flying everywhere.

The veins in his neck stood out and his Dragon was dangerously close to the surface. Had this woman been his mate? His lover?

"Our sister went on her own," Seth said quietly. "We knew nothing of it until it was far too late. I didn't see it coming."

The bile in my stomach rose and it was all I could do to hold back my own shift and go attack my father.

My God, I could end the regime on my own. No one else needed to die. My father wanted me dead. Maybe if I just showed up unexpectedly, I'd have a chance to kill him where he stood. I'd most likely die a violent death after the fact, but what was one life compared to all the lives he'd taken already? And I had something my father didn't have—something he'd never have. We both had hatred within us, but I had my son—and love was far stronger than hate. My son would always be loved and taken care of—I'd made sure of that. I just needed to make his world a safer place. That I could do. I had to.

I was now convinced my being here was wrong. Seth was the damn Seer. If he didn't see his own sister's death, why should I believe that he saw my help would end my father's reign of terror?

"It's not an exact science," Elaina said as she stood and put her hand on an ashen Seth's shoulder. "Seth's visions tend to the positive, not the negative. There is no way he could have known."

"I'm sorry," I said to Elaina and Seth. "Sorry is a paltry word, but it's all I have."

She nodded and sat back down.

"Blood is thick, Princess," Nicolai stated and stood his ground. "You have his blood. You have his ways."

"Actually it's not," I disagreed and went toe to toe with Nicolai. "It's rather watery and means little to nothing to my father. Ask my mother and my three brothers. Oh wait, you can't because he *murdered* them with his bare hands right in front of me. So if you believe my ways are similar to my father's, you are more of a fool than I thought you were to have insisted I come here in the first place."

Small fires began to ignite off of both Nicolai and me. Five more minutes and the entire room would be engulfed in flames.

"Stop it. Now," Seth said as he stood and came between his brother and myself. "My vision is clear. We will succeed together. It's the only way."

Silver smoke drifted ominously from Nicolai's nose and his eyes glowed a brilliant green. He wanted to tear my head off and I was feeling dangerously close to returning the favor.

He was dressed casually in jeans and a green t-shirt that matched his eyes. It was completely distracting and I stared at the table so I wouldn't kill him or jump him. The Dragons watched in rabid fascination wondering if someone—meaning me—was going to die.

Seth, Elaina and Lenny pulled Nicolai back while about a dozen more Dragons—male and female—sat forward and looked on.

The females watched Nicolai with hungry eyes, which infuriated me. We were here to figure out how to off my father, not get laid by an arrogant asshole.

Inhaling slowly and exhaling even slower, I made eye contact with Seth and decided to give it one more try. If they still refused to accept me I would leave—vision or no.

"My father's inner circle is solid," I said evenly, ignoring what had passed only moments ago. "They might not love him, but they're loyal."

"Why?" Seth asked.

I was no longer angry with Seth and he had regained my trust. He'd kept my secret about Daniel which was more than I'd expected. After a long talk, I'd realized he'd never led me to believe we were anything more than friends and he still treated me exactly the same as before.

He was a hugger and a hand holder. Seth was kind and affectionate with everyone. I wasn't jealous when he touched others. I just loved when he touched me. It was brotherly and protective. For him and for Daniel, I would try.

"Because he has something on everyone. That's how he works. If my father isn't blackmailing someone, he threatens the lives of the people his inner circle love. And they are not idle threats. He makes good on his promises."

I shuddered remembering how much pleasure he'd taken in tearing my older brothers and mother to shreds. It was hundreds of years ago, but the memory had played in my mind and my nightmares since the horrid day.

"So *she's* staying?" a leggy and obnoxious, beautiful blonde Dragon named Maria demanded, staring daggers at me.

Several Dragons around the large table hissed under their breath and I raised my eyebrows at the hostility. I had known it would be hard to win them over, but I was getting weary of the veiled threats. I'd been sleeping holding my knives the entire week. It was getting old fast. If Nicolai didn't show me respect, none of them would.

Maria was hot for teacher and saw me as a threat to her chances with Nicolai. I was very aware she didn't give a damn whose daughter I was. She was thinking with her crotch as most Dragons did. Maria and at least ten other horny female Dragons could not have been more wrong. I wanted nothing to do with the pig. The sexual chemistry between Nicolai and me was unavoidable and everyone had noticed, including Seth. Seth had even tried to talk to me about it, which didn't end well—for him.

"*She* has a name," I said calmly as I sat back in my chair and narrowed my eyes at her. "It's Dima and I'd suggest you use it...*Maria*. I'm equally as in charge as Nicolai and I will brook no insubordinate behavior. Are we clear...*Maria*?"

"I will listen to Nicolai, not her," she snapped angrily. "If *she* persists, I will challenge her."

The room went silent and my grin widened. Maybe I didn't have Nicolai's respect, but Maria had just given me the opening to get everyone else's. The entirety of the room watched with bloodthirsty interest. God, Dragons were so predictable.

"Ohhhh Maria, Maria, *Maria*, that's such a short sighted choice. However, I will accept your challenge. I've been itching to beat the hell out of someone the whole miserable week I've been here. Since it's not appropriate for me to kick Nicolai's ass being that we're partners and all, I suppose tearing you apart will suffice. Does sundown work for you?" I inquired politely.

Nicolai's audible grunt of displeasure at my show of disrespect for him somewhat satisfied my need to throat punch him—not completely, but enough to hold me over.

Elaina pressed her hand to her mouth to hide a small smile, but Lenny did no such thing. His grin was wide and his appreciation for me increased. That pleased me for some bizarre reason. He'd not spoken more than two words to me since we'd arrived at the compound, but I knew he was constantly watching.

"I didn't challenge you. I believe I said I was *going* to challenge you," Maria spat, but didn't completely back down.

"I beg to differ. I heard challenge, I accepted. And you will regret it," I explained slowly as if English was her second language. "Are you withdrawing?

"Of course not," she shot back angrily. "You have no idea what you've gotten yourself into."

Since what my kind understood most was violence, it was fitting that I fight someone to gain respect. Maria was an ideal choice. I didn't like her and she certainly didn't like me. However, she needed to respect me. They all did and if it took some bloodshed, far be it from me to decline.

"I look forward to it," I said. "Sundown or midnight?"

Maria wasn't quite as confident as she was only moments ago, but a Dragon never walked away from a challenge—ever.

"Sundown will be fine," she said with a sneer, making her attractive face ugly. "Dragon or human?"

Everyone waited in silence for my answer. Nicolai seemed particularly intrigued—he was most likely hoping I got my ass handed to me. He would be sorely disappointed.

I just shrugged. "Your choice," I told her. "I'll win either way."

Maria stood and turned her back on me—a blatant show of disdain. With a nod to Nicolai and the others, she left the room.

Slowly I let my glance scan the room, I made eye contact with every Dragon there. These were the lieutenants of the Resistance and if they didn't back me in here, they wouldn't back me in battle. I didn't know their pasts and I didn't care to, but they could not have been as violent and as horrific as mine. I didn't need their undying love, but I needed their trust and I needed to trust them in return.

"I'll say this once and then I'm done. I have been through hell and back so many times, I can't tell the difference anymore. The Marias in life don't bother me. I can tear them to shreds then go to a tea party. My heart is hard and I care about very little. However, my sense of justice and injustice is very clear. My life is dedicated to destroying my father like he destroyed my mother and brothers, along with countless others. I don't give a damn if any of you like me, but you will respect me or I will leave your petty Resistance and kill my father all by my lonesome." I took a deep breath and continued. "You have not succeeded alone, so I would suggest embracing my presence. According to Seth, without me you will continue to fail."

"I do believe you have not succeeded on your own either, *Princess*," Nicolai stated in measured tone as he watched me with an expression I could define.

It looked somewhat like begrudging respect, but I wouldn't lay money on it.

"This is true," I conceded. "But I have more reason than ever to destroy him. I have everything to lose. This makes me far more dangerous than I've been in all my 499 years, Asscrack."

"*What* did you just call me?" Nicolai asked with a disbelieving look of horror on his stupidly pretty face.

All eyes in the room were now wide with amused shock. Apparently irreverence *and* violence gained points with these fire breathers.

"Asscrack," I replied evenly. "However, if you're more comfortable with Assbucket or Asscanoe, I'll happily oblige. You stop with the *Princess* crap and I'll stop with the ass names."

Shaking his head and biting back a grin he nodded. "You win this round…*Dima*."

Damn it to hell, my name sounded like sex on his lips—and he knew it. I couldn't catch a break here if it bit me.

"So *Dima*, you say you're 499?" he asked with far too much interest for my liking.

"Are you deaf?" I shot back to titters from the peanut gallery of Dragons watching.

They were beginning to like me…maybe.

"Do you have a death wish?" he shot back with full laughter now coming from the occupants of the room.

"Some would say yes, but I would patently disagree," I said coolly—apparently I was a little hasty with the *like* thing. "The only death I wish for is that of my father. Anymore questions?"

"Just one," he said and crossed into my personal space.

His scent made me dizzy and I longed to either caress him or punch him—both would have satisfied. Although I was leaning toward the punch.

"Why do you have everything to lose? What is this *everything* you speak of?"

Me and my damn mouth. With a covert look at Seth, I raised my eyes to the man I couldn't stand and who made me want things I would never have. "That's for me to know and no one else to find out. Some secrets are meant to be kept, Nicolai. I'm quite sure you have some doozies."

"Does your secret affect the lives of my people?" he demanded with narrowed eyes.

"Only in that it will make me fight harder for the end of the man who wants all of us destroyed. And that's all any of you will ever need to know."

With that, I turned to walk out of the room. I was done playing nice with Dragons. The faster my father was eliminated, the faster I could leave and never lay eyes on any of these people again.

"One more thing, *Princess*," Nicolai said.

I ground my teeth at the repeated mention of my title and waited.

"Try not to kill Maria tonight. The Resistance can't afford to lose too many."

He raised an eyebrow and gave me a smirk that made me like him a little, not that he ever would know. I shrugged and gave him a mock salute.

"I'll do my best, but that will depend on her, Asslump," I replied as I turned on my heel and left.

The laughter and shocked gasps from the Dragons in the room were music to my ears—not to mention Nicolai's indignant, furious grunt. But this was too difficult to keep up for long. My inner Dragon had ideas about Nicolai that were not going to happen in this lifetime—tamping her down was becoming increasingly exhausting. Not to mention constantly watching my back sucked.

Being around so many of my own kind was waking up my sexual appetites—it wasn't Nicolai at all. Maybe I should find someone here to put out the fire. It might clear my head and make my inner Dragon shut the hell up. However, the best scenario was eliminating my father and getting out of here as quickly as possible before I did something stupid.

There were many reasons my being here was a bad idea…the very least of them was my attraction to the man who clearly hated me and I despised in return. They didn't want me here and I didn't want to be here, but I was practical enough to realize I needed them. They just had to realize they needed me as well.

My father's downfall could not come soon enough.

***

"You probably shouldn't kill her," Lenny said as came from out of nowhere and caught up with my brisk pace.

It was almost sundown as I made my way to the outdoor training area of the compound. It was enormous, as we were Dragons after all and needed an absurd amount of space when we shifted. Lenny's company was a welcome relief from my own jumbled thoughts.

Lenny shortened his stride. His legs were much longer than mine.

"Why's that?" I asked. "She's disrespectful and I'm losing ground here. I don't have time to slowly earn trust. One quick beheading and I'm in," I said half-joking half-not.

The thought was actually repugnant to me. In my long life, I'd only killed in self-defense or in defense of someone else. Sadly, I'd had to defend myself repeatedly over the years and I had become quite adept at ending lives. My father's assassins were never far behind me. I realized early on that you didn't have to like something to be good at it.

"You'll be sorry," Lenny said.

"Lenny, the cryptic stuff isn't really working for me. If you've got a point, then get to it. I would hazard a guess that Maria is going to go for the kill. I'd also guess that she's a sloppy and easily distracted fighter by the way she conducts herself in life. She's also stupid."

"Really?" Lenny asked with a slight grin.

"Yep. She's stupid because she's fighting me over a man. A man I don't want—a man who utterly disgusts me. She could die because of petty jealously. Men are simply not worth dying for."

"All men?" he asked, pulling me to a halt and making direct eye contact.

My stomach lurched as I wondered what he meant. Did he know about Daniel? He had powers I couldn't even begin to explain—could he read minds? I stared back evenly and considered my words carefully.

"There is one male I would die for. I'd die for him happily," I said holding his gaze. "Is that the answer you were looking for?"

"It is," he replied with a knowing smile.

"It's not Nicolai," I blurted, then smacked myself in the head and quickly resumed walking. Oh my God. Where in the hell did that come from?

Lenny chuckled, nodded and kept pace next to me. "No one knows what the future will hold."

"Lenny you're kind of a walking nightmare and you're starting to ride my nerves."

"Yes, well, I'm good like that," he replied. "But back to the matter at hand. Don't kill Maria."

"Is that all I'm going to get here?" Frustrated didn't begin to cover my feelings. I was almost ready to have a go at Lenny.

"Do you want more?"

"It might be a bit helpful," I snapped sarcastically as he tried to suppress a grin.

He failed.

"She's your niece."

He watched my horrified reaction for a brief moment and then vanished into thin air.

WTH?

Maria the leggy, rude, blonde pain in my ass who wanted to bang Nicolai was my niece? What were the odds of that? One of my brothers had a child? They were certainly of age to have mated when they were murdered, but wouldn't I have known about it?

Was Lenny full of shit?

Could my life get anymore complicated?

Actually, it would be easy to tell if Lenny was lying. I just needed to see Maria's mark. If the Warlock Dragon was telling the truth, it would match mine and Daniel's.

If Lenny lied, it wouldn't.

Chapter 9

God, she was stupid. Instead of readying herself for a fight that could potentially end her life, Maria was busy sucking up to Nicolai. If she was truly my relation, I prayed there weren't more of her.

The outdoor training area was well maintained and the covered bunkers that flanked the fields were stocked with weapons. The Resistance was definitely trained and prepared, but taking on a regime that had been around for at least a thousand years was no simple matter.

If I had to guess, I'd say all two hundred Dragons had come out to observe the match. This was going to be tricky. If Maria was my niece I wouldn't fight her. I couldn't.

There was one sure way to find out.

Without breaking or slowing my pace, I walked right up to the wildly inappropriate flirt-fest and grabbed Maria by the hair. Deciding to ignore my reaction to seeing Nicolai flirting with another woman, I focused on the tall blonde that might or might not be related to me. Nicolai was not mine and I didn't want him. I'd deal with my own stupidity later—or maybe never. Ignoring my underused girly parts was probably the safest way to go.

Taking Maria to the ground was simple. Holding her squirming body—not so much.

"Excuse me," I said politely to the gathering Dragons. "I have to check something before the showdown."

"Get off of me, bitch," she screamed as I put my knee on her spine to incapacitate her.

Damn she was strong.

"In a minute, sweetheart," I growled as I moved her hair aside to examine the base of her neck.

My vision narrowed to almost darkness as I stared at the mark of my family clearly embedded in her skin. I gasped and rolled off of her as I tried not to throw up. How was this possible? How was I unaware that one of my brothers had fathered a child?

In my shock, I didn't even see her coming. The blow to my head was impressive, but I didn't have time to deal with a headache or getting busted on by a woman I had no intention of fighting. I should have been protecting her my entire life. I wasn't about to spill her blood.

However, she wasn't on the same page.

She ran at me like a freight train from hell. She was sloppy and unfocused, just as I'd suspected. Who in the hell trained her to fight? She was a hot mess. Watching her, I was surprised she'd lived as long as she had.

With ease I moved to my right and stuck my foot out. She went tumbling like a mini tornado clear across the ring. I was going to have to educate this Dragon on how to defend herself.

"Enough," I shouted and willed crystal pink flames to burst from my hands and upper body much to her shock and the shock of the Dragons hoping for a bloody fight.

Maria stood several yards away, literally frothing at the mouth—highly unattractive.

"What's the matter?" she screamed, clearly furious and embarrassed, but thankfully not completely daft enough to run toward the deadly fire flowing out of me. "Are you afraid of me?"

"Hardly," I shot back as I searched for a resemblance to my long dead brothers. "Who is your father?"

The Dragons, very confused, began to murmur unhappily amongst themselves. They were primed for a bloodbath and it wasn't happening.

"None of your fucking business," she spat.

"Filthy language is not necessary," I hissed. Maria needed to learn some damn manners. "Don't make me repeat myself."

"I don't have to tell you anything," she shouted.

"Name your father," Nicolai demanded as he stepped up and stood next to me.

Startled that he'd taken my side I let the deadly flame recede a bit so I didn't blow him to Kingdom Come. That wouldn't go over well at all.

"What are you doing?" I hissed quietly, wondering if he was going to try to take me out.

"I'm not sure," he said with a half smirk and a shrug. "Call it Dragon intuition, but for the moment, I'm with you. And the pink fire is kind of hot."

Before I could process if Nicolai was making fun of me or hitting on me, Lenny poofed in from out of nowhere much to the delight of the antsy Dragons.

"You heard your leaders," Lenny stated with an eerie calm. The crowd hushed. Clearly they never heard him speak much either—or maybe it was fact that he'd referred me as their leader along with Nicolai. "Name your father."

The silence was long as I watched Maria struggle with the turn of events. Part of me wanted to take her in my arms, but that would be as welcome as death to her at the moment.

"I don't know," she whispered harshly. "I don't know who my father is."

"You mother?" I questioned.

She eyed me with hatred and looked to Nicolai who nodded curtly.

"My mother was Christina."

My fire receded completely and I dropped to my knees.

"How old are you?" I choked out as I realized which of my brothers she resembled.

"I'm 485," she said, now watching me strangely.

She was the daughter of my brother Sean. He'd loved Christina with a passion, but refused to mate and have children because of my father's deadly wrath—or so I'd thought.

"You said was. Is your mother alive?" I asked already knowing the answer.

"No," she hissed, furious again. "My mother was murdered by *your* father when I was a child."

"Shall I rephrase that last sentence for you?" I asked as I got back to my feet and pushed the nausea I felt aside.

"You make no sense," Maria snapped. She was ready to go at me again now that my flames were gone.

I didn't blame her. When she heard what I had to say next, she was going to burst into flames.

"You mother was killed by your grandfather and your father was my brother, Sean," I said flatly, waiting for a tirade of swearing from her or at the very least a spear of fire aimed at my head.

No such tirade came. Maria said nothing as her eyes rolled back in her head and she passed out cold on the ground.

Again I didn't blame her.

Our family lineage sucked.

"Well that certainly answers a few questions," Nicolai said as he snapped his fingers and several Dragons ran to attend to the unconscious Maria.

I wanted to go to her as well, but knew my welcome would be iffy.

"Her marking has always confounded me," he said as he lifted my hair and examined my neck.

Little shocks of heated desire shot though me at the touch of his warm fingers on my skin. Roughly I pulled away and turned to face him.

"I suppose you've been all up in Maria's neck," I snapped and then closed my eyes and pinched the bridge of my nose hoping everyone would disappear if I couldn't see them. I sounded like a jealous lover. This was all kinds of inappropriate and unprofessional.

"No," Nicolai said with a grin that made him ungodly beautiful. "All of my people's markings are known to me. Unfortunately the only neck I *want all up in* right now is yours," he added under his breath.

Stupidstupidstupid. I was making a mess of things and I needed to regain some kind of upper hand here. What the hell would distract a weyr of Dragons from sex and shocking revelations?

Blood.

I could do that. Violence would help me work out the forbidden sexual tension flowing through my veins.

"Since I will not fight my brother's child, I will accept challenges from anyone that would like to have a go at me," I called out.

Nicolai's eyebrows shot up. I was unsure if he was disappointed he wasn't going to get laid by a princess or if he was now positive I had a death wish. It didn't matter. Being around him right now was far more dangerous than slaying Dragons.

Fighting I understood. What was happening between me and Nicolai—not so much.

The challenges came fast and furious—four men and two women stepped forward. So much for thinking they were beginning to like me. Again, I didn't need their friendship. I needed their respect and after tonight, I would have it. It would come at a cost, but what in my life hadn't thus far?

"Dragon or human?" I shouted to my challengers.

"Dragon," the bloodthirsty crowd chanted.

"So be it," I muttered as I removed my clothing and let my body shift into my Dragon.

The feeling of freedom and rightness overwhelmed me as my body went from skin and fragile bone to massive gossamer wings and glittering golden scales. My vision was clearer and the air smelled sweeter. If I had my way, I'd spend all my time like this. Although, I wouldn't be fighting…I'd simply fly.

"You will engage with her one at a time," Nicolai instructed over the din of the excited Dragons. "And there will be no fight to the death. If *anyone*," he said giving me a narrowed eyed sideways glance, "goes for the kill they will be taking *me* on. Am I clear?"

His people nodded to him and went to their knees. For a guy who despised royalty, he had his people trained to a tight protocol.

"Begin," he shouted.

And we did.

The first four—two men and two women—were a breeze. I sustained some bloody injuries, but to me they were mere nuisances. The blood flow and damage to my challengers were far more severe, but they would live. If this was an accurate representation of the fighting prowess of the Resistance, it was no wonder they were losing the war.

"This is ridiculous," I huffed. Pink and purple flames left my jaws as I spoke. "This is child's play. These are the best you have?"

My large body shimmered in the quickly setting sun. A menagerie of rainbow colored points of light covered the ground around me as the sun bounced off my shiny scales and I knew I looked every inch the Princess I was. The Dragons pointed and whispered. A few danced in the sparkling lights. I was curious if Maria had gold in her hide when she shifted. I'd have to wait and see.

My last two challengers backed away. This was boring and the crowd echoed my sentiment. My Dragon itched for a real battle, but apparently it was not to be.

"I challenge you," came a familiar voice from below.

Oh shit...beware of what you wish for.

Nicolai removed his clothes and shifted quickly into his Dragon. It was fluid and gorgeous. I admired him and assessed him for weakness. I couldn't find any. His massive body gleamed and his silver makings seemed to dance along his skin. This would be satisfying and my Dragon approved.

"The rules remain the same," he said. His voice in his Dragon form was deeper and unfortunately even sexier. "We fight until I pin you."

"Or until I pin you," I corrected him to cheers and shouts from the crowd.

"Never happened. Never will," he shot back with a huff of laughter that produced an orange flame dotted with black and gold glitter.

"First time for everything, Big Boy," I said as I took to the air and waited. My body trembled with pent up aggression and sexual frustration. Nicolai was about to receive the brunt of it.

"Rule number one," I called down to him as he watched me hover above the tree line. "Never screw with a pissed off female Dragon."

"Oh I'll screw with you," he threatened as spread his massive wings and soared up to me. "But it will be in the privacy of my suite after I pin your golden ass to the ground, beautiful."

"And if I win?" I questioned, tamping down my excitement at the thought of laying underneath him.

"I'll still let you take me to my suite," he bargained arrogantly.

"In your dreams."

And so it began—on a dare and some innuendo.

The Dragons went wild. Neither Nicolai nor I held back. The massive fires and blood flow from both of us were proof. I'd never had such an equal adversary in my life and I'd not had fun like this in ages—granted it was painful fun, but fun for a Dragon was slightly different than it was for the average Shifter.

Nicolai fought with a viciousness that would have left me speechless if it didn't delight my inner Dragon to the point she wasn't sure if she wanted to fry him or mount him. Thankfully I was still in charge and we did neither.

Short of killing blows we went at each other like the animals we were. And it was glorious.

"You ready to call it?" Nicolai snarled as he took swipe at my midsection with the tip of his razor sharp wing.

He connected and I went hurtling backward in the air. A tree caught my trajectory and I bounced off and recouped. That was going to leave a scar even in my human form. I'd escaped most of his truly crushing blows as I was far more agile in the air with my smaller, sleeker form. Due to my speed and deadly accuracy, I'd gotten in just as many punishing blows as my cocky challenger.

"I won't ever call it, Dragon Boy," I hissed as I ran my talons down his back drawing blood and an enraged roar from him.

I laughed with joyous abandon knowing I had scarred him. Thinking too deeply about having left my mark was a mistake. However, enjoying my last blow was an even bigger error.

He came like a tsunami and knocked the breath out of me as we went hurtling to the ground. Clouds and trees zipped by at warp speed as I desperately tried to regain the upper hand. His body weight and size made it impossible. We landed with a jarring thud, but the impact was minimal.

WTH?

I opened my eyes and stared into the amused and victorious green eyes of the Dragon beneath me. He'd taken the brunt of the fall so he didn't crush me. While the girly part of me was all a flutter my Dragon part was miffed. I didn't need the arrogant leader of the Dragon Resistance to cushion my fall. I'd cushioned my own falls—always.

"I say we call it a draw," Nicolai said as he rolled me off of him and shifted back to human.

I followed suit and quickly searched the area for something to cover my nakedness. Nicolai just walked around butt to the wind shaking hands and speaking with his people. The simple fact that I was tentative about being naked was proof that I'd been away from normal Dragon life for too long. Nakedness was simply a nonissue for a Shifter. I was the odd one—or maybe it was because the idiot who had sort of let me win was watching me far too intently.

"Here you go, child," Elaina said with a twinkle in her eyes as she handed me a robe. "You're very impressive. I've never seen anyone but Lenny or Seth give Nicolai such a run for his money."

"He wussied out at the end," I said with a dismissive shrug. "He won, yet he lost by a technicality of a false landing."

"Sometimes you don't win by winning, my dear," Elaina said easily as she took my hand and led me into the chattering crowd. "Sometimes a consensus is far more beneficial."

"Consensus?" I asked as I noticed a distinct change in attitude from the Dragons toward me.

"Yes. Consensus. I like the word far better than compromise. In a compromise there is always a loser. In a consensus there are two winners." She smiled and slipped away.

I laughed. Elaina was another one who liked to drop bombs of wisdom and then walk away. Seth and Nicolai were very fortunate to have her as a mother. I definitely would remember the consensus versus compromise one. I would keep that handy for Daniel.

I was alone amidst Dragons who only an hour ago wanted to see my blood spilled on the ground. Now I was being asked pointers on fighting and getting compliments on my killer instinct and sparkling golden scales. It felt wonderful and for a brief moment I was grateful to the arrogant man who clearly knew what he was doing. He let me keep my pride for the most part, but demonstrated to his people that he had my back as well.

Crap. Staying pissy and rude to him was going to be childish now. However, I had a real child to think about and getting involved with a Dragon who had an ego the size of several states wouldn't fly. He would never accept my child and I would never accept a man—even for one night—who would not want my son.

Easy peasy.

Or not…

Chapter 10

"I will not open it. I will not open it. I will not it," I whispered frantically to myself as I tossed and turned in my enormous bed. "I. Will. Not. Open. It."

The knocks at the door of my suite came hourly all night long. And hourly I ignored them. I knew he could bust it down if he felt so inclined and I was fairly sure he had a key, but he waited for me to let him in—very un-Dragon like. His politeness, even though he was keeping me up all night, confused me. Nicolai was a mass of contradictions.

I couldn't let him in. If I did, I knew exactly what would happen. My focus had to be on the mission not the missionary position...not that I imagined something so bland would be Nicolai's position of choice.

Sleep was impossible, so I simply counted the minutes until the short sharp knocks would resume.

He didn't disappoint and he didn't give up.

This was going to be a problem.

***

The day dawned bright and chilly. I'd barely slept a wink, but for some reason my mind was clear. Most likely it was the newly acquired acceptance I'd gained from the

Dragons. It was a relief and now that I had their trust, it was time to come clean and give them mine.

I'd held back sharing the plans to empty my father's accounts and sell off his property holdings. I'd needed to withhold information incase the Resistance rejected me. Nicolai would be unhappy that I'd held such an important card close to my chest, but so be it. Maybe, he would get angry enough to leave me alone.

Doubtful but possible. Damn it, the thought of him giving up depressed me.

Hell, I was a mess and the day had just begun.

"Your fighting was impressive last night, Sir…I mean Ma'am…I mean Co-General," Cade stuttered as heat crawled up his neck and landed on his handsome and now mortified face.

"Dima. Call me Dima, Cade," I told him with a grin as I shook his hand and looked around the Command Room. Thankfully the animosity from the other Dragons toward me was gone. "I'll even answer to *hey you* as long as you're polite. But if you call me Princess, I'll take your ass out."

"I'm the only one allowed to call her Princess," Nicolai said as he came up behind me and deftly moved me away from Cade.

"What are you doing?" I hissed as he smiled and waved to the entering Dragons while pushing me across the room and away from everyone.

"Listen to me and listen to me carefully," he said tersely. "Not real sure what's happening here, but I just wanted to tear the head off of my best friend. I've known Cade for three hundred years. Because he was talking to you and you touched him, I wanted him dead where he stood. I don't like this. I don't understand it. But I'm having a *hard* time controlling it. Pun intended."

Glancing down, I realized he wasn't fibbing. The bulge in his pants was enormous and my knees went weak. However, he was insane if he thought I wasn't going to speak with the male lieutenants. I was one half of the team leading these people. I needed to have their backs and they needed to have mine.

"Um…not gonna fly, dude," I told him, slapping my hands on my hips and raising my defiant gaze to his. "I'm not hitting on anyone here, not that it would be any of your business if I was, but you will not tell me who I can speak with."

"Do you like Cade?" he inquired stiffly.

"He seems like a nice person," I replied with an eye roll.

"Well, I like him a lot and I *really* don't want to kill him. He's my closest friend other than my brother. So I would greatly appreciate if you're going to speak to him or any other male you keep at least six to ten feet between you and said male," he growled and then banged his head against the wall. "I can't even believe I'm saying this shit."

"Neither can I," I said. "Were you really going to kill him?"

"Yep, I was. I almost shifted right in the room, which would have blown the walls out. So until I figure out what the problem is, will you be a good girl and do as I ask?" he implored with his eyes closed and his hands in his hair.

"What about Seth?" I asked as I watched his brother enter the room.

"What about him?"

"Can I talk to him?" I snapped sarcastically.

Nicolai glanced over at his brother and winced. "Not sure. I think I'm good with Lenny, but that might be it at the moment."

"You know, this will be a clusterfuck in a battle," I said as I watched Maria enter the room and peer around warily.

I assumed she would avoid me. I would simply wait until she was ready to make the first move.

"Yes," he growled. "The thought has crossed my mind. I'll talk to Lenny and my mother after the meeting and I'll get this fixed. In the mean time, don't talk to the men."

"I can't…"

"Okay," he conceded with a groan. "You can talk, but at a distance. And for God's sake don't smile at any of them or touch them. That would equate to you being responsible for me having to burn them alive. We clear here?" he inquired with a pained expression.

"Yep," I told him as I very carefully walked away, hugging the wall so he didn't eliminate any of his friends—or God forbid, family.

"Dima," Seth called out as he crossed the room headed straight for me. "You were magnificent last night."

Oh hell no, he was coming in for a hug. I ducked and tried to avoid the incoming affection, but Seth was persistent.

"Stay away from her," Nicolai bellowed.

The room went silent and everyone stared at me and then Nicolai—then me and then Nicolai—as if we were opponents in a tennis match. If the stakes weren't so dire, I would have laughed.

"I'm sorry, what?" Seth asked, confused as he backed away from me cautiously.

"Dima has…" Nicolai started and clearly had no clue where to go.

"A cold kind of thingie…of sorts," I lied and then closed my eyes and shook my head in embarrassment.

Dragons were impervious to disease. I was thinking on my feet but my balance was way off because of the idiot with a monster erection who wanted to murder all the men in the room.

"She's somewhat claustrophobic." Nicolai came up with another appallingly ridiculous reason and I bit back my laugh with effort.

"Actually, it's that I'm, you know…um, dangerous because I sometimes light up like the Forth of July," I tried again, completely at a loss for anything that made sense. We were Dragons for God's sake. Fire didn't affect us at all.

"With no warning," Nicolai added. "So touching her could give someone a nasty um…booboo." He finished lamely and then banged his head on the wall again.

"You did not just say *booboo*," I choked out on a strangled giggle.

"Yes. Yes I did," Nicolai grumbled in disgust.

Seth's smile practically split his face and I thought I saw him give his mother and Lenny a look. What the hell was going on here? Did he know what Nicolai's murderous issue was about? If he did, he was going to fix it fast. I was clear that Nicolai preferred the male lieutenants in the room not be aware that they were at risk of being burnt to ash. I would respect that, but this had to end—immediately.

"All right then." Seth was still smiling. "Let's get down to business. I'd like to rearrange the seating a bit here so I can divide people into teams. Ladies, you'll be at the far end of the table and gentlemen you'll be on the near side. I'd like our Generals to take the ends of the table. Dima, please follow my mother. And Nicolai, you will come with me."

I heaved a sigh of relief and watched Nicolai do the same, for the moment everyone was safe. The Dragons stood and followed Seth's directive without complaint, but they were still giving Nicolai and me strange looks. I didn't blame them.

Seth clearly knew what was happening. I just hoped he could solve it quickly.

Maria was to my right and refused to make eye contact. Now that I knew she was my brother's child, the resemblance was uncanny. I longed to touch her, but I didn't dare. She would come to me in her own good time and I wouldn't force it. The thought that she'd survived over four hundred years without my protection clawed at my insides, but she would never go unprotected again. I also had plans to teach her how to fight. She was a disaster waiting to happen.

"I think we can make inroads if we can get to the King's finances," Cade said as he opened a laptop and began pulling up spreadsheets.

"That's next to impossible, we've tried," another lieutenant named John said. "His accounts are world wide and…"

"Can I stop you?" I asked as Nicolai tensed and watched me like a freakin' hawk. Ignoring his ridiculous behavior, I went on. "I was going to bring this up today. Until I had your trust, I held back some of the plans I already have in motion. I'm comfortable with including you now."

"Go on," Nicolai said as his lips thinned with displeasure.

Maybe I could piss him off so much he wouldn't want to kill his buddies…

"My father's accounts and properties are being hacked as we speak. My plan was to strip him of all assets and let his regime crumble. His wealth and properties are his hoard. Destroy the Dragon's hoard—destroy the Dragon. In the chaos that would ensue as his inner circle and army were no longer funded, I was going to strike."

"Alone?" Seth asked, appalled.

Nicolai's fist hit the table and he swore viciously. All eyes in the room turned to me. I wasn't sure if he was angry I'd withheld the information or if it was me going in Rambo style to kill my father.

111

"That's not the best plan I've ever heard, dear," Elaina said kindly as she patted my hand. "However, now you have the Resistance behind you and you've opened up a very fortuitous opportunity for us."

I smiled and let out an audible sigh of relief, but it was a bit premature.

"Let me get this straight," Nicolai said so calmly, most Dragons at the table blanched. "You were going to go in alone and take out your father."

"Yes," I said. "Your hearing is outstanding."

"Your death wish is extreme," he shot back angrily. "What the hell is wrong with you?"

I'd had about enough of the dictator at the end of the table. "I have a small window of time in which to accomplish my goal," I ground out. "As of a week ago, I was on my own just as I have been most of my life. Now, I have an army behind me. I'm no longer going in solo. Drop it and be happy that my father will be in financial ruin shortly."

"I won't drop it until you tell me why you have such a specific window," Nicolai stated as he sat back and crossed his arms over his massive chest.

"Not important and none of your business," I informed him and then ignored him. "Back to the matter at hand. My friend, Junior is a computer hacking genius. I had most of the passwords so it saved some time. We're also going after the land and all offshore accounts."

"Junior?" one of the females named Lena asked.

"He's an alpha Werewolf and before anyone makes a disparaging remark, please understand I will smackdown hard on any of you who speak poorly of my friends. I'm part of a very mismatched pack including Werewolves, Vampyres and Were Cows. They accepted me and my...I mean me when no one else would and I would die for them."

"Did she say *Were Cows*?" I heard someone whisper.

"She did," another whispered back.

"I did. They exist, no thanks to my father's hatred of them, and they're wonderful," I informed the room. "I also think at this point I should ask Junior to come here. It would be faster and safer for all of us for me not to be communicating with him by phone. I'm using an untraceable burner, but still…"

"So you'll be quite rich when all is said and done, Princess," Nicolai commented in an unpleasant tone.

I put my head down for a brief moment so I didn't zap his ass to hell with a fiery blast. "I'm already rich," I countered coldly. "I've earned every cent I have, legally. Every last bit of money that's gained by wiping out the monarchy is going to charity and to research a cure for the wolves that my father had a hand in trapping in their shifted form, Asshole."

Lenny's eyes shot to mine and he looked at me curiously. In fact, all eyes were on me and they were baffled.

"What the hell is the problem here?" I demanded. "Are all of you so prejudiced that you have a problem with the Wolves? They're saving our asses."

"I can vouch for the Wolves and the Vampyre," Seth said, much to my relief. "They're trustworthy and have no issue with us."

Looks were traded amongst the Dragons. A few questions were asked and even though they were wary they also seemed fine with the strange turn of events.

"So with your blessing, I'd like to have Junior come here," I told the table.

"You don't need our blessing, child," Elaina said. "You're leading us along with Nicolai and we will follow."

"Is Junior the big one that hugged you on the beach?" Nicolai demanded as he stood up looking quite murderous.

"Yep," said with a grin and my middle finger lifted. "He sure is."

"Meeting adjourned," Seth said quickly as he pushed his brother back down in his chair. "Cade, I want you to run drills with our people. After the less than stellar performance last night, I'm concerned many of them are not ready to fight."

"Yes, sir." Cade bowed and then saluted. "Dima, I'm very glad you're here and I'd like to personally apologize for any disrespect that I've shown."

The others nodded in agreement with Cade's statement of regret.

"Thank you," I said. "However, trust must be earned and I probably would have behaved the same. We're not a race that puts faith in much."

"And that needs to change," Lenny said as he stepped up next to me and put a hand on my shoulder.

My head whipped to Nicolai who was watching with narrowed eyes. His audible sigh of relief at being fine with Lenny near me was a good sign that he might be getting over his bizarre problem.

"Lenny, Mother, Nicolai and Dima," Seth said. "Please stay."

As the Dragons dispersed, Maria approached me tentatively. "Can I talk to you?" she asked.

My heart soared, but I kept my expression neutral. "Yes. I can arrange that."

"Now?"

She looked like a lost child to me—not the man-magnet I'd thought her to be. Turning to Seth, I implored him with my eyes. If she wanted me, I was going. She might change her mind if I put her off.

"Go," Seth said with a smile and a nod. "I will speak with you later."

"*I* will speak with her," Nicolai cut in and gave his brother a glare. "*Not you*. Dima go with Maria to your suite. Talk to her and then lock yourself in."

"Are you serious?" I asked as sparks of fire began to burst from my fingers.

"Completely," he shot back with sparks of his own bouncing around the room. "If you have a problem with that, I'd be happy to put you in lockdown for a few hours. Your choice."

"Here's what you can lock down, little mister," I growled. "You can lock down your big, fat, ridiculous ego or you can shove it up your ass. Either will work for me."

Grabbing a confused Maria by the hand, I stomped from the room. I was sure I heard Elaina and Lenny's laughter following us out, but I was too furious to take any pleasure in it.

Nicolai was treading on very thin ice.

No one was the boss of me except *me*.

Chapter 11

"So what's the deal with you and Nicolai?" Maria asked as we sat awkwardly together on the couch in my suite.

That was certainly a loaded question to start our relationship off. Buying time, I fluffed all four pillows on the couch and then hopped up and grabbed two bottles of water. What the hell was the *deal* with me and Nicolai? My Dragon and my human had completely different opinions on the subject. Avoidance was silly so I sat back down and examined the floral material of the couch while I figured out how to answer Maria's query.

The living quarters at the compound were nice and I was very aware I'd been given a coveted suite. It was comfortable and quiet and worked for me. Thankfully there was a kitchenette because I'd been eating alone due to my overwhelming lack of popularity. However, now that everything was changing for the better, I was excited to go to the mess hall. But mostly I was excited to be sitting with my niece even though her question made me uncomfortable.

I'd considered talking to her outside on a bench to shove it in Nicolai's face, but the lives of real people were possibly at stake and I wasn't that heartless or stupid.

"Well," I replied, tilting my head to the side and considering my response carefully. "I could ask you the same question."

"Me and Nicolai?" She snorted with laughter. "Oh no, that would never be. We all vie for his attention, but he treats us like sisters."

"You're not in love with him?"

"Not in the real sense of the word. I love him because he saved my life, but I'm not *in love* with him," Maria explained. "He's not my true mate. I'm waiting for my true mate."

Ignoring my confusing sense of relief that she wasn't in love with Nicolai, I hesitated to tell her she might be waiting a very long time for her true mate. And I also realized I owed Nicolai a huge debt for the life of my niece. Freakin' great—more complications I didn't need.

There were also a few things she had to know…today.

"Maria, rarely does a Dragon ever mate with their destined one. We're too violent. Most of the time our true mate is dead long before we have the chance to meet."

"I know this," she agreed, pulling her knees to her chest and wrapping her arms around them. "But I have a feeling my mate is out there."

"You have to mate with someone before you turn 500 or you die," I told her, blocking out the fact that I was only months away.

"Why? This is news to me." Her eyes grew wide with surprise and she sat forward in doubt and anger.

"I don't know why," I told her, pressing my temples and giving her the same answer my mother had given me hundreds of years ago. "But for those in our line, it's just the way it is. The Royal Dragons got stuck with the short end of the stick in more ways than I can count."

"That's ludicrous." She was outraged.

I couldn't have agreed with her more. However, knowledge was power and she needed to know.

"Yep, but it's true. You still have time."

"How many of us are of the Royal Dragon line?"

"Um...me and you," I lied.

Telling her about Daniel was risky at this point. I wanted her to know, but she was still too new to me. The thought of him having real family after I was gone was heartening, but I needed more time with her.

She nodded and picked at her fingernails.

Should I just start talking? Did I wait for her to start? I'd just dropped a bomb on her and sadly I had plenty more where that came from.

Crap, this was uncharted territory. Parenting— especially a 485 year old niece—was the hardest job I'd ever had. Taking on an army of Dragons was easier than this.

"You know, you can ask me anything," I told her quietly.

Again she nodded. "I'm not sure I'm ready to hear things that will make me upset yet. The whole *you're going to die at 500 thing* will take a while to digest. I kind of just want to be with you."

"I get that," I said thankful not to have to go into anymore horrid stories today. "I will tell you this, your father was an amazing man and I knew your mother as well. She was lovely and they adored each other."

"I remember my mother saying my father was her true mate. It's another reason I want to wait for mine. Not that their story turned out so great, but..."

"I hear that finding your true mate is like nothing we can imagine. It's supposed to be absolute perfection," I said wanting her to have solace that her parents were happy for whatever little time they had together. "However," I added with a laugh as I remembered the distant past. "They knocked heads tremendously in the beginning. Eventually your mom had my big bad brother eating out of the palm of her hand. It was all kinds of awesome."

Maria's smile brightened my day considerably.

"Do you know what happens when you find your true mate?" she asked as she unfolded her long body and scooted close.

"Nope, not a clue. I've heard stories over the years, but it kind of sounds like fiction to me."

We sat in comfortable silence and stared at each other until we both started to giggle. She touched the mark at the base of my neck that matched hers and laid her head on my shoulder. She was a beautiful woman and I longed to know her story, but she would tell me when she was ready.

"Can I hug you?" I asked.

"Yes, I would like that," she replied.

I took her in my arms and I could swear I felt my brother Sean smiling down on me. It was surreal and so moving my eyes filled with tears. I would keep Maria close for the rest of the time I had and then I would make sure there was someone to watch over her.

"You hug like a mom should," Maria whispered as she buried her face in my neck.

"That's because I am a mom," I said and then stiffened and froze.

"I have a cousin?" she asked pulling back with a grin of excitement and wide eyes.

My stomach clenched. The more people that knew about Daniel, the more danger he was in, but she was of his blood—and mine.

"Yes," I said slowly. "You do. He's four and he's my world. But no one knows of him. Until my father is dead it has to stay that way. Please."

"You have my word," Maria said solemnly. "I swear to you on my life."

"Thank you." I was still distressed I'd let Daniel's identity slip, but my gut told me she could be trusted.

"When this is all over, can I meet him?"

"Absolutely. He had blond hair just like you."

"And his father?" she asked and then blanched. "Oh my God, does Nicolai know you're *mated*?"

"Um...Nicolai is not privy to my private business nor will he ever be," I stated firmly. "And, no. I was not mated to Daniel's father. He was a lovely man I barely knew. My father had him killed when he discovered I'd shown interest in someone. Daniel's father never even knew I was pregnant. Some might argue that Daniel was an accident. He's not. He's my greatest accomplishment."

"You father is a fuck," Maria hissed as she swiped at a few stray tears that had escaped her eyes.

"This is true," I agreed, not chastising her for her language or reminding her the abomination was also her grandfather. In this particular case she was accurate.

"Was Daniel's father your true mate?" she asked as she placed her hand on my cheek for comfort.

It reminded me so much of Daniel that I sighed with longing for him.

"No, he wasn't. He was kind and we were attracted to each other. End of story. But he wasn't my true mate. I think I could have been happy with him, but I wasn't given the chance to find out."

"I'm really sorry," Maria said and took my hands in hers. "However, as strange and alarming as all this is, I think I'm glad you found me. The whole dying at 500 thing is a bit unsettling, but at least I know."

Her wording was on target and I agreed wholeheartedly. The Universe had an unusual way of bringing people together. The timing wasn't what I would have chosen, but I was grateful all the same.

"I *know* I'm very glad I found you. It was Lenny who actually brought us together so we owe him a beer."

"Lenny has spoken more in the time you've been here than in all the years I've known him," Maria said with pursed lips and little laugh. "And he drinks scotch, not beer."

"I'll keep that in mind," I replied. "He's an odd duck, but I like him. I'd always thought Warlock Dragons were a myth."

"Lenny was held prisoner and tortured by your...my...the son of a bitch King for hundreds of years. Nicolai freed him about seventy-five years ago and they've been a team with Seth and Elaina ever since."

I stared down at my hands and inhaled deeply to hold onto my composure. Was there any Dragon alive that my father's despicable ways hadn't touched? I was beginning to think not. How could one single man have wielded so much power for so long?

"That makes me ill, but I'm glad you told me," I said running my hands through my hair. "How about I join you for dinner tonight in the mess hall? Right now I need a little time to think. And I need to make plans to bring a Wolf into the Dragons' den."

"Can I call you Aunt Dima?" Maria asked with a chuckle.

"I answer to pretty much anything," I told her with a grin. "But Aunt Dima sounds damn fine to me."

After my niece left, I locked, chained and bolted the door behind her. I didn't need any more surprises today. Talking about my father made every muscle in my body tense.

A nice long hot shower wouldn't solve my problems, but it might relax the ball of tension that had been my constant companion as of late.

***

"I'm glad to see you can follow directions."

"Oh my God," I screeched as I wrapped the towel I was wearing tighter around my naked, wet body. "How in the hell did you get in here?"

My eyes flew to the door. It was still locked, chained and bolted. Nicolai was as smug as I'd ever seen him and he'd made himself far too comfortable on my couch. Unfortunately he also looked hotter than hell—all sexy bad boy Dragon.

"You didn't lock the window," he said with a casual shrug and a lopsided grin. "When you didn't answer your door, I became concerned for your welfare and took it upon myself to protect you."

"I call bullshit. You do this for all your people?" I snapped.

"But of course," he replied silkily. "Especially the ones I want to see naked."

"You're disgusting," I spat, torn between wanting to tear his head from his shoulders or drop my towel and dive on top of him. "And you can show your manwhore ass to the door immediately before I zap it so hard you won't sit for a week."

"That's not nice," he said as he reclined on my couch and put his feet up.

He looked ridiculous. My couch was small and floral. He was enormous and all male. I had to bite back my grin at his audacity. There was no way I was going to let him win anything.

"I'm not a manwhore. You can ask anyone here."

"The status of your sex life is not my concern, Dragon," I lied through my teeth.

My inner Dragon was furious with me. She wanted to jump the sexy god on the couch and she was making no bones about it. The rational side of my brain began to reason out why it wouldn't be such a bad idea. I mean who would know? Our attraction was off the scale and I hadn't been with a man since Daniel's father. If I was going to die in the near future, why shouldn't I have a little fun?

What in the hell was happening to me?

Never in my life had I thought with my lower region. I was practical. I was a *mom*, for the love of Pete. I had no time to dally with an arrogant Dragon. It didn't matter that he had a damn eight-pack stomach, stupidly kissable lips or a bulge in his jeans that was mindboggling. He was my partner in a war, not in the bedroom. Sex would make things messy.

"What's going on in that devious mind of yours?" Nicolai asked

His eyes followed me with undisguised lust and his lopsided grin made my tummy flip.

"Nothing," I said as I dropped the towel and yanked on some sweat pants and a t-shirt. If he was rude enough to break in, I'd be rude—or stupid enough—to show him exactly what he couldn't have.

Nicolai sat up ramrod straight and swallowed hard.

"Women don't think about nothing," he said calmly, but his glowing eyes belied his unfazed tone. "Only men do."

"Why are you here?" I demanded as I took the seat across the room from him. My strip show had kind of backfired. I was so wildly turned on I no longer trusted myself. He needed to say his piece and get the hell out. "Are you over your Cro-Magnon thing?"

"Interesting you should ask." He stood and began to pace the room. "The short answer is no and apparently I won't be over it any time soon unless…"

"Unless what?" I asked warily as I sat on my hands to keep them from pulling my shirt over my head and begging him to touch me.

I closed my eyes tightly to ward off the lightheadedness that had come over me. My body felt like one large heartbeat. Had I started to die before my 500th birthday? Shit, this was not in my plan. My father was alive and I needed to see Daniel and say goodbye if this was the end. But first, the man I wanted and could never have needed to leave. It would be all kinds of horrific if I croaked during illicit sex with a Dragon I didn't even like.

"Seth says we're mating."

"I'm sorry, *what?*" I choked out. "That's bullshit."

Death was more welcome than this news. I couldn't mate with Nicolai. My God, if my life was spent avoiding speaking to men at all costs, I'd rather be six feet under. And Daniel…would he kill my son out of jealousy?

"Yes, my thoughts exactly. However, I've been convinced that we have no choice so I'm good with it."

"*You're what?*" I shouted as I jumped to my feet. This was not happening.

"Do you have water in your ears from your shower?" His eyebrows were raised and he was trying not to smile. "I said we're in the beginning stages of a true mating. I'm fine with this and think we should seal the deal."

"You think we should *seal the deal?*" I growled as my hands lit up on fire and thin tendrils of smoke wafted from my nose.

"Um…maybe another time?" he offered with a delighted grin. He didn't even attempt to hold back his laughter.

"You are *not* my true mate. I don't even like you," I shouted. "You don't like me. We hate each other."

Nicolai shrugged and chuckled. "Thin line between love and hate, Princess. I hope you're half as much of a spitfire in bed as you are out of it. As for liking each other…you're growing on me and I've wanted you from the moment I saw you. You're mine—like it or not."

"Not," I hissed. "If you were my true mate, you would respect me. You wouldn't try to kill every man who said hello."

"I beg to differ," Nicolai said tightly as he clenched his fists. "Apparently that's exactly what happens until we mate according to my mother and Seth. They've warned the weyr of our situation."

"You're kidding me," I screeched as I backed up and overturned the chair I'd been sitting on. "We're a *situation* now?"

Sparks were flying all over the room and I had to duck as an aggressive flame shot from my fingers and bounced right back at me. This was all wrong. Yes, I was physically attracted to him. Yes, I secretly respected him. Yes, I wondered what he looked like naked fairly often. Yes, my inner Dragon wanted to claim him, but...when he found out I had a son...

"No," I said as I backed farther away from him even though every instinct I had was to run to him.

Was this love? No. This was lust.

I was horny and he was hot. Period. Love was earned just like respect. I couldn't love someone I didn't know and could barely tolerate. Ridiculous.

It was Nicolai's turn to be shocked. "Did you say *no?*"

"Yes."

"Wait," he said, pressing his temples and letting his head fall back on his shoulders. "You said no and then you said yes. Most of my blood has left my brain and is visiting my dick at the moment. You need to be a bit more clear."

I let my chin drop to my chest and I bit down hard on my lip so I didn't laugh. This was *not* funny. The very fact that I was enjoying this ludicrous exchange meant I needed my head examined.

"No, I will not mate with you."

"You can do that?" he asked wildly confused.

"I just did," I replied as my insides rioted, furious I was going against nature and fate.

"Do you have any clue how many women would be delighted to be my mate?" he bellowed as burning energy flowed off of him and added to the stream of fire dancing around the room. "I'm a very good catch and I'm hung like a damned horse."

"Oh my God," I shouted back. "Are you really trying to woo me with your dick size and the list of women you've bedded?"

"No," he shouted and then banged his head against the wall in frustration. "I was just...um...I don't think that came out right."

"You *think*?" I snapped.

Righting the chair, I glanced around the room and cringed. It was scorched and smoking. We were dangerous together. The longer we were trapped in here the more chance we had of burning the entire compound to the ground.

"I've got it," Nicolai announced grandly. "You want to be wooed. Then I shall woo you. I have no idea how to do this because I've never had to, but how hard can it be?"

I was stunned to silence. Was he insane?

"I'll get my mother to help me. She's a woman. I will woo the living hell out of you and then you'll have no choice to straddle me and ride me until we're both blind," he said, very satisfied with his appalling plan.

"Um..."

"Great. I will meet you for dinner and we will have a date in the mess hall. Wear something baggy and unattractive so the men won't stare. Until we exchange Dragon Fire and mate, no one is safe. Did you by any chance bring a ski mask where only your eyes show?"

"Are you serious?" I asked in a strangled tone— shocked my voice worked at all.

"Very. No worries. I have one and you will wear it."

With that he walked to my door and yanked it open. In his sheer excitement over his horrifying plan, he ripped it clean off its hinges and barely noticed.

I sunk down in the chair and let my head fall to my hands. The thought of being wooed by the crazy idiot was the most terrifyingly wonderful thing I'd ever experienced, but the timing was beyond bad.

No matter how much I was tempted to let the powerful Dragon clumsily woo me, I couldn't let this happen. Something this monumental took time—years of time and I only had a few months.

I also had a son from another Dragon and that would be a sticking point that had no happy ending.

My inner Dragon hissed and snarled reminding me that if I mated with Nicolai I would have eternity, not simply a few more months.

I was willing to mate with Seth because he accepted Daniel. He wasn't attracted to me in the normal sense and if I was honest with myself, I was never really physically attracted to him either. It was his spirit and his kindness that appealed to me.

But I was attracted to Nicolai and maybe there was a chance that if Seth accepted Daniel that Nicolai would as well... Wait. Who was I kidding? Seth never had a thought in his mind to mate with me and that's why Daniel posed no issue.

There would be no mating.

As soon as my father was dead, I was leaving. All the men in Nicolai's life would be safe if I left. It was a shitty plan for more reasons than I would ever admit to myself, but it was the only one I could come up with at the moment.

Ignore what you can't have or change, and deal with what you can.

I needed to get Junior up here. I needed his help and I needed someone to talk to. God forbid getting any kind of rational advice about men and women from Junior, but it would be better than nothing.

Focus on the goal.

God, please help me focus on the goal.

Chapter 12

The mess hall was completely empty. What the hell time was it?

I was sure the paperwork in the folder I'd received when I'd arrived said dinner was from six until eight. It was now 6:15 and no one was here. Why was it deserted?

And then it all became alarmingly clear…

In the middle of the room was a table set for two. There were candles and roses and wine.

Silver domes covered the fine china plates and the food smelled heavenly.

It was beautiful and I was sure Nicolai had no hand in the décor. However, I was certain he had a hand in the absence of the other Dragons.

I pressed the bridge of my nose and tried not to laugh as the deadliest Dragon in the world popped up from behind the table and flexed his considerable muscles while grinning like a dumbass.

He was wearing his usual jeans that hugged his backside to perfection, but tonight he'd paired them with a green tailored shirt—and it was sinful.

Damn it.

"How am I doing?" he yelled across the mess hall. "It's a romantic dinner for two. My mother said this was the way to go. Personally I think it's somewhat ridiculous, but if this is the way into your pants... I mean heart, we will do it everyday."

"You meant pants," I corrected him. He was right out of his mind.

"You are correct. However, I'm sure that's not romantic so let's pretend I didn't say it. Or at least don't tell my mother."

"Don't the other Dragons need someplace to eat?" I asked with an eye roll and a laugh as I glanced around the empty mess hall.

"No worries, I ordered pizza and they're all in the Recreation Area. I though it would be nice for the weyr to see us together, but my killing any male who looks at you could put a damper on things."

"I can see how that wouldn't appeal," I said as I crossed the large dining room and approached the beautifully set table. "You did this for me?"

"I did," he announced proudly. "Actually my mother, Maria, and Lenny did it while I ransacked my living quarters for a gift for you. However, I will take credit for everything."

"Of course you will," I muttered.

"Look at me, Dima. This may be funny to you, but trust me—I'm not playing any games here."

Silly charming Dragon Guy disappeared and in his place stood the man I couldn't get out of my head. He went from goofy dude to lady-killer on a freakin' dime.

It made me dizzy and it made me want to run.

"Nicolai, we really need to deal with my father and then we can discuss this...um, thing that might be happening here," I said backing away as he came around the table stalking me like prey.

Ignoring my halfhearted protests, he gently took my arm and led me to the table. His hand on my bare skin sent pulses of heat just south of my bellybutton.

He pulled out the chair and seated me. Brushing my long, wild red curls aside he pressed his lips to my neck and my body jerked violently in response.

"Just imagine what would happen if my lips got to know the rest of your body," he whispered in my ear.

I gripped the table in sexually frustrated terror. His breath was warm and minty and his scent drove me to distraction.

Holy hell, with no one in here but us, there was a very fine chance I was going to tackle him and ride him like a human cowboy.

"This is a bad idea."

"It's an outstanding idea," Nicolai countered as he poured me a glass of wine and a bourbon for himself. "You have to eat and you've been holed up in your suite all week. I'm excellent company. It's a win-win."

"For who?"

"For my true mate and myself," he stated as a smile pulled at his lips.

I was riveted to his mouth as he raised his glass and took a sip of his drink. He was gorgeous, powerful and he was good. Not kind like Seth, but as arrogant as Nicolai was, he made me feel safe.

Shit.

"You've gone from being *okay* with the mate thing to actually wanting it?" I squinted my eyes at him and tried to figure out his game.

To give my nervous hands something to do, I removed the domes from the plates and put them aside.

The food was even prettier than the table—rare filet mignon with risotto and green beans with slivered almonds. I was ready to inhale the food. It was far more appealing than the microwave dinners I'd been eating all week.

"Yep," he said as he sipped his bourbon and watched me over the rim of his glass. "I actually had a suspicion you were mine when I was choking you in the parking lot in Chicago."

"That's certainly a lovely memory," I said with a grunt of disgust.

"It will be an interesting story to tell our children some day," he agreed and placed his glass on the table.

I ignored his statement completely and played with my food. My appetite was gone and my skin felt clammy.

"You don't like children?" he asked, noticing my uncomfortable silence.

"I love children," I said a little louder than I'd intended. "I wouldn't have guessed you would like them."

"You guessed wrong, Princess."

"Anyway, we need to just put this on hold and..."

"I'm a very good multi-tasker," Nicolai said smoothly cutting me off. "I've waited my whole life for my true mate but never really believing I would find her. You're here and you're mine."

"Why have you been so hateful?" I demanded and then shook my head and put my hand up to halt his answer. "Don't answer that. I don't want to know. I'm sorry that fate has given you me, but I can't do this."

"Can't or wont?"

"Both."

We silently stared at each other for a long moment and then he smiled.

"I'm winning," he said as he rested his elbows on the table and steepled his fingers.

"No you're not."

"Am."

"Not," I shot back with a giggle. "God, you're like a four year old."

"With an enormous dick," he amended my description with a humble shrug and a wicked sexy grin. "You really should see him. He's dying to meet you."

"You refer to your dick as a separate person?" I grimaced and laughed.

"I do since he has his own zip code."

Nicolai's eyes gleamed with humor, but I'd seen the bulge and he was fairly accurate.

"As to why I was so hateful...I didn't expect my true mate to be the daughter of the man who killed my sister. I didn't want it to be you."

I smiled humorlessly at the irony and took a healthy sip of wine. It was very difficult for a Dragon to tie one on, but I was going to give it a shot.

"I'm not a prize. You should find someone better suited," I said, dropping my gaze to my lap. My father had killed my siblings as well. I lived with my hatred daily. I didn't even blame him for the way he felt about me.

"Fate doesn't work that way, Dima. I want you. I wanted you when I thought I hated you. I couldn't understand it and it infuriated me," he said as he refilled my now empty wine glass. "My need has increased to something almost uncontrollable. My instinct is to pick you up, throw you over my shoulder, take you to my room and make you mine...right now."

"You wouldn't dare," I huffed as I downed my wine and poured myself another. What the hell was wrong with me that his caveman scenario turned me on? I was a modern woman, not a damsel in need of a man.

"Actually I would, but Seth and mother were quite clear that I'd be in the dog house with you for several hundred years if I tried that method."

"Thank God for that," I muttered and chugged the wine like it was water.

Damn it, I wasn't even tipsy. I grabbed the bottle of bourbon and took a swig.

"You can deny it all you want, but I can feel you Dima. You want me as much as I want you. Stop playing games. It's beneath you," Nicolai said as he took the bottle of liquor from my hands and put it out of reach. "It's the really good stuff," he said referring to the bourbon. "It gives me pain to watch you chug it. So get over whatever it is you have to get over and let's go fuck."

"Wow, that's the most romantic proposition I've ever received," I snapped sarcastically. "Is that how you usually get the gals?"

"I usually don't have to *get* the gal," he replied with a shrug and a lopsided grin. "You've made me work much harder than I normally would."

"Too bad, so sad. But *we* are not happening."

"Dima, Dima, Dima," he said with pure delight in his voice. "You have challenged me and we are *definitely* happening. Clearly not tonight, because I have never forced a woman to come to my bed and I never will."

"How noble of you."

"It is, isn't it? And just so we're clear here, I will never force you even though my Dragon is all but insisting on it."

"Again, how noble of you," I said rudely while my inner Dragon danced inside me with joy at his crude plan.

"You see, *my true mate*...I won't have to force you because *you* will come to me."

Nicolai sat back in his chair, crossed his arms over his chest and grinned with smug satisfaction.

"You're going to be waiting a very long time," I hissed and stood, knocking my empty wine glass to the floor with a crash. Normally I would clean up the mess, but I had to go. Now.

I didn't trust myself to stay without making his appalling desire come to fruition. Every instinct I had roared through me and insisted I make him mine. It was terrifying and couldn't happen.

"God you're hot when you're pissed," he yelled after me as I stomped out of the mess hall. "I'll leave my door unlocked."

He was an epic asshole and hell would have to freeze over before I would beg him.

Chapter 13

"Now lemme get somethin' straight here," Junior said as he walked around the outdoor training ring with me. "I need to keep how much distance between us when we talk?"

"Six to ten feet," I told him with an embarrassed shake of my head.

"Goddangit, I'm gonna use that one on the pack at home," he said with a whistle of appreciation. "It craws at my butt when I see guys talking to Sandy."

"Oh my God." I gasped and stopped dead in my tracks. "Do you think he's bullshitting me?"

Junior mulled it over for a moment and shook his head. "Nah, you Dragons have got some weird shit going on. I'd have to guess that your Nicolai is real serious."

"He's not my Nicolai," I insisted. "He's an arrogant ass."

"Whatever you say, Dima." Junior smiled and kept walking.

He wasn't on my side either.

Initially the Dragons were wary of Junior until he let loose with his theory on how to return my father's land to all of the Dragons it had been stolen from over the centuries. Some of the Dragons my father had robbed were right here and part of the Resistance. Junior had already obtained a good portion of the deeds and was in the process of reclaiming all of them.

The re-division of land was solely Junior's idea. I wished I'd thought of it myself. It was brilliant and the right thing to do.

Those in doubt of his MENSA status shut the hell up when they discovered he was the genius behind the solution that prohibited the Dragon shift. It made a few very uncomfortable, but in the end everyone understood why another species would want to have a trick up their sleeve to defend themselves against us.

We weren't the most popular houseguests.

"I'm getting close to ruining the bastard, but probably need about a week to have it finished up. Working from here is a good idea. Lot of sensitive info coming through now and I want you to see it," Junior told me as he stopped and took a seat on a bench. "Nothing is obvious to them yet and I'm keeping it that way. Even if they went looking, it's all status quo at the moment."

"How'd you do that?" I asked, impressed.

Glancing around and not spotting Nicolai anywhere, I considered taking a seat next to Junior, but he was my friend and I wouldn't risk his life. I settled myself on the grass about fifteen feet away.

"I'm just that good," Junior explained with a humble shrug. "And to be honest, this is fun. Your dad's a damned bloodthirsty little peckerhead with no balls. Watching him fall will be a pleasure."

I'd never heard that description attributed to my father before—I'd never heard it used to describe anyone, for that matter. It was all kinds of awesome and would make my father go ballistic. I tucked it away and prayed I'd get a chance to use that gem.

"So our plan is once we bankrupt his organization and they're in chaos, we go in and take him out," I told Junior.

"We would never have had this chance without you. You've made it possible for Dragons to live normal lives."

"Now *normal* is a relative word," Junior teased as he shrugged off my praise with a chuckle. "You fire breathers wouldn't know normal if it bit you in the ass."

"You are correct, my friend," Lenny said as he poofed in to our conversation in a blast of smoke and fire. "I've been looking forward to your presence. You intrigue me."

"Damn, that was a fine entrance. I almost peed my goddurn pants," Junior bellowed as he hopped up and shook hands with an amused Lenny. "You're one sneaky mother humper."

I had to agree. Lenny scared the hell out of me often—and seemed to enjoy the fact immensely.

"Would you be available to have a chat with me later this afternoon?" Lenny asked politely.

"Well, my calendar is pretty free seein' as I'm here to help y'all out, so I'd be happy to," Junior said with a twinkle in his eye. "I've got some questions for you too."

"Two o'clock?" Lenny asked.

"Works for me," Junior replied.

Lenny nodded to Junior and me and then exited the same way he'd arrived—in a cloud of purple smoke. His magic was awe inspiring to even me—and I turned into a golden fire breathing Dragon.

"That is one powerful sumbitch," he said with respect.

No one I knew could swear with as much reverence as Junior. He brought cursing to a new level of esteem. They broke the mold after he was born and I was so very grateful he was my friend.

"You talked with Dwayne?" he asked softly.

"Yesterday," I whispered back with a smile. "He said Daniel is doing well and the Cows are besotted with him. From what Dwayne said, Daniel is running the show."

"Everyone I know is in love with that little man. You done good with him, Dima."

"Thank you."

We sat in silence for a few minutes. I could see Junior's brain working a mile a minute. Several times he started to speak, but stopped himself. After the third time, I was too curious to stay mute.

"Out with it, Wolf," I said. "You clearly have something to say."

"I do," he agreed with a little wince. "But you gotta promise not to set fire to my ass when you hear it."

"Shit," I muttered and then heaved a huge sigh. This was going to be a doozy. It always was with Junior. "I swear on my life not to set you on fire. Can I hold onto the option to punch you in the head?"

"Sure can," Junior said with a grunt of laughter. "I'll survive a head butt. The fire—not so much."

"Shoot."

"Well, Essie and I had a little talk before I came up here and …"

"And?" I asked, readying my left hook.

"And, we know that you're gonna die in a few months if you don't mate. I was hopin' Seth was your man and then it turned out he's a Seer. Unless he's gonna do a Thornbirds thing and turn his back on his calling, we're barking up the wrong tree on that one."

"We're?" I asked, confused and slightly annoyed.

"You're one of us, Dima. Once you join our pack, we crawl so far up your ass and into your business there ain't no way out," he explained as if this was logical occurrence.

"While the sentiment is lovely, the analogy was gross," I replied and tried not to let him see how moved I was by the fact that he cared enough to tell me something that could end in his getting throat punched.

"So the way I see it, you should mate with Nicolai. Essie and Granny are convinced he's your true mate. You're wasting precious time here, girlie."

"I can't."

"You're startin' to sound like my Sandy," Junior said, eyeing me with raised eyebrows. "You and me both know it's just a matter of time and me keeping my willy in my pants before she says yes. Is Nicolai a manwhore?" he asked seriously.

A burst of laughter flew from my lips and I laid back in the grass and grinned. Even when Junior was serious, he was funny. Sandy was lucky.

"No," I said as I stared at the puffy clouds. "Nicolai is not a manwhore."

"Um…small man tool?" he suggested with a wink.

"No," I said as I turned over on my stomach and gave my friend the middle finger. "His man tool is just fine."

"You attracted to him?"

"Yes."

"Think about him all the time?"

"Yes."

"Is he a good person?"

"Yes."

"An arrogant jackhole?"

"Why would that be a good thing?" I asked confused.

"Cause you're too strong to be with some wimpy girlie-man," Junior explained.

Damn it, I had to agree with that one.

"Can you imagine your life without him in it?" he went on.

"Shit," I mumbled. The answer was no. I couldn't imagine my life without him, but…

"Then what's the damn problem here?"

"The problem is Daniel. Wait. That came out wrong. Daniel is my miracle, but he'd be a problem for Nicolai," I snapped and got to my feet.

"Explain," Junior said as he tensed.

"It doesn't matter what I want, or even what fate intended, if it's not good for my son. There is no way in hell a Dragon would willingly raise another Dragon's son. All through our history stepchildren have been killed by the new male in order for his line to be pure. No Dragon is worth the life of my son."

"Are you freakin' serious. You people kill children?" Junior shouted, completely offended and pissed off.

"Well," I hedged. "My father did it to my mother's child from another mating. So yes, it has happened and I won't risk it."

"Stop me if I've missed something here," he said as he slowly sat back down and put his elbows on his knees. "We're comparing your psychotic sperm donor's behavior to the behavior of all other men?"

"No," I insisted, wondering for a moment if I was. Junior didn't understand Dragons. How could he? He was a Wolf.

"You don't actually know if that bull honkey you just spouted would apply to anyone other than the sick fuck who sired you. Correct?" he asked.

"Well…um…"

"I'm correct," he answered for me. "Have you even told Nicolai about Daniel? Have you given him a chance to make a decision about this himself?"

"Well…um…"

"I'm gonna go with a nope on that one," Junior said as he shook his head at me like a disappointed parent.

"Junior, while I appreciate you being all up my butt, I'm Daniel's mother and if there's even a small chance that my mating would harm him—even if it was fated to be—I won't do it."

He was quiet for a few moments as he absently stared at the sky.

"I'm not a Seer. I can't read the future. But I'm gonna tell you right here, right now that you're making a mistake."

"Junior I…"

He held up his hand to stop me. "Hang on. I'll support any decision you make because that's what a pack does, but I need to say my piece and I want you to think about it. Give Nicolai a chance to know about Daniel. Don't make his decisions for him."

Picking at the blades of grass, I avoided my friend's gaze. He had no children and couldn't understand my fear.

"What if Sandy had a child by another man?" I questioned wondering how he would feel if the tables were turned.

He didn't miss a beat. "I'd defend the child with my life," he said simply. "I love Sandy and therefore I love anything that is a part of her."

He was telling the truth—I was sure of it, but he was a Wolf. Dragons were different.

"You know something I don't?" he asked with a smirk on his handsome face.

"No," I said with a laugh. "I don't think Sandy is hiding a hoard of children from you. But what I do know is that she is one lucky mother humper."

"Can I get that in writing?" Junior asked with a silly grin. "I need all the help I can get."

"How about I call her?" I suggested as I got to my feet and scanned the area.

It was clear.

"Junior, stay where you are. I'm coming in for a quick hug because I need some affection from a friend. You okay with that? I'll back off fast just incase anyone is watching."

He smiled and put his arms out. "Get over here, little Dragon. Your Alpha wants a hug."

I giggled and wrapped my arms around him in the same way I wished I could wrap my arms around my long dead brothers. It felt so nice and warm and safe.

"Unhand her. Now," Nicolai's furious voice bellowed across the field. "I like you Junior, but I can't control this shit right now. I'd hate to send you back to Georgia in a box."

Junior backed away quickly with a laugh. He raised his hands in the air to prove he meant no harm.

"She's all yours, Dragon," Junior called out as he walked away. "And she's a handful. Good luck."

Thankfully Lenny and Seth were holding the seething Nicolai back. I'd never forgive myself if something happened to Junior or anyone else here because of me.

Taking a deep breath, I made a decision and crossed the field. Taking advice from others had never been my forte, but a couple of the things Junior had said made sense.

At least I hoped they did.

I stopped in front of the angry Dragon. My presence seemed to calm him.

"Seth, Lenny, thank you," I said. "Could you give us a minute here?"

They nodded and left. Nicolai eyed me cautiously. He was still ready to blow, but I could tell he was fine as long as I was near.

"I want you to meet me in my suite at seven tonight. Can you do that?"

He was speechless as he narrowed his eyes in confusion. I watched him search for the catch.

"Cat got your tongue?" I asked with a smirk. My calm tone belied my churning insides.

"No," he said slowly. "I'm just trying to figure out if I'm being played here."

"You're not."

"You're sure?" he asked, meaning far more than just the fact I'd asked him to my suite.

"Very," I said as I turned and walked away. I was aware that his eyes were glued to my ass, but I'd have done the same to him.

I could be making a grave mistake, but I was going in with eyes wide open. If it went poorly, Daniel was nowhere near and he would always be safe.

My baby was my first and most important concern— and that would never change.

Chapter 14

"Does this look okay?" I asked Maria as I stood in front of the mirror and stared at my image with a critical eye. The fitted green dress matched my eyes and showed just enough cleavage to be sexy, not slutty. It was quite short and flirty and—shit...what in the hell was I doing?

Maria laughed at me as she valiantly tried to rearrange the pillows and throws in my suite to cover the scorch marks all over the furniture.

"You could wear a garbage bag and you'd be gorgeous," she replied, finally satisfied that she'd covered the worst of the damage that Nicolai and I had caused to my living quarters the other day.

"You're just silly," I said as I flopped down on a chair and began to second-guess my hasty decision to invite Nicolai into my lair.

"Nope, I'm honest. And while I'm being honest, I'd really like to borrow those shoes at some point. They fucking rock."

"You can borrow anything you want if you clean up that mouth of yours," I told her with a laugh as I glanced down at the fabulous nude Chanel stilettos my niece so admired.

"You sound like a mother," she shot back with an eye roll.

"I am a mother."

Her observation made my stomach sink. Could I really tell Nicolai about Daniel? If he was furious would he go after my child? In my heart I didn't think so, but I also didn't think fathers were capable of murdering mothers and sons—or chasing their daughter for hundreds of years to kill her. My warped version of family life haunted me endlessly. I suppose it colored everything I did.

"So you're going to tell him about Daniel?" Maria asked as she sat on the arm of my chair and smoothed my wild curls out of my face.

"I think so."

"What does it feel like to find your true mate?" she asked with huge eyes and a grin.

"It's fucked up," I muttered.

"Wait, I'm not allowed to talk like that, but you are?" she demanded as she shoved me over and wedged herself into the chair with me.

"You're right. I'm sorry. That was uncalled for, but it's still accurate," I told her, turning my body sideways so we could both fit.

We were smushed, but it was wonderful. I was nose to nose with my brother's beautiful, foul mouthed, precious child. Never in my wildest dreams did I think this moment would happen.

"I want you to mate with him," she whispered as she traced my nose with her finger. "I just found you. I don't want you to die."

"It's not that simple," I told her, closing my eyes and enjoying her touch. "If it was, I would have followed my instincts immediately."

"Do you love him?"

"I'm not sure I even know what that means," I admitted. "I know I love Daniel and I love you. That I understand."

Maria's eyes misted and she pressed her forehead to mine. "I love you too. Do you know how I know?"

"How?"

"There is no doubt in my mind that I would die for you—and Daniel. I've not laid eyes on him, but I feel a possessiveness that I've never known."

I sat up and pulled her with me. Putting my arms around her I hugged her. I would do the same for her and Essie and my friends in Hung. Slowly I let my mind consider if I would step willingly into peril for Nicolai…Would I?

The thought of harm coming to him made me breathless and agitated. My Dragon perked up and slid close to the surface, confirming that she too would let nothing happen to the leader of the Resistance. God, was this what love felt like?

It was terrifying, annoying, horrible and wonderful.

Pushing the thoughts away I stood and checked my reflection one last time. The armor was in place. However, the woman underneath was a mess.

"I'm leaving. Nicolai will be here soon," Maria said as she stood next to me and caught my eyes in the reflective glass. "Follow you instincts and your heart. If it's not meant to be, I will take care of you at the end and then I will watch over Daniel."

I stared at the floor because words wouldn't come.

"But please remember that I want you to stay."

Silently, Maria let herself out as I was still trying to pull myself together.

***

I'd had three glasses of wine that did little to nothing to calm my nerves when the knock at the door I'd been expecting came. I stood on shaky legs that I couldn't blame on the alcohol and slowly approached it.

"Who is it?" I called out and then smacked myself in the head.

"Are you serious?" Nicolai sounded amused, but tense.

Opening the door, I stepped back and let him in. I was glad I had something to hold onto because he'd dressed up and my knees became jelly in response. He wore his usual jeans, but he'd added a navy sport coat and a pinstriped green tailored shirt. His sheer beauty simply wasn't fair.

"You take my breath away, Dima," he said as he stared at me.

"Back at you," I said shakily. "Would you like something to drink?"

I moved away so I didn't lay my head on his chest and pour out my story all at once. Timing was crucial.

"Water would be good," he said as he moved into the living room taking up all the space.

He was large, but it wasn't just his size. It was everything about him.

"Here you go," I said as I handed him a glass of water and then crossed to the other side of the room.

"I don't bite," he said with a chuckle as he sat on the couch and patted the seat next to him.

"I beg to differ," I shot back with a grin remembering how he'd chomped on my fingers the first time we met.

I carefully made my way to the couch and sat. His weight depressed the cushions so much so that we were thigh to thigh and there was very little I could do about it. Of course I could get up and move...but I didn't want to. I wanted to be exactly where I was.

"You stuck them in my mouth. What was I supposed to do?" he asked with a sexy laugh that pleased my inner Dragon.

"I was trying to gouge out your eyes," I told him truthfully with an unapologetic shrug.

"Now there's a lovely thought."

The heat that was generated by us touching jumbled my train of thought. I was close enough to his lips to lean in and kiss him. I smiled at the thought.

"What are you thinking?" he asked. "And don't say nothing."

His eyes were hooded and the energy in the room was electric. I'd never wanted a man more in my long life. I didn't know if it was nature's way of bringing true mates together or if it was something akin to love. I just knew it was overwhelming and wildly exciting.

"I was wondering what your lips taste like."

"My lips would be very pleased for you to find out." He leaned in close and until we were a mere breath apart.

I closed my eyes and pressed my mouth to his. He tasted even better than he smelled. I opened my lips to his exploring tongue and felt such a sense of completion it made me dizzy.

"Mine," he whispered into my open mouth. "You were made for me."

His hands were everywhere at once and I matched his frenzied need to memorize each other's bodies. Never had anything felt like this. It was as spiritual as it was carnal. With each touch I was catapulted into needing more. He was like a drug.

"I need all of you," he demanded, looking as desperate as I felt.

"Yes," I whispered as yanked my dress over my head. His hissed intake of breath was music to my ears and I tore at his shirt and coat. "I want you to touch me and I want to touch you."

"Ask and you shall receive," he murmured as he helped me with his clothes.

His hot mouth paved a wicked trail from my lips to my neck and I shuddered with delight. With little bites and nips that made me see stars, I wasn't even aware that he'd somehow removed his jeans. We were now skin to skin except for my barely there panties and his white boxer briefs. I knew we should slow down, but I couldn't remember why.

"You work fast," I giggled. I watched his eyes begin to glow a brilliant green.

"I know what I want," he whispered huskily as his hungry mouth latched on to my breast and sucked hard.

"Oh God," I cried out as I arched into him, my body begging for more. "Shouldn't we talk first and get to know each other better?"

His laugh went straight to the hot coil of need spiraling out of control in my lower body. "Do you want to know if I put the toilet seat down? Or if I snore?"

"Um...sure," I gasped out as he went to work on my other breast and pinched the sensitive nipple of the one he'd just finished with.

"Yes to number one and no to number two." His mouth moved greedily to my neck and he bit down in a spot that sent little shock waves through my body.

I screamed and realized I had no clue what I'd just asked him or what his answers were—and I didn't care. I laced my fingers in his hair and pulled his lips to my mouth. Our tongues and teeth clashed as the kiss danced in a dangerously sexual rhythm.

"Tell me now if you want me to stop. I can't guarantee I can, but if we go any farther I won't be able to."

"I don't want to stop," I said as I crawled on top of him and straddled his legs.

His hands clamped onto my ass and pulled me forward to feel his desire. I'd thought his temperature was hot before, but he was now positively volcanic. I rocked against his huge erection and felt my body go liquid.

"Goddamn, I want you so badly I can't see straight," he growled as he tore my panties from my body and plunged two fingers into my willing body while he pressed the heel of the same hand against my clitoris. "Gorgeous," he said as my body jerked in orgasmic response to his expertise.

"Nicolai." I gasped as he hit the spot that made my vision narrow. "We can't mate yet."

My Dragon Fire was dangerously close to flowing from my body and entering his. My words were rational, but my body was not on the same page. It was with my inner Dragon one hundred percent. I writhed against him like I was trying to crawl inside him. Control was nowhere to be found.

"Damn it, why?" he hissed as he pulled back with Herculean effort. "You want this as much as I do. Why are you fighting it?"

For a brief second I had no idea why I was fighting something that was so perfect—so right.

"If you want to say something, for the love of God, say it now," Nicolai ground out holding on to his sanity by a thread.

And then I remembered. There was no good time to say it. And this was a particularly bad time, but the opening presented itself and I had to take it.

I should have spoken before we'd gone this far. What the hell was wrong with me?

"I have a son and if we mate I need to know you won't kill him," I blurted out on one terrified breath.

Time stood still as Nicolai's green eyes burned into mine with an expression I couldn't decipher. I was unsure what was happening, but it felt very wrong.

Nicolai's body stiffened in shocked rage and he pushed me off of him in disgust. I fell ungracefully to the floor and buried my head in my knees. My heart shredded into tiny pieces. I should have trusted my gut. I was right and everyone else was wrong. This Dragon would never accept my child.

Nicolai wasn't the man for me. Fate was a bitch and she lied.

"What exactly do you think of me?" he asked coldly taking me by surprise as he picked up his clothes and yanked them on jerkily. "You think me capable of taking the life of a child because I want his mother?"

My head jerked up and I stared at him strangely. What was he saying?

"It's been done," I said flatly. "My father did it to my mother's first child from another mating."

"You're comparing me to your father? To the man who *skinned my sister alive*?" he asked so calmly the hair on my neck stood up.

His roar shook the walls of my suite and his fire shot furiously around the room. I stood up and faced him as my own fire erupted and tangled with his. I was very aware I'd possibly just made an enormous mistake, but it was out on the table and he hadn't directly answered my question.

Throwing my own needs and hopes to the wind, I asked my question and I needed an answer. "Would my son be safe with you?"

Nicolai barely moved as an icy coldness came over him. I watched him drift from me even as he stood only feet away. Tears blurred my eyes and I wanted to curl into a ball and sob, but I wouldn't. He would not see me break.

"I am many things, *Princess*. I am arrogant and selfish. I am not good with what humans would call polite social behavior. I'm jealous and possessive, and I don't like being played for a fool. I may be deadly—and trust me, I am—but I have never killed for any reason other than defense of my people or myself. *I'm a goddamn Dragon, not a monster*," he shouted with so much anger directed at me, I blanched in shame.

He waited for a response, but I didn't have one. My fire was extinguished. I was empty of everything and felt numb. Death couldn't be more painful than this and I wished it would take me now.

"Your disrespect, your lineage, your insane power—all that I could take, but this…" He shook his head sadly then turned and put his clenched fist through my wall. The veins in his neck bulged and he took a deep breath to regain control. "This I cannot take. Your son would have been as safe in my arms as any other child we had together. He is part of you and that is enough for me. However, there is no need to test that theory because I no longer want his mother."

My knees weakened and I fell back onto the couch and dropped my face to my hands.

"Any woman—including the one fate decreed for me—that thinks me capable of the barbarism that your father enjoyed during his soon to be ended life is not a woman I can love or want. Ever," he hissed in disgust.

"Nicolai," I whispered brokenly.

"Stop. Please just stop," he said, refusing to look at me. "Whatever we had, you broke it. You have killed fate with words so vile I don't ever want to hear them again. After we eliminate your father, you will leave. I can't see you or be near you."

He turned to go and I wanted to crawl out of my skin. I was so sorry, but it was something I had to ask. Daniel's welfare was more important than mine. I'd grossly misjudged him and I knew it, but time would not rewind. I'd made my lonely bed and I would die in it.

He was not the first man that hated me. I'd known hatred my entire life. I just hoped he would be the last.

"We will work together civilly," Nicolai said tonelessly with his back to me. "Because of nature, you will still stay away from the men when I'm present. I'd rather die than kill one of my own over you. Junior says he needs a week to be ready. Stay out of my way and I shall stay out of yours. We can communicate through Lenny or my mother. Am I clear?"

"Yes," I whispered. "You are very clear."

"Good," he said without turning around.

And then he walked out the door—and out of my life.

Chapter 15

"Oh my God," Maria gasped as I pinned her to the ground. "I didn't see that coming. I want to try again." She hopped up and took a defensive stance.

I'd gone on autopilot after my devastating exchange with Nicolai. I hadn't seen him in days, but I'd stayed so busy that I fell into bed exhausted every night. I was training the Dragons to fight like killers. It was what I knew best and I was shockingly good at it.

I fought and bled all day and then at night I spoke to Daniel until sleep took me. I was existing for two reasons only—to kill my father and to see my son.

Even the male Dragons were in awe of my deadly skills and everyone picked up the new methods I taught quickly. Lenny was always hovering nearby, but he hadn't spoken a word to me since I'd seen him with Junior. He just watched with knowing eyes and then disappeared when he felt like it. He was probably pissed at me too.

Whatever. I had more important things to worry about.

Thankfully, Maria was a good student. I needed her to be ready and strong. If I'd known about her, she'd never have been so woefully unprepared to protect herself. A week wasn't long enough to teach her everything I wanted her to know, but it was all we had.

Junior respected my desire not to talk about anything that had happened. After asking me once if I wanted him to kill Nicolai, he dropped it. If it was possible, I loved Junior even more. It was difficult to tell him that it was me, *not Nicolai* he should kill, but I told him anyway. He laughed and pulled me into a hug that I desperately needed.

We were on track to bankrupt my father. It was only days away now. It was the only thing that kept me going along with my burning desire to see Daniel. A huge part of me wanted to run away from this place, but these Dragons had done nothing to me. Everything that was wrong in my life was my own fault.

I replayed the scene with Nicolai over and over again in my mind. Sadly, I knew I still would have asked him the same question. In my world fathers *did* kill their sons...Soon I would come to terms that we were not meant to be. Right now it ate at my insides like a cancer.

"Dima, did you hear what I said?" Maria asked as she took my chin in her hand and raised my eyes to hers.

"No, I'm sorry, I didn't," I replied. "What do you need?"

"I don't need anything. You do. When did you last eat?" she asked with concern.

"Um..." I couldn't remember.

I'd avoided the mess hall and most open areas so I wouldn't run into Nicolai. The compound was huge and I'd been successful.

"Come on, you're going to eat or you'll drop. We have a son of a bitch to kill soon and we need you," Maria insisted as she dragged me from the training area.

"Let me go to my room and change," I said as I glanced down and winced at my blood spattered workout clothes.

While the training was relatively safe, it wasn't without a few wounds here and there. I refused to eat looking like an axe murderer.

"Fine," Maria said as she hugged my tired body. "I'll meet you there in a half hour. If I don't see you I will come get you and drag you over by your pretty red hair."

"Can you speak to your aunt like that?" I asked as a small smile pulled at my lips.

"I just did, didn't I?" she answered cheekily and flounced off to get changed.

I realized that all the pain was worth it because I now had my niece in my life. I'd only have her for a short time, but it was better than not having known she existed at all.

Maria was right. I needed to eat. It was ridiculous for me to keep avoiding Nicolai. We'd be together in battle. I may as well get used to his presence here so it wouldn't be distracting when our lives were on the line.

***

I rounded the corner to the mess hall and stopped dead in my tracks. There was an argument in full swing and I was the subject.

Shit.

"You're a stupid asshole," I heard Maria shout at the top of her lungs.

Oh dear God, please don't let her be yelling at Nicolai.

"Why would she think differently?" she went on at full volume. "Most of her life she's hidden among the humans while running for her life. Before that, she watched her father murder her mother and her brothers. Tell me, O great and compassionate leader, how would she know to think differently?"

My stomach dropped to my toes. My niece was accosting Nicolai in my defense. This was a clusterfuck. As much as I tried to move forward, my feet were stuck to the ground. Literally. I couldn't lift them.

Someone touched my shoulder and I would have screamed if Lenny hadn't gently put his hand over my mouth. He put his finger to his lips and indicated for me to be silent. He was all kinds of crazy and I was all kind of out of here.

Did I really have to relive the horror from a few days ago?

"Let me leave, Lenny," I hissed. "I don't want to hear this. I have to stop her. I fight my own battles."

"Shhh, child. Some battles are not meant to be fought alone."

"You're an ass."

"I've been called far worse."

"I'm not like her father," Nicolai bellowed angrily. "She should know that."

"You are the dumbest man alive right now. I'd kill for a mother like her—someone who put me before her own happiness. Hell, I want to be just like her someday, but because you're such a pigheaded jackass, she won't be around to see it."

"Explain yourself," Nicolai demanded furiously. "And refrain from calling me every foul name you can think of."

"I'll call you what you deserve, assface," Maria informed him rudely.

She was definitely my niece, but I didn't want her to be banished from her weyr for defending me. I wasn't going to be around much longer and these people were her family.

"I will ask you once again," Nicolai ground out through clenched teeth. "Why won't that *woman* see you as a mother?"

God, could he not even say my name?

"Because when she turns 500, she'll die unless she's mated, you canker sore. She's from the fucked up Royal

Dragon Line. Apparently we have some very stupid rules to contend with. I have to follow the same fucked up edict, but I have time. Dima doesn't because you screwed everything up."

"I did no such thing," Nicolai snarled. "She did that herself by putting me in the same category as the cold blooded killer who murdered my sister."

He was correct and Maria had overstepped her bounds. She needed to stop, but Lenny's magic had encased my feet. He was going to get an ass kicking very soon.

"If you'd pull your self righteous head out of your Dragon ass for a moment, you'd understand her fear," Maria snapped.

"Maria's right," I heard Elaina say. "Dima has lived in fear her entire existence. She knows very little of love and trust. She's only recently found it and it wasn't even with her own kind. It was the Wolves and Vampyres that accepted her—not us."

Kill me now. Was everyone going to put their two cents in about my pathetic existence?

"I'd have to say you're pretty much a jackhole," Junior chimed in. "You need to get down on your knees and beg."

"She thought I would kill her son," Nicolai shouted.

"Would you?" Elaina asked.

"Are you out of you ever loving mind?" Nicolai snarled. "I would never kill her son. My God, does everyone think I'm murdering imbecile?"

"No, my child," Elaina said calmly. "But with Dima's past, the question was fair. It doesn't reflect on you or your character. It reflects what she's gone through. You need to tell her you would never harm her child."

"I did tell her that," Nicolai growled and then swore viciously. "I might have added a few other things as well."

"Awful things?" Maria demanded.

"Possibly," he admitted.

"You are such a douche," Maria added somewhat quieter, but still loud enough to be heard. "She will die because of you."

"No, she won't," Nicolai said. "I will find her and make this right."

Oh God no. I would not mate with him out of pity. I was better off alone. Everyone's time was up eventually and mine was up in a few months. If I mated with him because he didn't want to be responsible for my death, my heart would wither and die...

I'd much rather spend my final months with my friends and my son. An eternity with a man who despised me but felt it was his duty would be a death worse than the real thing.

Grabbing Lenny by the collar, I got in his face. "Let me go now or I will come back and haunt your ass for the rest of you unnatural life. And trust me, it won't be pleasant."

"As you wish," he said and then disappeared in a cloud of smoke.

I was free and I didn't waste a second. I turned and ran as if the devil was chasing me. I knew I couldn't go back to my suite—that was the first place Nicolai would look. I didn't want to be cooped up inside anyway. I knew exactly what I needed to do.

Tearing at my clothes, I let my Dragon come out. She was giddy with joy and I launched myself into the air with reckless abandon. I needed to fly. I needed to soar above the clouds and be away from all the anger and confusion.

A couple of hours—that was all I would take. But when I came back, I would be whole. I would be a strong Dragon who just happened to be a single mother. The wind and the sun would give me the strength I needed to get through the next few days. I didn't need a mate. I didn't want a mate. And I certainly didn't want a mate that was forced to accept me.

My father needed to be taken down so he could no longer hurt anyone. I wanted to hold my son in my arms and hear him laugh. I wanted my niece to visit me and meet her cousin.

All of that did not include a man. Nothing I'd done worth anything had ever included a man. I was well aware that Daniel's father had helped in his creation, but he never even knew. We weren't trying for a child. The child came after he was gone, so the child was all mine.

The wind on my scales was glorious.

I would live out the rest of my days like the wind—carefree and wild.

Chapter 16

I'd successfully avoided being alone with Nicolai. It was difficult, as everyone I knew was trying to make it happen, but I'd been running my entire life. I was very adept at getting away. My inner dragon was livid with me, but I was beginning to think she was more trouble than she was worth.

"I've drawn out maps of my father's compound. I haven't been there in quite some time, but he's not one known for change. We'll have to go on the assumption that these are correct," I said in a business like tone as I addressed the lieutenants. "Have your people memorize the floor plans, but make them aware that they might not be one hundred percent accurate."

"They're also *your* people as well," Nicolai added from across the table as he stared at me with frustration clearly written on his face.

"Semantics. They're people and I don't want them to die." I replied to the top of his head.

To all in the room, it appeared I was speaking to Nicolai. He was the only one aware I wouldn't make eye contact. As childish as it seemed, it wasn't. It was self-preservation on my part. I wanted him even more than I had before and falling into his pitying gaze would break me.

"It's all going to happen at once," Junior said as he typed away on his laptop. "Everything will go down on Friday about nine am Eastern Standard Time. I'd suggest waiting until Sunday to strike."

"Will that short amount of time be enough to throw everything into chaos?" Nicolai asked the same question that was on my mind.

"Technically no, but I've got national exposure on this puppy," Junior replied with an enormous and evil grin.

"Explain," Seth said.

"King Jackhole's wealth is very mixed in with mainstream human society's financial structure. That sumbitch is possibly the richest man in the world in the human realm. They have no idea about the Dragon shit. I have buddies at every major news outlet in the world and they plan to hit this mother humper hard about two hours after it goes down. It will be on every TV station, newspaper and online presence from here to hell and back," Junior said as he jumped up in excitement and knocked about six glasses of water and three computers off the table.

The Dragons didn't blink. After the first day when Junior accidentally took out the electrical system in his excitement about getting to fly on Seth's back, the weyr turned a blind eye to the odd MENSA Wolf's destructive ways. He was brilliant and clumsy. That was not a sin here.

"How do you know all of these people? Are they Weres?" Elaina asked, sitting forward as she caught Junior's contagious glee.

"Weres of every kind and a few humans in the mix," Junior told her. "I game online with most of them. Basically we're just a bunch of nerds."

"Fascinating," Lenny said with admiration for the Wolf who had inadvertently demolished more items at the compound in five days than any Dragon had in a year.

"So you believe that will cause his inner circle to splinter?" I asked, still worried about the time frame.

"It should do it, but a few geeks who want to join my secret online gaming group are CFO's of some of the top banks worldwide," Junior explained.

"Mmmkay, that's all kinds of weird. How does that help?" I asked patiently.

Junior's mind often worked so fast, he tended to leave out details.

"Oh right," Junior said with a laugh and a shrug. "Every major bank in the world he's connected with will be calling in notes immediately. They're all blocking the possibility of new loans as well and have promised to go public with the information immediately. It's gonna get ugly real fast. I've told the guys and one gal, who I think might actually be a guy—not sure on that one, that whoever causes the most shit to fly has an open invite into the club."

"I'm interested in this online gaming club," Lenny announced. "I want in."

Small conversations broke out in the room. Dragons did not mix with other species. Ever.

"Well," Junior said as he sat back down, grinned wide and gave Lenny an assessing look. "We ain't never had a Dragon in the club yet. But let me tell you somethin' now, boy, you use any of your magic hoodoo to cheat and we'll come down on your Dragon ass like white on rice."

The gasps in the room were loud and I bit down on my lip to stifle my laugh. Out of the corner of my eye, I saw Nicolai do the same. Lenny was positively ecstatic. No one had the balls to speak to him as Junior did. It was clear he found it refreshing.

"You have my word," Lenny said extending his hand to Junior who took it and pumped it with gusto.

"All right buddy, I plan to kick your online ass every Tuesday at nine pm for the foreseeable future," Junior told him.

Lenny's delighted laugh rang out and startled the room to silence. It was heartwarmingly bizarre and I was certain no one had ever heard him laugh before.

"The units have been decided," Nicolai said, pulling the conversation back to business as he examined the sheet of paper in front of him. "Unit A will be first in. It consists of me, Cade and twenty-five others. Seth will lead unit B. Lenny will lead C. My mother will lead D. Dima will lead E. Units B, C, D and E will surround the compound and enter in ten minute intervals unless the lieutenant is notified otherwise."

"That's a bad plan," I said staring at the table.

"Really?" Nicolai demanded angrily, startled to be questioned.

"Unit A should consist of you, me, Seth, Cade, Lenny and Elaina. We send the strongest in first and then there's a very fine chance the others will not have to come in at all. Far fewer people will die," I said with no feeling in my voice even though my insides were a riot of emotion.

I firmly believed what I said. Nicolai's plan had deadly holes. The first battle would be the deciding factor and it had to be the strongest. If my father found a weak link he would exploit it and win. Would the other Dragons even fight if Nicolai was taken prisoner and then ransomed for their withdrawal?

If I were being completely forthcoming—which I wasn't—I would admit that I wanted to be there to make sure nothing happened to Nicolai. I did not want him for a mate, but I refused to let him die. I knew how truly vicious my father was and there was a fine chance some of his most loyal would stay with him even in his financial ruin.

"Dima is correct," Lenny said. "I know what you're doing, Nicolai, but it's shortsighted and too many will perish. You cannot save Dima and the rest of us by going in first. It will fail."

Nicolai's head fell back on his shoulders and his upper body began to spark dangerously. "Fine," he conceded angrily. "But Dima goes with Unit B."

"Wrong," I said, firmly pushing aside the realization that he had the same instincts about my safety as I had about his. "I know the compound better than any of you and I know how my father works. Personally, I think I should go in alone. I have very little time left as it is and getting rid of my father is paramount to my son's safety. I'm the most expendable here. I say let me go in first and then the rest come in as back up."

"You have a son?" Cade asked, shocked as the others murmured their surprise.

"I do. He's my world and other than Maria and myself, he's the last of the Royal Dragon line. Only we three bear the Royal Dragon Mark. My father wants us gone so his rule will never be disputed."

"You are not expendable," Nicolai roared and threw his computer across the room.

The Dragons watched with rabid interest as I stood up, picked up the smashed electronic and tossed it in the trash. I walked up to Nicolai and looked him right in the eye. "I am very expendable. I know it and you know it."

With my head held high I turned and left him standing there speechless.

"Hold on one cotton pickin' freakin' second," Junior shouted as he jumped up and paced the room in agitation, knocking pictures off the walls and lamps from their tables. "Your father doesn't have the Royal Dragon mark?"

"No. My mother did. And my brothers did, which is why Maria has it as well."

The room stared at me like I had three heads, but Lenny just sat back and smiled.

"He's not even the rightful leader," Elaina gasped in anger and paled. "Dima is."

"I am no one's leader except my own," I told the room harshly. "I want nothing to do with leading a violent and fucked up race. You people can decide on a democratic government after my father is gone. I want peace and to be with my son until I die."

"Dragons would not survive in a democratic society," Lenny commented and put his hand up to silence the heated conversation that had broken out in the room. "We have been a matriarchal society for thousands of years. It wasn't until your father killed your mother's true mate and forcibly took the crown that we've ever been led by a man."

"This is true," Elaina said quietly. "All of it, including the sad fact we would destroy each other without some kind of ironclad but fair leadership in the form of a monarchy. Our history is what it is and our future depends on embracing what is good and right of our past, but making it better. The monarchy will live on. Dragons, even in the enlightened age, will understand and accept no less."

"I've seen this," Seth said quietly. "I've seen the words carved in blood on stone and trees and in water."

"What words have you seen?" Lenny asked. "Is it a prophecy?"

Seth nodded and closed his eyes. A golden aura suddenly surrounded him and it bathed the room in a magical glow. The Dragons all dropped to their knees, even Nicolai. I was the only one who stood.

Seth's voice was devoid of emotion, yet it filled the room like a full symphony. A strange buzzing started in my ears and I held on to the table for purchase. Part of me felt like I'd left my body and was floating freely in the room.

"The true Queen will wear the mark of the Royal Dragon line. She will link the nations and by her side will stand the most physically powerful of us all. Together they will lead us to prosperity and peace."

The silence was reverent and I could feel the age-old magic, but all I wanted to do was scream.

"No," I said loudly and decisively as I gripped the table with white knuckles. "Prophecies are possibilities, not fact. No one knows the future. Even Seth will tell you that fate is fickle and can change her mind."

"While you have a point, I respectfully disagree," Lenny said as the spiritual glow from Seth receded and the atmosphere went back to the way it had been only minutes ago.

"That's your option," I shot back.

"Yes, Dima. It is," Lenny replied and then went to Seth whose eyes were closed in exhaustion from sharing his vision.

I refused to deal with any of this. It wasn't pertinent to the plan we needed to focus on. It was a fairytale and I didn't believe in fiction.

"First things first," I said, cutting off anymore hypothetical conversation. "We need to get rid of the piece of shit in power and then you people can figure out what's next. If my father stays on all of these conversations are moot."

"Dima is correct," Nicolai backed me in a curt tone. "She's right about the new plan and about focusing on the matter at hand. The meeting is dismissed. We will gather again this evening after you have gone to our people and apprised them of the situation."

"Are we free to be candid about everything discussed today?" Cade asked.

"No," I said before Nicolai could speak. "My son is off limits. Everything else is fine."

"As you wish," Cade said as he bowed respectfully to me.

Thankfully he was about six feet away. I was unsure if Nicolai still had his murderous issue where I was concerned.

"Dima, you will stay," Nicolai commanded as the Dragons left the Command Room.

"No, I can't," I said as I quickly made for the door.

"We have strategy to work out. You are one half of the leadership of this mission. Are you too busy to ensure the safety of your people?" he asked silkily knowing he had me by the metaphoric balls.

"I'll give you a few minutes," I ground out as I silently implored Junior to stay with me.

"You'll be fine, little Dragon. It's time for you talk to him," he whispered as he passed. "You'll be in battle soon. Talk now before it's too late."

It was already too late, but I would stay as long we discussed the mission.

Anything personal...I was out of here.

Chapter 17

"You heard the prophecy," Nicolai said evenly when the room was empty.

"The prophecy is crap," I shot back as I took a seat on the far end of the table from him.

"And you know this because you're a secret Seer in your spare time?" he inquired coolly with raised brows.

My groan was internal, but my sigh was audible. "Look Nicolai, none of it's relevant until my father is gone. Let it go and focus on what's real and in front of us."

"You are in front of me and you are very real," he said.

Part of me melted at his words and part of me wanted to destroy him for uttering them. The boat had sailed and we'd missed it. He was just reopening barely healed wounds.

"I'm in front of you because you forced my hand, not because I want to be here."

I pressed the bridge of my nose and closed my eyes for a brief second as I considered what I wanted to say, but as usual he beat me to it.

"I'm sorry," he said quietly. "I'm sorry I behaved the way I did. I didn't take into account your past."

"Thank you," I said with sincerity. "However, it changes nothing. I told you of my past when I asked you if you would harm my child. I don't see what's different now."

"You accused me of being capable of killing your son," he bellowed and then dropped his head to his hands. "I would never kill your child—or any part of you."

"I really do know that now," I said with remorse. "And I'm truly sorry that I used the words I did, but in the same situation I would ask the same question. My words can't be erased—and neither can yours."

"I don't even remember what I said," he told me in agitation as he got up and rounded the table. "I was so angry that you would think that of me I couldn't see straight."

"You said that I killed fate with my vile words. You said I broke it," I reminded him quietly. Repeating the words tore at my insides like a hot knife shredding my internal organs, but we needed to get all of this out of the way to move on. "And you were right. It's okay, Nicolai. We will both be okay."

"You will *not* be okay," he hissed as his fists clenched at his sides. "You will die."

"Everyone dies eventually," I said with a brittle smile that came nowhere near to reaching my eyes. "My time has come and I will not prolong it because you pity me. I have far more pride and self-worth than that."

"You think I pity you?" he demanded with an angry and confused shake of his head.

"I don't think. I know."

"There is a whole lot you don't know, Dima…You'd have more time with your son. You'd choose death over your son?" he asked with narrowed eyes as he continued to move into my personal space.

"I choose my son above all else," I said in an icy tone as I put my hand up in warning to stop him from coming closer. "You should know that better than anyone."

"I can give you all the time in the world with your son if you mate with me." He stopped his forward movement, but I could feel the heat from his body even five feet away.

"I'd rather my son see me at my strongest than a broken woman with a dead heart because she'd tethered herself to someone that despised and pitied her."

"And that's where you're wrong, Princess. This is not easy for me because I'm *rarely* wrong, but...I was. I was very wrong," he said as he ignored my hand and walked to me.

"Stop." The agonized cry ripped from my chest. "Lies are beneath you. I don't want you. This ended days ago. It's not up for discussion."

"Lies are beneath you as well," Nicolai said as he took my hand and pulled me out of the chair.

We were face to face and it was terrifying because it felt so right.

"You still want me as badly as I want you. I can scent your desire and need. I can still taste your mouth," he purred as he ran his calloused fingers over my trembling lips.

"Those are hormones," I snapped and pulled away. "Lust means nothing. It sucks and so do you."

I rolled my eyes at my adolescent response and dropped my head to my chest. I couldn't win for losing at the moment. All I wanted to do was leave, but this had to be dealt with now. I wasn't strong enough to leave it hanging anymore.

His laugh filled the room and I fought harder than I'd ever fought not to smile.

I succeeded.

"Let's look at this a different way," Nicolai suggested, clearly not giving up. "If you're willing to waltz into your father's chambers alone and possibly die for Daniel and our people, why wouldn't you put your pride aside to live for your son and all Dragon kind?" he asked.

His logic was quite sneaky, but I was tired of playing this game.

"Because you would be part of it," I lied even though it was brutally painful.

"Interesting," he allowed as he sat down in the seat next to the one he'd pulled me out of. "I call bullshit on that, but we won't discuss that falsehood at the moment. What if I agreed to leave you alone after we kill your father? You could live a happy long life with your son and I would be nowhere in it."

"Why would you do that?" I demanded. "What do you have to gain?"

"I'd sleep better at night knowing my true mate was alive and happy."

I slapped my hands down on the table in a rage. "We would be miserable apart, you idiot. If we mated and parted it would destroy us both."

"Your death will undo me far more," he growled.

"We're not mated," I shouted. "My death will not affect you. Are you daft?"

"As far as I'm concerned we're already bonded except for the exchange of Dragon Fire. You are my every waking thought. Fate made us for each other. I do not accept your answer. I may have fucked up, but you have to give me the chance to make it right."

"I can't do this," I muttered as pulled on my hair and paced the length of the room. "This is insanity."

"Not to mention, it would be tragic if I killed Cade, Seth and Lenny because they were near you in the battle when my target is supposed to be your father."

"I thought you were fine with Lenny," I said, perplexed.

"Whoops, my bad. I meant Seth and Cade," he amended and then scrubbed his hand over his face trying to hide his smug grin.

He failed.

"So now you're resorting to blackmail to get what you want?" My feet stopped and I stared at him with an open mouth. He was every kind of crazy.

"It's sounds a little harsh when you put it that way," Nicolai said, feigning offense.

"Is there another way to put it?" I asked as involuntary deep pink and gold sparks began to fly from my hands.

"Hmmm, I like gentle persuasion better," he explained with a careless shrug. "It's a win-win for everyone."

"Except you," I told him as I aimed and shot a spear of pink fire at his head.

The laugh that escaped his lips as he ducked my incoming shot made me shoot two others out of spite. The second one hit his shoulder and his loud curse made me giggle.

"So is this what I have to endure to make you smile?" he asked with a bemused grin as he tamped out the fire on his smoldering sleeve.

"Possibly," I shot back flippantly. "And it's not a win-win for you, Nicolai. It's a lose-lose."

"That depends entirely on your definition of those two words," he replied as he crossed the room and pinned my arms over my head so I couldn't get another cheap shot in.

He pressed his hard body against mine and it was all I could do to remain stiff and unyielding. He knew it and it infuriated me. My nipples hardened to painful points and I felt a dampness between my legs. I was tempted to fight fire with fire, rubbing up against him and then leaving him high and dry, but I wasn't stupid. That would backfire in a big bad way.

"Everything I've said makes complete and total sense," he whispered into my ear. "What I offer to you is simple. Take it…I know you want to."

My breathing was labored as I fought the war raging between my body, my brain, my heart and my pride. He was right and I knew deep down inside I would accept, but I was accepting for all the wrong reasons. I was going to accept because it's what my heart wanted.

I'd fallen in love with the horrible man. The arrogant man who was willing to give up his own happiness for me to live and raise my son. The terrible person who wanted me to be happy so he could sleep at night. The despicable man who was blackmailing me so our friends wouldn't die while we saved our entire race from my father's tyranny. The man I was fated to spend eternity with…

He would never know my reasoning. It would be my downfall. Giving him my body was one thing. Letting him know he also owned my heart would never happen.

"You win," I said.

"*What?*" he sputtered as he stepped back and stared at me with delighted but wary shock.

"I said, you win."

"Is there a catch?" he asked as he narrowed his eyes and pushed me up against the wall.

"No. No catch."

He was silent for a moment while his eyes searched my face for deceit. There was none to be found because I wasn't lying. I would let him make me his and I would make him mine. Parting from him would be hell, but I'd lived in hell on this earth for so long it really didn't matter. I would raise my son and I would live. It would be an empty and sad life, but…

"Come with me now," he insisted as he grabbed my hand and pulled me toward the door.

"Where are we going?" I gasped as I tried to keep up with his long stride.

"To my suite. I'm taking no chances of you changing your mind," he said tersely as he shoved the door open with his shoulder. "You have a problem with this?"

"Um...no, I guess not," I stuttered. My brain was all over the place and my inner Dragon was jumping for joy.

"Good. In five hours you'll be mine."

"Oh my God. It takes five hours to mate?" I'd never heard that.

"No, as far as I know it takes a few minutes. It will take me five hours to make you come so many times you'll agree to a renegotiation of the terms."

"Oh God."

"You can call me that, but I prefer Nicolai."

And thus my true mating began.

Chapter 18

As Nicolai dragged me across the compound, Dragons waved and cheered. I was mortified. We may as well have been wearing a sign that said we were off to live out a pornographic fantasy. Nicolai accepted the congratulations with a shit-eating grin and very few words. He was on a mission and the mission was me.

Practically throwing me through the door of his suite, he began to disrobe immediately. He was frantic and little sparks flew off his body and danced on his skin.

I was stunned to silence when the man was totally nude. He made all the Greek statues look like wimps. His perfectly muscled chest was lightly dusted with black hair that veed down to his stomach and pointed to the most alarmingly large and beautiful erection I'd ever seen.

My breasts grew heavy and my need for him overwhelmed me. My breath came in small uneven pants and my mouth felt dry. Holy hell, I wasn't even sure if he would fit. This was so stupid, but there was no turning back now. My Dragon would fry me from the inside out if I ran.

Nicolai's decidedly masculine chuckle pulled my eyes from his lower region back to his face. His eyes burned green and he approached me with the intent of ending my single life forever.

"You're over dressed," he said as he solved the issue by stripping me naked almost as quickly as he stripped himself. "Damn, you are perfection."

His hands roamed my body and I tried to steel my heart against him, but I knew it was too late. The only thing I could hold back were the words and I would never give him those. Tentatively, I ran my hands over his skin and gloried in the way his body contracted as I discovered it.

"Touch me like you mean it, Dima. Because trust me, I mean everything I'm doing to you," he said in a dark voice as his lips slid from my neck to my aching breasts.

I tangled my fingers in his black hair and arched into his hungry mouth. All rational thought was gone and I felt a lava-like heat begin to wind its way through my limbs.

"Nicolai," I gasped as his mouth moved lower. "Too hot. I think I'm too hot."

"It's the Dragon Fire," he hissed as he found the spot between my legs that made my vision go white. "It's okay, baby. I feel it too."

He worked my body like he'd known it forever and I was certain the entire weyr could hear my screams of ecstasy, but I didn't care. His mouth made me come so hard I sobbed, but we weren't done. We'd only just begun.

"My turn," I demanded as I pushed at him and made him lay back.

His eyes were hooded with lust. He looked dangerous and sexier than hell. I ran my tongue along his skin and nipped at him as I moved down his body to happily return the favor. He tasted like he was mine and my Dragon writhed inside my body with satisfaction.

"Only for a second, Dima," he growled as he grabbed my hair and guided me to his cock. "The first time I come with you will be inside your body. Do you understand me?"

"I hear you," I said with a coy smile as I looked up at him and winked. "But it doesn't mean I'm going to obey. Besides, my mouth is part of my body."

"You're killing me here," he said as his body jerked with pleasure when my tongue slid over the broad head.

"You're a big boy. I'm sure you'll be just fine." Again, I wondered if he would fit inside me, but I decided to cross that bridge when we got to it.

Taking him into my mouth, I ran my tongue around the soft skin that covered his rock hard desire. It felt powerful to have him coming apart under my lips. The sounds that came from deep in his chest spurred me on. I wanted to make him feel as good as he'd made me feel.

"Enough," he ground out harshly as he pulled me off of him and easily slid me up his body until we were nose to nose. "I have no clue how this works, but just stay with me."

I nodded as the heat in my body ramped up to the point of pain. My Dragon Fire was close and it wanted a new home inside Nicolai's body. His eyes were wild and his hands gripped my ass in a vise like hold as he ground himself against my squirming body.

"I think I'm on fire," I gasped as I felt the head of his cock at my softened entrance. "I think we're going to blow up. Can that happen?"

"I sure as hell hope not," he said as he flipped me to my back and spread my legs open wide. "I haven't come yet."

His grin was huge and I laughed despite the fact I felt like I would implode any second. My need to be connected to him, both physically and spiritually was indescribable. I pulled at him so hard he fell forward on top of me. The weight of his body made it difficult to breathe, but it was so good at the same time.

"I need you," I hissed as I bit at his lips in desperation. "If you don't help me put this fire out I will zap your ass to hell."

"You're idea of foreplay is a little violent, but I like it," he said with a sexy smirk. His voice was even, but I could feel he was getting as desperate as me. "When you feel it coming, kiss me. The flow will be less painful."

"It's going to hurt?" I asked and felt my eyes go wide.

"I have no idea, but if it's anything like what's boiling up inside of me it's going to be explosive," he said as he pushed the head of his cock into my writhing body and groaned. "You feel so good—so fucking perfect."

Ready or not I was going to do this. I was fearful of the pain from both the Dragon Fire and Nicolai's sheer size, but that didn't stop my body from wantonly inviting both in.

With a thrust of his hips Nicolai buried himself to the hilt inside. I cried out at the initial invasion and then cried out again as an orgasm much more intense than the first ripped though my body and brought the Dragon Fire to the surface.

"Kiss me," Nicolai shouted as he crushed my lips with his and rocked his hips with such speed I was sure I would pass out.

My body undulated beneath his and I met him thrust for thrust with wild and joyous abandon. I never though anything would compare to the freedom of flying, but making love with my true mate beat it hands down.

I felt my fire leave my body and flow into his as he plowed into me like a freight train. The pain was outweighed by the surreal feeling of becoming one with him. I couldn't tell where I began or where he ended. I was Nicolai and he was me. Our auras blended and meshed as one. It was sexual, emotional and right out of this world.

As his fire raced through my veins, my body bucked wildly, begging to be even closer. There was no way I could get close enough.

"Deeper, I need to be deeper," he mumbled almost incoherently as he pulled out of me and flipped me to my stomach.

180

Yanking my hips up off the bed, he plunged into me with such a ferocious need it left me breathless. His body hammered at mine and we had sex like the animals we were. It was perfect, frightening and life changing. I felt the beginnings of another orgasm grip me as Nicolai bent forward and planted little bite-kisses all over my neck and shoulders.

"I'm going to come. I want you to come with me," he instructed in a hoarse voice.

"Yes," I said roughly as I pushed back against his strong thrusts.

Using one hand to hold himself up, he pressed the other to the same spot where his mouth had been only a short while ago. I felt him grow larger inside me and my desire spiraled to a point I didn't know existed. My scream echoed in my ears as if it had come from someone else and Nicolai's roar of satisfaction rang in my ears.

It was if I was floating above my body and I closed my eyes as the orgasmic aftershocks continued to make me shudder. Nicolai stayed buried deep within me but rolled us to our sides so we were spooning.

"Are you alive?" he asked as he worked to catch his breath.

"No. I don't think so," I replied with an exhausted giggle. "Are you?"

"No, but death was fucking great," he said.

I could feel his heart beating like a machine gun pressed against my back and his chest still heaved to take in enough air. However, the most shocking thing was I felt him grow hard again within me.

"You've got to be kidding," I muttered on a laugh.

"Um...nope," he said with an absurd amount of male pride. "You do it for me like no one in my life has ever done. I don't think I'm going to be able to get enough of you."

"You can really go again?" I asked as I peeked at him over my shoulder.

"And again and again. You up for it?" he asked with a lopsided grin and a thrust of his hips.

I was surprised at how fast my desire for the insane Dragon ramped up again. Thankfully it was different than the painfully hot lava feeling I'd had before we'd mated, but it was no less intense.

"Is that a challenge?" I asked as I ground my backside against him.

"It is," he agreed readily. "I hear a Dragon can't resist a challenge."

"You heard right," I purred as I began to rock my hips in earnest.

"God, I love being a Dragon," Nicolai shouted.

I did too.

And I accepted his challenge again and again and again because far be it from me to run from a dare.

Chapter 19

"Do you want to tell us anything?" Maria asked with a wide smile she couldn't hide and didn't even try to.

My suite was filled with Dragons and a Wolf. I'd slipped away when Nicolai fell asleep. I realized he'd lied a little about the snoring thing. I just hoped he hadn't exaggerated his prowess with putting the toilet seat down.

"Um…no?" I said as I popped open a bottle of water and downed it.

Sex made me thirsty. A marathon of sex made me feel like the Sahara Dessert.

I was not about to give a blow by blow to my niece, my mate's brother and mother, the nutty Warlock Dragon and an Alpha Wolf—pun kind of intended. It was very clear they knew what happened by the embarrassingly enormous grins on their faces. I didn't need to add to their fun.

"I'm so happy," Maria screamed and tackle hugged me. "Can I call Nicolai Uncle Nicolai now?"

"You'll have to take that up with him," I grunted as I crawled out from underneath her with the tiny bit of dignity I had left.

"Welcome to our family," Elaina said with outstretched arms and tears in her eyes.

This was so wildly uncomfortable for me. It was bad enough that Elaina knew I'd boffed her son for a few hours, but it was even harder for me to accept that I had a family who didn't want to kill me.

"Thank you," I mumbled as I hugged her back.

"I saw all of this, my sister," Seth said as he took my hands in his and squeezed them tight.

"A heads up might have been nice," I said with a laugh and a wince.

"That's not how it works. Fate has to play out on its own terms," he said as he kissed my forehead and smoothed back the hair that I was sure was far more out of control that usual.

"Essie is downright beside herself with joy, little Dragon. And I am too," Junior crowed as he picked me up and swung me around the room like a rag doll. "We're gonna have a big dadgum party when all this shee-ot is over. And by the way, I think that call you made to Sandy is helpin'. She talked on the phone for a full seven minutes before she got pissed and hung up on me. I should probably quit comparing her ass to the moon and stars. I figured that crap was poetic, but she thought I was sayin' she had a big butt."

As usual, Junior left me speechless, but I'd come to expect that and wouldn't have it any other way.

Lenny was the most sedate of the group. He touched my face and then turned his back on me and lifted his shoulder length hair. I was confused by his bizarre action until I saw what he wanted me to see. Thankfully I was near a chair because my knees buckled and I gasped so loud the entire room quieted.

Lenny's mark matched mine. It matched Daniel's and it matched Maria's. Who in the hell was he?

He let his hair fall back into place and turned back to face me. He tilted his head to the side and was silent as he watched the plethora of emotions cross my face.

"Who are you?" I whispered.

"My name is Leonardo and I'm of your line."

"No. I mean who are you to me?" I asked a bit louder.

Maria slowly walked over and stood next to me. She'd seen the same thing I had and was just as confused.

"I suppose you would call me your grandfather," he said with a small shrug. "I'm your mother's father."

"Wait," Junior said trying to piece the puzzle together that had so many missing pieces it was ridiculous. "Why in tarnation aren't you the King?"

"We're a matriarchal society," Lenny answered quietly. "My mother ruled for thousands of years and then my daughter should have ruled next. However, this did not happen."

"Because my father killed her," I finished the horrid tale. "And you're the Dragon Warlock that he imprisoned."

Lenny nodded.

"Is your voodoo handed down?" Junior asked a question I hadn't even thought of. "Is that why Dima can poof places?"

Again Lenny nodded and watched me carefully.

"Wait," Maria said as she sat down beside me with a thud. "Can I poof too?"

"You can and so can Daniel," Lenny said.

"Well, this certainly explains why you knew Maria was my brother's child."

Lenny shrugged and smiled.

"So are you just going to answer the questions we come up with or are you going to shed some real light here?" I asked getting frustrated. I was still digesting that Lenny was my grandfather and his cryptic ways were driving me nuts.

"For now I'll answer questions. You're very much like children at the moment. You'll ask the questions when you're ready for the answers," Lenny explained.

"Oh my God," Maria gushed. "Can I call you Great-Grandpa?"

"If that is what you wish," Lenny said with a chuckle.

"This is fucking unbelievable," Maria shouted, clearly forgetting we were all right next to her. "In just over a week, I got an aunt, a cousin, an uncle and a great-grandfather. I mean who in the hell would have guessed that?"

The door to my suite flew open and a half dressed, wildly upset Nicolai burst into the room. "Where is she? Did she leave?" he roared as his eyes scanned the room in desperation.

As soon as they landed on me, he calmed. He ran his hands through his hair and audibly sighed with relief. My company slipped quietly from my suite and closed the door behind them as Nicolai and I stared at each other.

"You thought I would run?"

"Yes...no. I didn't know," he answered honestly.

I'd never seen him so vulnerable and it made my heart hurt.

"I'm still here," I said and grabbed two bottles of water. I tossed him one and he downed it in one sip.

"God, I was thirsty," he muttered and he stood in the middle of the room, still unsure what to do with himself. "I just thought..."

"Thought what?"

"I thought I might have scared you with the renegotiation of terms thing. I swear to you I'll honor the deal we made. You'll be free to go when your father is dead. I was just kidding about making you come until I got what I wanted—well, kind of. I mean I did make you come…" His grin was all kinds of sexy, but his eyes belied his bravado.

"What if I don't want to go?" I asked as I popped open my water and chugged it. I knew the mature adult thing to do was to maintain eye contact, but I was putting it all on the line and I chickened out. It was so much easier to kill stuff than it was to talk.

"You want me to go?" he asked, now completely confused.

I rolled my eyes and looked up at the ceiling. Did I have to spell it all out for him?

"Noooo," I said slowly as if I were talking to Daniel. "What if I wanted to stay and I wanted you to stay too?"

"Would we have separate living quarters?" he asked still not following.

Clearly, I had to spell it out.

"Um, no. I was thinking maybe we could live together."

"Like *together*-together?"

"Is that a problem for you?"

Oh my God, had I misinterpreted all this? Did he *want* me to leave?

"Hell no, that's not a problem," he said in a voice better suited for the outdoors. "Are you sure?"

I looked at the half clothed Dragon standing in my room taking up most of the air and space and I sighed. He was beautiful when he was in control and just as stunning when he was unsure of himself. I knew he didn't he loved me the way I loved him, but that didn't matter. I'd been so deprived of love my entire life I had enough for both of us.

Fate had handed me several gifts—Daniel and now Nicolai. I was certain she expected me to cherish what she'd bestowed and I accepted her challenge. I *was* a Dragon after all.

ROBYN PETERMAN

"I'm sure."

Before I could utter another word, his lips crushed mine. I wrapped my arms around his huge frame and moaned happily into his mouth.

"I promise to make you happy," he whispered as he planted little kisses all over my face. "And I will love Daniel, too."

"Too? You mean you love me?" I asked, startled as I pulled back and searched his face for a sign he was lying.

"Um…yes. Is that okay?" he asked cautiously, trying to gauge if he'd said the wrong thing to the crazy woman.

Tears filled my eyes and I dropped my head into my hands.

"I swear to God I'll never say it again. I'll only think it," he bargained, totally at a loss on how to handle the sobbing Dragon who was now on the floor. "Oh shit," he muttered as he sat down on the carpet next to me and took me in his arms. "I'm in new territory here. My mom—whose ass I'll kick later—said I was supposed to be honest with my emotions. I didn't even know I had any emotions until you came along."

He waited for a response, but I was still choking on my tears.

"Would it help if I let you zap my ass with that pink fire you have? How about I keep letting you call me names with ass in it. I've grown partial to Asscanoe. However, I'll fry the living hell out of anyone that dares to call me that but you. Dima, please stop crying. I didn't mean it."

"You didn't?" I asked as I peeked at him through splayed fingers.

"Fuck." He let his head fall back on his shoulders and he groaned at the ceiling. "Yes, I did mean it, but if it upsets you this much we can pretend that I don't like you at all. Will that work?"

"No, Asscanoe. That won't work," I said as a little grin pulled at my still trembling lips.

"Help me out," he said, removing my hands from my face. "Not real sure how to proceed here."

"I love you," I said.

Nicolai looked terrified and I laughed.

"Call me crazy, but I'm just going to ask you exactly what I'm supposed to do," he said warily.

"You say you love me too."

"Will that result in a sob-fest again?"

"Those were happy tears," I told him with a giggle as I wiped away a few stray droplets.

"Sweet Jesus, this is far more complicated than I'd anticipated."

"Do you want out?" I asked as I scooted closer and smoothed my hand over his wrinkled brow.

"No. I do not want out," he informed me in the same tone he used to talk to his lieutenants. "However, a comprehensive list of what you mean as opposed to what your words and actions imply would be extremely helpful."

"I don't come with an instruction manual."

He stared at me with a bemused expression for a long moment. "Well, this certainly won't be boring."

He was right. Our life together would be anything but boring.

Chapter 20

"The shit has hit the fan. I repeat. The shee-ot has hit the fan," Junior shouted with glee as he typed on his computer like he was hopped up on a vat of caffeine.

"It's working?" Nicolai asked as he looked over Junior's shoulder with a wicked grin on his handsome face.

"Like a goddang dream," Junior said. "Going faster than I thought. The press is all over it and the King has made a statement that it's sabotage. Says he knows who did it and he's going after them. The world thinks he's right off his rocker."

"The world is right," I muttered. "How is it being explained in the press?"

"Basically they're telling a version of the truth and leaving off the fact that the bastard is over a thousand years old. It's being reported that every cent he had was gained through blackmail and extortion and then invested through questionably legal means," Junior explained as he texted on his phone and answered emails on his laptop, while watching several other computer screens at the same time. "We might have doctored the proof just a bit, but no one was gonna buy nine hundred year old cases."

190

"You're multi-tasking skills exceed mine," Nicolai commented as he gestured for all the lieutenants to be seated.

It was Friday evening and our mission was a Go in a little over twenty-four hours. I was antsy to get started. I wanted it over with and I wanted to have my happy ever after—the very one I never thought I would have.

"The Cows and Vamps will be here tomorrow morning," Junior said, not looking up from the computer.

Looks were exchanged between the Dragons, but they stayed silent. However, I did not.

"What do you mean the Cows and the Vamps are coming?" I growled. "They're watching over Daniel. They can't come here."

"I asked them to come," Nicolai said calmly. "Now that everything is about to go down, they'll be safer here. We have a bunker that goes several stories underground and we'll be leaving a contingency of Dragons behind for protection."

"Don't you think I should have been consulted about this?" I asked in a tone that made everyone in the room duck for cover.

"I did this for you," Nicolai said not backing down. "I want our child to be safe."

The *our child* thing secretly thrilled me, but he wasn't our child. He was mine and I made the decisions for him.

"You will tell them to turn around now," I said. "You had no right to do this without my permission."

"It was a group decision," Seth cut in before I could shoot a fireball at Nicolai and singe the eyebrows off his face. "I had a vision and I'm the one who put the plan into action, not Nicolai."

"What did you see?" I demanded. "Did you see Daniel being harmed where he is now?"

The thought made me ill.

"No, my visions are mostly positive. I saw you holding Daniel in your arms and kissing him before you went into battle. I took it as a sign that he should be here."

I took three deep breaths and got a handle on my need to blow up the Command Room. I needed to speak and I needed to be understood.

"Look here's the deal guys, I'm not used to people making decisions for me or even giving a shit about my welfare, for that matter. While it's alarmingly nice, you can *never* make a decision about my son without my knowledge again. Are we clear?" My tone was terse and I was holding onto my temper with difficulty, but I was okay with it this time. Next time…

"I told you we should have checked with her," Lenny said giving Nicolai a look.

"Fine," Nicolai shouted. "When I knew what was happening, I ordered everyone to stay quiet. I wanted to surprise you."

"Manual item number one," I said as I got right up in my Dragon's face. "Do. Not. Surprise. Me. When. My. Son's. Life. Is. Involved."

"Cade, write that down and put it in a file called Understanding Dima," Nicolai snapped in frustration. "I will never get women," he muttered.

"Alrightyroo," Junior said with a relieved whistle. "Now that we got that solved with no bloodshed, you should know that the Cows plan to fight along side you."

"Why?" Elaina asked. "This is not their battle."

"With all due respect, I beg to differ," Junior said as he stopped typing and glanced up at the shocked faces in the room. "The sumbitch who's soon to be dead is the same peckerhead who ordered the mass destruction of their species. Over ninety-nine percent of their population was taken out because of the Dragon King. They want revenge and trust me, you want them on your side in this battle. However, I'd just like to put it out there that everyone should get a nose plug."

"Why?" Seth asked as he paled a bit.

"Dima, you wanna clue them in or should I?" Junior asked, snickering like a middle school boy.

"Well," I hedged trying to figure out a way to explain the Cow's methods without using the word fart in a sentence. "They, um...emit lethal explosions that are, um... pungent."

"Oh for God's sake," Junior laughed and shook his head. "She means they blow deadly butt farts."

"I'm sorry. What?" Elaina asked with a scrunched nose and an appalled expression.

"They can singe the hair off your head and blind you with their bottoms." I winced and threw my hands in the air. "Junior's correct. They fart and it's the most horrendous thing I've ever seen."

"You mean smelled," Junior added, helping me out.

"Yes, smelled. As long as you're upwind or next to them it's tolerable, but if you're in the line of fire, you're dead."

"Is this a joke?" Nicolai asked as he gaped open-mouthed at me and Junior.

"No, it's not," I said.

There was about five minutes of silence while the Dragons mulled this new stinky twist over.

"I've heard of this," Lenny said trying not to laugh and failing miserably. "At this point I say we accept their generous offer and let them help avenge their race."

"Seriously?" Nicolai asked with a grimace.

"Yes, I agree with Lenny. They're lovely people and they deserve to be there as much as we do." I finished my piece and took a seat. My stomach was flipping with excitement at the thought of seeing Daniel and I began counting the minutes until tomorrow morning.

"I agree as well," Elaina said. "The King's tyranny has been devastating to our race, but we're still here. The Cows are not. I will fight along side them proudly."

"Make sure you stay beside and not in front of," Junior recommended in total seriousness as he went back to his computers.

"Will do," Elaina said.

"As you know," Nicolai said, staring at the maps I'd provided of my father's compound. "We have no intel on the inside. We do have spies surrounding the area, but we've been banking on the fact that he'll stay there. That could prove to be our downfall."

The silence was loaded as everyone considered this possible clusterfuck of a wrinkle.

"The press is tracking his every move at this point," I said, speaking my thoughts aloud as they formed in my head. "If he moves it will be publicized and we'll just be ready to abort mission one and move on mission two."

Nicolai nodded. "It's the best we can do. We've never had such a brilliant opening until now. We'll make it work no matter where we have to go."

"It has to stay covert so the humans don't figure anything out that could harm them or reveal us," Seth added.

"Agreed," Nicolai said with a curt nod. "We want as few casualties as possible. I don't want the humans even remotely involved, but if it comes down to getting the King or losing him—we get him. Clear?"

"The King—for lack of a better word—will be at the compound. He won't leave his hoard behind," Lenny said with more anger than I'd seen in the brief time I'd known him.

"Um, news flash here, guys," Junior said, glancing up from the computer in alarm. "I'm destroying his hoard as we speak."

"You're destroying *part* of his hoard," Lenny corrected him. "You're bringing down a very public and important part of his hoard that will throw his army and loyalists into chaos, but a Dragon always keeps the most valuable part of his hoard very close."

"You know what his hoard is?" I asked, unable to imagine what other horrible thing my father had done to have something more valuable than the billions of ill-gotten dollars in his hoard.

"I have my suspicions," Lenny said tightly.

"And that's all we're going to get?" I was so frustrated with my *grandfather's* cryptic ways. But Lenny only would let you know what he wanted you to know when he was ready to share it.

"Is there anything I can do to destroy the rest of his hoard?" Junior asked. "I have a lot of great minds at my disposal right now."

"No," Lenny said. "The false king has already done much to harm this section of his hoard."

"Do we need to search out this treasure and destroy it when we're in the compound?" I asked wanting to make sure if my father somehow escaped us, we could completely decimate everything of value to him.

Lenny stared at me for a bizarrely long beat and then shook his head. "No. I'll be keeping this part of the hoard if it still exists."

"Fine," Nicolai said. "You deserve to have whatever you want from that bastard after being tortured in his dungeon for hundreds of years. I will personally help you find this treasure and kill anyone who tries to take it from you."

"I'm in too," Maria vowed. "I will kill the fucking shit out of anyone who messes with you, Great-Grandpa."

God, I really had to have a talk with her about her language. She was a hot mess of profanity.

"Thank you, child," Lenny said as he stood and kissed Maria on the head. "You do your father and mother proud."

Maria bowed her head and was silent. Hell, we all were.

"We must sleep," Elaina said, breaking the silence. "We have much to accomplish in the next twenty-four hours and rest is imperative."

With nods, handshakes and hugs we parted.

"You're coming with me," Nicolai said with a gleam of childlike excitement in his eyes.

"Am I?" I asked as I squinted at him and tried not to smile.

"Yep, you are."

He drove me nuts and made me feel loved.

I'd follow him to the ends of the earth.

Chapter 21

"Close your eyes," Nicolai said, barely able to contain himself as he led me into his quarters.

Having the deadliest Dragon alive behave like an excited child on Christmas morning was a little disconcerting, but I was going with it.

"Okay…open," he said.

I opened my eyes and my hand flew to my mouth. My ever-present tears of late filled my eyes and I gasped with joy. This was impossible. How did he do this?

"Please tell me those are happy tears," Nicolai pleaded as he backed away in fear of the unknown mood swings of the female Dragon named Dima.

I nodded and gave him a watery smile as I slowly walked around the main living area touching all the colorful treasures. It was filled with toys—trains and trucks and coloring books and so much more I couldn't even take it all in. It looked liked ten toy stores had exploded in his suite. It was the most beautiful thing I'd ever seen.

"This is incredible," I whispered in awe.

"I also baby proofed everything," he informed with so much pride I giggled. "I had no idea what the hell that even meant, but my mother said I had to do it since our son was coming. Junior looked it up online and we baby proofed the living hell out of this place. I can't even open the damn cabinets now."

"I think I just fell in love with you a little more," I said as I stared in wonder at the man I'd been blessed enough for fate to hand me.

"I can baby proof the entire compound if it will get me laid," he offered with a wicked sexy grin.

"I'd have to say this is probably good enough to make your wish come true," I told him as I picked up a stuffed dragon and hugged it to my chest.

"Wait. Does this mean I'm getting lucky tonight?" he asked with a laugh as he began to disrobe, obviously very sure of his odds.

"You are so getting lucky tonight," I said as I dragged him toward the bedroom.

"More than once?" he asked as he picked me up and sprinted the rest of the way.

"As many times as you want, baby... As many times as you want."

***

"Should I just talk to him like a regular person?" Nicolai asked as he paced the grounds while we waited for the arrival of Daniel, the Cows, Dwayne and Granny. "Damn it, what do I do if he doesn't like me?"

"Yes, Nicolai, you just talk to him. He doesn't bite. Well, not anymore. When he was teething he almost took my fingers off a couple of times, but we're over that now," I told him and laughed at his horrified expression.

"You'll be fine," Elaina assured her nervous son. "I'm more worried about accidentally getting downwind of the Cows."

"And don't forget we have Vampyres coming as well," Seth reminded us.

"More than just Dwayne and Granny?" I asked as I scanned the horizon for cars.

"Hell, yeah," Junior said. "The Cows are bringing their undead husbands."

"Shut the front fucking door," Maria snorted. "The Cows are mated to Vampyres?"

"Yep, and they eloped, which almost killed Dwayne even though he's already technically dead," I told the group. "He had adopted the Cows and was furious he didn't get to plan their weddings."

"Vampyres like to plan weddings?" Lenny asked skeptically.

"Dwayne does. Dwayne's not your everyday Vamp," I told Lenny cryptically. God it felt good to give him some of his own medicine.

Lenny waited for more and when it didn't come he winked at me and gave me a thumbs up. I was taking after the old man and it felt good.

"Here they come," Maria yelled as she ran toward the approaching caravan.

Dwayne, Granny and Daniel led the cavalcade in a brand spanking new, cherry red Hummer. I rolled my eyes. Essie had told me Dwayne liked to drive Hummers because he enjoyed being able to say the word hummer in polite company without getting in trouble. However, the Cows made the most spectacular entrance I'd ever seen. The Dragons watched with raised brows and amused expressions.

Eight huge, loud, and shiny Harley motorcycles trailed behind the Hummer each carrying one Cow and one besotted Vampyre. They waved to the crowd of open-mouthed Dragons and the cheering started. I marveled at the unbelievable irony. Never had Dragons partnered with any species other than their own. It was a new time and a new day.

"I thought the Cows were women," Nicolai whispered in my ear. "I'd swear on a stack of bibles that each of those bikes are carrying two men."

"They're women," I said as I watched them drive in. "Masculine, wonderful women."

"Jesus," Nicolai muttered with a grunt of disbelief. "They scare me and I'm a freakin' Dragon."

"If they offer you milk, drink it," Junior advised under his breath as he waved at the incoming parade of strange.

"They brought milk with them?" Nicolai asked, confused.

"Dude, they are the milk."

Junior laughed like a loon and he moved off toward the Cows as Nicolai slapped his hand over his mouth and gagged. This was going to be fun...

I ran over to the Hummer, yanked open the back door and smothered my son with kisses as he laughed and squealed.

"I've missed you so much," I said as I unbuckled his seatbelt and pulled him out of his booster seat. "Have you been a good boy?"

"He certainly has," Granny said with a big smile. "Them Cows don't want to give him back. He's got those girls doin' his every bidding."

"Me love the Cows," Daniel said with a long put upon sigh. "I asked them to mawry me, but they are alweady mawried."

"You've asked a lot of women to marry you in your four short years," I said as I bit back my smile. "Do you think that's wise?"

"Yes, I do. There are so many giwrls I wove."

"Our boy is a Romeo," Dwayne said as he bent down and gave Daniel a big kiss and a hug. "We're going to miss having you around."

"What do you say to Dwayne?" I asked Daniel.

"Thank you for letting me stay wif you, O Gweat Uncle Dwayne the Best Gaga Ever."

"Seriously?" I gave Dwayne a look and he just grinned and shrugged.

"He only calls me that in public. At home I'm just Uncle Dwayne."

I laughed as I put Daniel on the ground and took his hand.

"I have some very good friends I want you to meet. Would you like that?"

"Yep," he said as he pulled me toward the waiting group. "Is Seff over there?"

"He is and he's so excited to see you. His mom and his brother Nicolai are over there too."

"Awesome," Daniel yelled and squeezed my hand. "Will they wike me?"

"They're going to love you," I promised as we approached. "Guys, this is my son, Daniel."

I introduced him to Maria who was thankfully able to rein in her dirty mouth. Elaina and Lenny gave him warm hugs and promises of letting him fly on their backs. Daniel was wildly ecstatic that he had a new grandpa *and* a cousin. Maria cried and Lenny just beamed.

Junior tossed my little man in the air and Seth took him in his arms and hugged him tight. The only one left was Nicolai. He stood off to the side not quite sure what to do. In the end he had to do nothing…four year olds were very good that way.

"Who are you?" Daniel asked as he walked right over pointed at Nicolai with open curiosity.

"Um…I'm Nicolai and I like your mommy a whole lot," Nicolai said and held out his hand for a shake.

"I wike my mommy too," Daniel told him and then lifted his chubby arms for Nicolai to pick him up. "You is huge. When I gwow up I wanna be big as you."

"Well, you just have to eat right and...um, eat a lot," Nicolai said and then rolled his eyes at his lame answer.

Daniel didn't seem to care a bit. He was quite impressed with the big Dragon's reply.

"How much do you wike my mommy?" Daniel inquired as he poked at Nicolai's massive arm muscles.

"I like your mommy a whole bunch. Is that okay with you?" Nicolai asked with a grin as he flexed to impress my boy.

Daniel considered Nicolai's statement seriously while he stared the deadly Dragon right in the eye. "I wike a lot of girwls and I ask them to mawry me. Will you ask my mommy to mawry you?"

I closed my eyes and stifled my laugh, but I was the only one who held back. The rest of my friends found my son's lack of candor quite amusing—including Nicolai.

"I think that could definitely be arranged," Nicolai said, swinging Daniel up onto his broad shoulders, much to my son's delight. "In fact, maybe you should ask her for me. I might have a better chance of getting a yes."

"I can do that for you, Nicowai. My mommy needs a big stwong man cause sometimes she cwies," Daniel whispered the way a four year old does...loudly.

"Mommies cry sometimes, but how about I promise to only make her cry happy tears?" Nicolai suggested as he looked at me with so much adoration in his eyes that I almost proved my son correct by crying on the spot.

My big bad Dragon was a total softy.

"I think our little man needs a nap," Granny said as she and Dwayne finished meeting the group. "Do you want us to keep him in our room?" she asked with waggling eyebrows.

"Nope," Nicolai said as he started off for his suite. "Our boy is coming with us."

"I'm gonna be big like Nicowai," Daniel shouted as Nicolai trotted them off to the suite.

Daniel was going to lose his mind when he saw the surprises that Nicolai had gotten.

"Dima, I want to have a chat with you later today if you can find the time," Lenny said as everyone went over to greet the Cows.

"Of course."

"Meet me at two in your former suite. I'd like it very much for it to be just you and me."

"Not a problem, Len...Grandpa," I mumbled awkwardly, trying to get used to the word.

Lenny beamed and gave me a quick bow. "Till then," he said and poofed away.

Shaking my head at his oddities, I waved to the Cows who were holding court with the Dragons. The semi-terrified Dragons, some of whom were covertly holding their noses as a precaution, were doing their best to stand directly in front of the Cows. The visual of the constantly dodging Dragons as the Cows unloaded their gear was absurd.

I turned and picked up my pace. I was ready to play trucks, trains and cars with my boys. Life couldn't get much better than this very moment. I pushed aside the thought that tomorrow would be very different and decided to enjoy today to its fullest.

Today was the first day of the very happy rest of my new life.

Chapter 22

After rousing games of Hide and Seek, Candy Land and Old Maid, we consumed an enormous amount of both macaroni and cheese and chocolate cake, compliments of the chefs in the mess hall. Daniel was so wiped out he couldn't keep his eyes open. We had family time at warp speed and Nicolai kept up just fine. I hadn't heard my big deadly Dragon laugh so much in the entire time I'd known him and Daniel was in heaven. He'd found a new hero to worship and followed Nicolai all over the suite, copying every one of his mannerisms.

"I'm going to put Mr. Sleepyhead down for a nap. Lenny wants to talk with me. Will you watch Daniel?" I asked quietly as the little man in question fell asleep on my shoulder.

"Give him to me," Nicolai whispered. "He wore my ass out. I'll nap with him."

I gave my baby a kiss on his head and Nicolai a soft kiss on his lips and then I handed Daniel over.

"I won't be long."

"Take your time. I have a feeling your guys are going to be asleep for a few hours," he said with a grin and a yawn.

"Thank you," I said softly.

"No Dima, thank you," he replied as he turned and walked back to our bedroom with my child cradled safely in his strong arms.

***

"Can I ask you a question?" Lenny inquired as he seated himself on the couch and sipped on the hot tea I'd made.

"Sure. Do I get to ask you some questions in return?" I bargained with pursed lips and raised brows.

"But of course." Lenny laughed and placed his teacup carefully back in the saucer. "I might not answer them, but you are free to ask."

I rolled my eyes and sat down next to him. "Shoot."

"Your powers...have you tried anything other than transport?" he asked.

"I had no clue I could do anything other than that," I told him truthfully. "My mother taught me to do it and I'd only ever done it once for practice before I did it in Chicago." I froze. My stomach contracted like a hot knife had been shoved into it and I felt dizzy and ill. "That's not true," I whispered in a strangled voice. "There was one other time, but I think I forgot about it because it was..."

"When?" Lenny prodded gently. "When was the other time you transported?"

"It was the day they died. It was how I got away. She screamed for me to transport and I did. I left them all there to die."

"Your mother told you to go?"

"Yes."

I stood up and began to pace. I'd not spoken my nightmare aloud to anyone. Ever. But Lenny was my Grandfather. He had a right to know.

"Go on child. I need to hear this," Lenny said as he sat forward and gently rocked back and forth.

There was no way to sugarcoat any of it. It was the most awful day of my existence and it would forever be with me.

"I heard yelling and screaming and I ran toward it. I knew it was my mother…when I opened the door all four of them were bound in heavy rope and chains and there was blood. There was so much blood and my father had huge knives and hatchets in his hands. He was hacking away at my brothers."

"And were your brothers dead at that point?" he asked as he raised his tea to his lips with shaking hands.

"Yes…no, I'm not sure. There was blood everywhere. I focused on my mother because she was yelling at me."

"To go?"

I nodded and sat back down. My knees had gone weak and my body felt as if it weighed thousands of pounds.

"I went in to try and save them, but I was so small and my mother kept screaming at me."

"How old were you?"

"Ten. I was ten."

"My God." Lenny swore harshly and pressed his hands to his temples. "Where did you go? What did you do? You were just a child."

I heard his question, but I had no intention of answering it. It was over four hundred years ago and it was in the best forgotten past. It was a lonely and desolate time. I tried to never give it a thought anymore. I knew it defined who I was to a certain degree, but it was so damned depressing and degrading. I didn't feel sorry for myself and I didn't want Lenny to feel sorry for me either.

How could I tell the man who was the father of my slain mother that his granddaughter had lived as a Dragon in the wild for a hundred years before she was brave enough to take her human form and try to live among society?

What would he think if I told him I'd been a homeless human and had to prostitute myself for food and shelter? How do you tell the man who would have wanted my life to have been idyllic that it took me decades before I could talk to people or to be around men?

Could I explain to my grandfather that once I did find a weyr of Dragons, they beat me so brutally when they discovered my identity that death would have been kinder? Did I explain to him that the reason I was so deadly was because I'd had absolutely no choice? Should I tell him that before I had Daniel I'd considered taking my own life more times than I could count?

No. I shouldn't.

So I didn't tell him. I told him the softer parts—the better parts—the parts that wouldn't upset him.

"It took a long time," I said hesitantly. "Eventually I realized that knowledge was power and once I'd earned enough money I educated myself. I've been to every Ivy League school at least twice—some, three times. I have more degrees and doctorates than I have sense. Of course when you're immortal, you have a lot of time on your hands and…"

"It was awful, wasn't it? The parts you're withholding…they were awful," he pressed.

I inhaled slowly and closed my eyes. I knew tendrils of smoke had escaped from my nose, but I didn't care. "It's unspeakable. I'll leave it at that. But probably no more unspeakable than the years of torture you endured at my father's hands. Would you tell me about that if I asked?"

"No," he said quietly. "I would not."

I nodded and poured him a fresh cup of tea as his was now cold. We sat in silence lost in our own thoughts of the past.

"Are you sure they were dead?" he asked, pulling my mind back to the present.

"How could you even ask me that?" I demanded as I jumped up in distress. My teacup clattered to the table and broke in to tiny pieces. "Don't you think if they weren't dead they would have found me?" I yelled as flashes of my wretched existence passed before my eyes. "My mother would have found me—she loved me. My brothers would have saved me from the horrific hell on earth I lived for hundreds of years. That is the most hateful question you could ask me. Why would you say that?"

Lenny went ashen and looked like a very old man for a brief moment. He stood and wrapped his strong arms around me as guttural, animalistic sounds left my mouth. His soft words sounded like white noise as I tried to get a grip on my rioting emotions.

"I'm sorry," he whispered over and over into my hair as I shook and tried not to be ill. "I'm so sorry. You will never be alone again. You have my promise and my love. I'm so sorry."

I held on to the man whose life had been just as affected as mine by what happened on that day. His tears mixed with my own as he pressed his cheek to mine. In my heart, I understood his question. I'd prayed for hundreds of years that my mother and brothers had somehow survived my father's brutality, but I'd given up hope. Hope can kill you just as easily as a blade. It takes longer though, and is far more painful.

"It's okay," I said as I held tightly to my grandfather. "I prayed for the same for so many years until I couldn't pray anymore. I'm sorry that I…"

"No, child. I'm sorry. I had no right to open up painful wounds. It's just an old Dragon's wishful thinking…It's inexcusable. It will never happen again."

"No Lenny, it will happen again and it should. At some point I will have to tell Maria and Daniel these stories and I want you with me. Never in my life did I think I would have a family. I have one now and I will defend it with my life. And that means you, too. I know you're a magical freak," I said with a weak laugh, "but you need our family as much as I do."

"You are correct." He sighed heavily. "And just so you're aware, you are a magical freak yourself. Over time, I will teach you just exactly how freaky you are."

"I look forward to it."

"As do I," he said with a smile. "Now go back to your boys. I have some work to do."

Lenny kissed my forehead, helped me clean the broken pieces of the cup and then left in a poof of purple smoke. I had to sit for a bit before I had the energy to put on a happy face for my guys. I could fool Daniel, but not Nicolai.

Taking some cleansing breaths, I made a promise to myself. Most of the time I tried not to think about my mother and brothers anymore—that was wrong. I would honor them by being happy. They would want that for me just as I would have wanted it for them if the tables were turned. I had everything to live for and after tomorrow their deaths would be avenged.

Tomorrow couldn't come soon enough.

Chapter 23

"We'll go in first," Pat said as she and her Cow sisters did jumping jacks and pushups. "We can clear every outside guard and sniper off their perch with a few well aimed assbombs."

"Any that don't disintegrate after the first gaseous anal attack, we'll nail with machine gun like farts that will kill em dead as a doornail," Francis added with a grunt and a thumbs up.

"Shouldn't take more than six minutes and thirty-four seconds," Pat told us as she did some nightmare inducing leg lifts.

"Outstanding," Lenny said much to the delight of the Cows while the Dragons were utterly dumbfounded and stunned.

We'd left Daniel with Granny, Dwayne, Junior and a contingent of fifty well trained Dragons in New York two hours ago and flew to Michigan where my Father's main compound was located. Lenny had provided magical cover for the hundred and fifty members of our Dragon army so we could fly undetected in daylight. The eight Cows rode on our backs and their Vampyre mates flew along side.

It was difficult leaving my baby, but I knew I was doing what had to be done. I prayed that I would come back to him, but if my father was dead, Daniel's future would be safe. I would trade my life for my son's in a heartbeat.

"Are you positive they're women?" Nicolai whispered in my ear. "I just don't see it."

"Maybe they're both," Maria offered with a shrug. "They do have boobs."

I elbowed both of them in the gut and swallowed my laugh. We were lucky to have them. It would save lives and hours of fighting. We had the chance to take out the outer protection ring in one enormous and odiferous blast. My father would never expect it and the plan, as bizarre as it was, bought us time.

We were about three miles from the compound and we'd all gone back to human form.

"Now, I'm just gonna suggest all of you good people either hold your noses or you can take one of these here handy dandy gas masks we brought along," Pat offered politely as she nodded to her undead mate.

The Vamp blew her a kiss and began passing out the masks. The Dragons accepted them gratefully and whipped them on so fast it was funny.

"Four minutes after the initial blast, it's safe. You can't die from the aroma anymore," Francis explained. "That's when you shift and strike."

"Will the um…aroma be gone then?" Elaina inquired.

"Oh hell no," Pat said with a snort of laughter. "It's gonna smell like butt-hell for about a week round here."

"I'm sorry, did you just say butt-hell?" Elaina asked in a choked voice.

"Yep, she sure did. Thankfully we don't have taste buds so we can't smell it. You people aren't as lucky," Francis chimed in as we all smiled and nodded numbly. "A word to the wise. Stay behind us until we give the okay. I'd hate to kill someone on our team if an air biscuit misfires."

That left us all speechless—and kind of green. We were the deadliest species alive and we were terrified of butt-hell...

"All right then," Nicolai said with a slightly detectable wince. "Everyone will stay back until the Cows secure the outer perimeter. As soon as we get the go ahead, the units will divide and surround the main compound. That's where we expect he will be."

"He'll be there," I said. "His War Room is in there."

"Unit A is in first," Nicolai continued. "The rest will follow in ten minute intervals unless otherwise instructed. Unit E will stay outside with the Cows the entire time and take out anyone who runs from the buildings. Stay Dragon when you're outside the structure and go back to human when you enter. Am I clear?"

The army nodded their assent. Pat raised her hand and waited patiently to be called on.

"Yes, Pat?" Nicolai asked.

"You want a few of us inside with you? It can get a little dangerous with the anal acoustics indoors, but it can be done," she said.

"We did it by accident once at an AC/DC concert. Blew the back wall completely off the auditorium," Harley, one of the tougher looking Cows, volunteered. "Course the irony there was it was during *You Shook Me All Night Long*."

"Oh my God," I choked out through my laughter. "Are you serious?"

"Nah," Harley said with a chuckle and a shrug. "But it's a great story. Right?"

"That it is," I agreed with a shudder.

"It was actually during *Back in Black*, but Harley just loves irony so she likes to put a little spin on it for fun," Pat added as she gave Harley an affectionate punch in the arm. "She's a real jokester."

"Okay then," Nicolai said as he scrubbed his hands over his face and tried to move the conversation back to business. "Ten minutes and we move. Make sure all of your chips are in the on position and you're dialed to the correct frequency for your unit."

Junior's brilliance knew no bounds whatsoever. He'd developed insertable chips that allowed us to communicate with each other. He was concerned because they were a prototype and hadn't been tested, but Nicolai convinced him to let us be the guinea pigs for his experiment. The chips were placed under the skin of our inner wrists and stayed in our bodies even through a shift. All we had to do was talk into our palm area and we could communicate.

Tapping the device put us on different channels. It was fallible, but it was the best we could do. Because the Resistance had been together as long as they had, Nicolai was able to communicate to everyone through mind speak. However, the Dragons weren't capable of answering back.

Nicolai hadn't been successful with touching my mind yet, but I assumed that would come with time. At the very least Nicolai could let our people know when to strike if the chips went down.

Cade landed in the middle of the group along with several other Dragons and quickly shifted back to human. "It seems there are quite a few loyalists staying with the King. I'd estimate about fifty on the outside alone," he reported. "Fully armed and ready for an attack."

"Weapons won't work on us," Seth said with a shake of his head. "What is he thinking?"

"I think they're anticipating an attack by all sorts of Weres—or possibly humans," Lenny said. "God knows our reputation among the other species is nothing to be proud of."

"He's right," Nicolai said tersely. "Did you spot any Shifters other than Dragons?"

"No," Cade said. "We combed the area. If anyone else was here we would know."

"What about the press?" I asked.

"Junior's people sent out some false information and every news outlet that was here is now on their way to Idaho," Maria said with a grin.

"Why Idaho?" I asked, perplexed.

"Why not?" she shot back.

"You know, fifty flying freaks shouldn't be any problem at all," Pat said. "I've personally taken down thirty all by my lonesome. With all eight of us blowing stinkies, they don't stand a chance."

It was all I could do not to laugh. We were talking life and death here, but the Cows' pride in their bizarre weapon lightened the somber mood and I embraced it as a good omen.

"If there are fifty on the outside there's a very good chance there are fewer than that on the inside," Elaina said as she studied the maps of the interior. "I'd have a difficult time believing he'd be able to keep a large group now that he's in total financial ruin. If the map is accurate, we only have the foyer and one large hallway to get through if he's in the War Room."

"If he's not there now, he will be once the explosions go off," I said with confidence. "Creatures of habit like my father rarely try something new."

"We just have to hope there's less than fifty inside," Nicolai said. "Get to your Units. Lenny are you ready to fly over and cover the area?"

"I'll do my best. I'm going for the five mile surrounding radius. If we can glamour that much ground well enough we don't have to worry about the US Military coming in," Lenny said.

"Am I capable of helping you?" I asked. "Do I possess that magic?"

214

"No," Nicolai said and the same time Lenny said, "Yes."

"If I have the ability, I'll use it," I said evenly to Nicolai. "I do not need your permission or protection. If our combined magic will hide the area more thoroughly, we stand less of a chance of killing a huge number of human military units who think we're a terrorist attack on the United States."

Nicolai's lips thinned in displeasure, but he nodded curtly.

"What do I have to do?" I asked Lenny.

"Take my hand," he instructed.

I took his hand and immediately convulsed forward as a blast of searing hot magic entered my system like a runaway freight train from hell. I clamped my lips shut so I didn't scream. I'd endured plenty of pain in my life. This sucked, but I could take it.

"Is that it?" I asked with an agonized wince as I tried to play off the fact that a fiery bomb had just blown up in my gut. I was so hoping there wasn't a second surprise.

"Yes," Lenny said with a proud smile. "I've never seen anyone take that so well."

"Well, I'm not just *anyone*," I shot back with a weak smile as the pain began to ebb.

Nicolai stood three feet away with his fists clenched at sides. His neck veins were pronounced and he looked ready to blow. He clearly wanted to kill something. I wouldn't have wanted to watch him receive the magic any more than he enjoyed watching me jack knife forward in excruciating pain. However, this was simply the way it had to be.

"No pain, no gain," I told him with a wink.

"While I understand it, I don't like it," Nicolai ground out. "You're my mate."

"Today, I'm your co-leader and a deadly killing machine. I'm very adept at what I do. Tonight, I will be your mate. Are we clear?" I asked.

"We are," he said with a hiss of angry frustration. "Cows please move now. As soon as you're in position Lenny and Dima will fly over and cover the area."

"The guards on the ground will be alerted to our presence when Lenny and I are in the air. As soon as we're out of your sightline, you shoot," I told the Cows.

"Roger that," Pat said, hopping around with barely contained excitement. "We've waited many years for this day. Thousands of my people—including our mamma and daddy will be smiling down from heaven," she said reverently. "We thank you for having us."

"Who in the hell woulda thunk the same species that destroyed us would be our partners in killing the mother humper who started the hate?" Francis said, verbalizing the bizarre irony of our pairing. "We really are honored to fight along side you crazy fire breathing freak shows."

"No," Nicolai said as he knelt down on one knee to Pat and Francis. "We are honored and blessed that you have come. United we stand...divided we fall."

The Cows gasped as every Dragon went to their knee in respect for the unusual bovine Shifters with the strange powers. The times were changing and no matter what the outcome of today was, there would be no going back. The Dragons had officially joined the Were race.

"Are we ready?" Nicolai questioned the troops as the Cows left and got into position in the tree line around the compound.

"We are," a chorus of voices called out.

"Then move," Nicolai shouted. "Today the King dies!"

The cheers were loud and my skin broke out in goose bumps. The day of reckoning had come. Quickly and silently, the units dispersed. Lenny took my hand and kissed my forehead.

"Come child, we have work to do."

I nodded, shifted and launched myself into the air with my grandfather. The magic welled inside me and I marveled that I instinctively knew how to use it. I *was* a magical freak just like Lenny—it was in my DNA. The good side of my DNA.

The evil side was about to go down and my Dragon couldn't wait to make it happen.

Today was a very good day.

Chapter 24

As we soared over the compound, covering the area with the magical smoke, I glared down at the massive, spired building below. It was a palace that could have come straight out of medieval times with gargoyles and a damn moat. Actually it had. My father had the identical castle rebuilt many times over the centuries in different parts of the world. He was a creature of habit and tradition and needed the trappings of the old world to keep his vise-like hold on the new one.

It was somewhat of a miracle that the Resistance ever came to be. We were a race of tradition and tyranny, seldom did anyone challenge it. My admiration for my mate and our people was enormous. The bravery it took to challenge the monarchy even slightly was unheard of. What we were doing today, would be mind bogglingly impossible for most of our kind.

But we weren't most of our kind.

"Dima, I have waited for you for centuries. You've given me the chance to come back here and do something that will change everything," Lenny said, bowing his huge head to me.

Lenny's Dragon was beautiful. His hide had flecks of gold that matched mine, but the majority of his body was a brilliant purple.

"We'll do it together," I huffed out blowing pink fire with my words.

"You don't understand," he insisted. "This is the day I get my life back."

"We all do," I told him.

Lenny looked at me with the eyes of a very old and wise Dragon. I thought he was going to explain what he meant, but he just stared for a long moment and then bowed his head in submission. It was odd and uncomfortable. I didn't want my grandfather bowing to me like I was his superior, but we'd discuss that another time. Whatever Lenny wanted to say he would say it when he was ready.

He was Lenny the Cryptic after all.

"Let's get back to the unit," I said in a puff of pink and silver smoke. "The area is sufficiently covered and we have about four minutes. You lead. I'll follow."

"My pleasure."

***

"It's too quiet," I said as we entered the main doors with extreme caution.

Something wasn't right. My stomach churned as I took in the ornate and overblown interior of the grand foyer. Marble floors inlaid with gold leaf shone just as I'd remembered. Tall, intricate ivory columns and a curved grand staircase were the focal points of this particular room. As I child I'd slid down the banister until my rear end was raw. Granted, the castle I'd lived in all those centuries ago in wasn't in Michigan, but its newest incarnation was the same in every way.

The horrifying blasts from the Cows had taken out every Dragon on the outer perimeter just as they'd promised. The stench of the explosion coupled with the burning flesh of the flame engulfed Dragons was something I hoped to never experience again.

"Is anyone even here?" Seth asked as he and Elaina expertly secured the rooms to our right.

"He's here," Lenny said as he and Nicolai secured the rooms on our left. "I feel him."

"The War Room is about eight hundred feet straight ahead. Follow me. Stay low and close to the walls," I instructed.

"I'm calling in B and C," Nicolai said softly. "I don't like this. Something is off."

I turned to check my unit and couldn't find Lenny. Where in the hell had he gone? He was desperate to get inside and now he'd disappeared.

"Um...did Lenny decide to ditch us?"

"No," Nicolai said. "He's gone after the hoard."

"By himself?" I hissed. I'd just found my grandfather. I wanted to keep the crazy old man.

"He was imprisoned here for hundreds of years. He says he knows where he's going," Elaina relayed with an angry headshake. "He's been odd since we arrived."

"Back up is in the building," Nicolai reported.

"Tell them to move to the north side of the palace. There's another entrance into the War Room from the library. I'm pretty sure there are sky lights," I said as memories of old flooded my brain. "Have Unit D fly to the roof and be ready to break through the glass."

"Will do," Nicolai said as he closed his eyes and communicated through mind speak.

It was safer and more reliable than the chip, but...

"Lenny, can you hear me?" I asked my palm.

"Yes," his clipped reply came back through the chip in my arm.

"What in the hell do you think you're doing?" I hissed. "The party is on the main floor."

"I'm getting the hoard. I have to find it."

"We're here to kill the King. I think his fucking hoard can wait," I growled.

"You've been keeping company with your niece," Lenny replied.

"What the hell are you talking about?"

"Your language, dear child. It's appalling."

"Whatever," I snapped. "We need you up here."

"No, you don't. If he sees me he will know I've come for his hoard. It will ruin everything. You are more than capable without me. Please trust me."

I bit down hard on my lips to keep myself from ordering him back. As one of the commanders of the mission I had every right to do so and he would have no choice but to obey. However, my gut told me otherwise. He'd been in my father's presence more recently than I had and if he thought the hoard was that damned important, I had to trust his judgment. I didn't want to—but I would.

"Fine," I ground out. "But find the hoard and get your ass back up here."

"I'm going to give the go ahead to the units as we enter the War Room. We'll enter simultaneously from all sides and improv once we're in there," Nicolai said with a bloodthirsty grin that I found wildly sexy.

"Works for me," I said with my own grin that matched his perfectly.

My mate looked like the angel of death with so much lethal power rolling off of him it was frightening. Fate had led me to this man and together we would change the direction of our kind. I clasped his hand in mine and felt the exchange of our Dragon Fire. I inhaled deeply as I absorbed some of his power and gave him some of my own. My body felt volcanic and my Dragon was so close to the surface it was painful.

She danced a macabre rhythm inside my body. My need for blood and vengeance was all consuming. I was at home in this state. I shook my head and realized no matter how much we might try, we would never fit into normal society. Even somewhat tamed, we were an innately violent race.

"Now or never. Let's go," I said as my Dragon begged to come out and play. I tamped her down and moved with inhuman speed down the hallway. Nicolai was right next to me and Elaina and Seth brought up the rear.

Without any communication needed, we burst through the door in a blaze of fire, smoke and untapped rage. Units B and C coordinated with us to perfection as if we'd done this particular maneuver a thousand times. D came crashing through the skylights with such force, shards of sparkling glass flew like bullets all over the enormous room ricocheting off the marble floor.

And then everything just stopped.

Every Dragon in the room froze in confusion and looked to Nicolai and me for direction. There was no army to fight us. There were no weapons. There was no one at all to stop us from incinerating the man who sat on a gilded throne watching the scene with a small smile on his hideously handsome face.

"Very impressive," my father said flatly and clapped his hands as if he was bored to tears. "I knew it was you," he continued calmly, tilting his head to the side and narrowing his eyes at me.

He was a devastatingly striking man. However, he was smaller than I'd remembered. For the briefest second I was overcome with terror—just as I'd always been as a child. But I was no longer a child. I was a grown woman— I was damaged, but I was still here. Holding my head high, I proudly stood next to the man who *did* love me. The odds were stacked heavily against my father. There were at least seventy-five Dragons surrounding him and no way out.

This was far too easy. It shouldn't be this simple.

Had he given up? Had the loss of his fortune made him lose his mind?

"I'd always hoped the next time I saw you, you would be ash. Your skill at avoiding me for all these centuries has been stunning, *Dima*," he said in an icy tone as he gave me a condescending salute. "But then again you are my daughter…"

"I stopped being your daughter the day you killed my family," I snarled as fire lit my fingertips and I took a step toward him.

I put my hand up to halt the forward movement from the Dragons. My father was mine and I was going to have the pleasure of killing him myself.

"Ahhh yes, the day you ran like a coward leaving your mother and brothers to die." He eyed me with mock pity as little tsk-ing sounds fell from his lips.

It made me want to wrap my hands around his throat and tear his head from his shoulders.

"Such a weak Dragon…leaving your poor hacked up family like that."

"I was just a child, you monster," I hissed and I took several more steps forward.

He was still a good three hundred feet away, but close enough to kill.

"You've certainly become a lovely woman. So much tougher than I remember," he said as he stood and kicked aside the four emaciated, barely alive Dragons at his feet.

I hadn't even noticed them and couldn't make out if they were men or women. They were so far beyond repair the most humane thing to do would be to kill them and put them out of their misery. My father was a sick fuck. I'd kill him first and then deal with the tragedy at his feet.

"Stronger, no thanks to you," I said.

"Touché," he replied with a hollow laugh.

I stared at him hard as I tried like hell to decipher what the catch was. The simplicity of the scene was all wrong. It was too easy.

I'd just wing it. There was no other option.

"You have two choices here," I told him with a smile on my lips and hatred lacing my words. "You can die quickly or you can die slowly. Technically you deserve no choice whatsoever considering the sins you committed, but I'm quite sure they have a special place in hell for people like you. Not to mention, I'm polite. Pick now or I'll pick for you."

"Oh Dima, Dima, Dima, you amuse me so. Do you *really* think you can kill me?"

"Yes. Yes, I *really* think I can."

"Well, before we get to that gruesome part of our daddy-daughter visit, I'd like to let you know my terms."

Again he kicked the filthy pathetic people at his feet. I heard a faint feminine cry and it chilled me to the bone.

"*Your* terms?" Nicolai laughed with no humor in his voice. "You will make no terms."

"I beg to disagree," my father said in such a mild tone the hair on my neck stood up. "And you are?"

"Dima's mate."

My father clapped his hands, but this time with far more gusto. "Welcome to the family. We're a delightful bunch. PS," he whispered, leaning forward as if he was letting us in on a secret. "I know exactly who you are *Nicolai*. You'll be pleased to know your sister only screamed a little bit when we skinned her. Such a mess."

Nicolai's roar of pain bounced off the walls and he dove for my father with a rage that was as magnificent as it was horrifying. Every Dragon in the room went for the soulless King. Through the melee, my father's eyes never strayed from mine. He winked at me as all movement seemed to morph into slow motion.

And then the shoe I was searching for dropped.

With a careless wave of his hands a circular wall of translucent fire dropped down around him, shielding him and the four dying Dragons on the ground from the onslaught. All it took was a second for more than forty of our Dragons to burn to ash as they came into contact with the fire wall.

The scream that left my throat was animalistic as I searched frantically for Nicolai amidst the carnage. The relief that powered through me as I saw him yanking Dragons back from the wall brought me to my knees. My father had once destroyed my world there was no way in hell I would let him do it a second time.

My vision narrowed with fury as I heard my father's laugh above the cries of agony for so many lost in the blink of an eye. The bastard possessed magic. It was impossible since he wasn't of the Royal Dragon line, but I suspected he'd tortured it out of my grandfather.

However, my father didn't yet know the true meaning of torture. I just needed to get through the wall and I would teach him. The only way to fight magic was with magic. I had no real clue what the hell I was going to do, I just knew I was going to do it.

"Stop," Lenny roared harshly as he entered the room in an enormous cloud of smoke. "Everyone stand back. Now."

"Is that you Lenny?" my father asked. "I had a feeling you would be here! I've missed you so much. It's wonderful of you to come back. The dungeon hasn't been the same without you. So many people scream when I play with them. It was so refreshing to have someone who could take it in such stoic silence."

I swallowed back the bile in my throat as I glared at the abomination who'd sired me. There was nothing about him that I could even call Dragon. He was pure evil.

"Let him make his terms," Lenny yelled to the crowd. He wore a strange expression and appeared to have aged dramatically.

I was so flabbergasted by Lenny's order to cave in to my father's demands that I didn't notice Maria, Seth and Elaina surround me. Maria touched my shoulder and helped me to my feet. I sagged forward into her arms with relief. At this point I had no clear idea who'd perished, but was wildly grateful that my closest had been spared.

"He is fucking insane," Maria hissed as sparks of fire danced on her skin. "There is no way in hell we're related to that piece of shit."

"Who? Lenny or the King?" I asked.

"Well, right now, both of them," she snarled.

Maria was correct. This was bullshit and wasn't going to happen.

"There will be no terms," I shouted over the din.

"There will be terms," Lenny contradicted me savagely. "He has the hoard."

I was dumbfounded that while almost half of our army lay dead on the floor, Lenny was concerned with money or jewels or whatever the hell my father had. Disgust didn't begin to cover how I felt. Lenny's selfish materialism was staggering. I clearly didn't know the man at all—and now I didn't want to.

Nicolai caught my eye. He was shocked and confused as I was.

"Ahhh yes, the *hoard*. I just knew they would come in handy some day," my father sneered and grabbed two of the half dead Dragons by the hair in one hand the second two in his other. "And today is the lucky day."

He held them high as if they weighed nothing—they did weigh next to nothing. They were completely skin and bones. My heart jumped to my throat as I imagined the unspeakable horror the Dragons must have suffered. I'd seen many awful things in my life, but these poor people were up there with the worst. They'd clearly been treated like animals.

My father's eye's lit up with maniacal excitement as he held their faces close to the deadly wall of fire. "Dima, darling I'm surprised you haven't said hello to your mother and your brothers yet. I thought your manners were far better than that."

"Wh...what?" I asked in a small voice that seemed to be coming from very far away. What was he saying? They were dead. His games were so vicious.

The half-dead Dragon woman look up and me and cried out raggedly, "Go. You must leave. He will kill you. Go."

Her voice sounded so familiar. I'd heard those words before. I tilted my head as my body began to shake violently. She was dead. She wasn't talking to me. That wasn't possible. A keening wail filled my ears and I wanted it to stop, but it wouldn't stop.

I glanced around sharply to see who was making the awful noise and I realized it was me. I tried to stop but the sound kept coming. Why couldn't I stop?

Maria dropped to the ground beside me and vomited. Lenny walked toward me, but his face was distorted. He looked so odd. I thought I heard Elaina scream for Nicolai, but surely I was mistaken. The room was floating. We should probably leave. It was getting dark and it would be time for dinner soon. My mother was a wonderful cook. I wondered if she would be upset if I brought my friends home with me. She never got mad.

I pressed at my eyelids and tried to stop my eyes from moving so fast. It was so hard to see when they kept rolling back in my head. Oh thank goodness, Nicolai was here. I wanted him to meet my brothers. They would like him.

The feel of a large hand connecting to my cheek violently jerked me out of the hell I'd descended into. Nicolai stood over me. His eyes were wild with concern and I knew he had pulled me back from the abyss. The burning sting was nothing compared to the pain of reentering reality and having to absorb the horror of what was before my eyes.

My father hadn't killed them. They were alive— barely—and he'd kept them to use against me one day. I now understood my grandfather's obsession with the hoard. My mother and brothers were my father's hoard. Not because he loved them, but because he hated *me*.

I would listen to his terms. And I would probably agree to them.

"So here's how it's going to go," he purred as dropped my precious broken family to the ground and clasped his blood stained hands in front of him. "You will restore my finances and my reputation. I don't care how you accomplish this, but I'm sure you'll figure it out. I was very impressed with how quickly you ruined me."

My voice was hoarse from wailing so I nodded my assent.

"You will alert the press that I was sabotaged by a group that goes by The Resistance. You will see to it that all of your names hit the press—every single last one of you. I will then give you a twenty-four hour head start and I will methodically hunt each and every one of you down and kill you."

"He's fucking crazy," Nicolai muttered under his breath.

I couldn't have agreed more, but I had one last plan up my sleeve.

"My mother and my brothers. You will give them to me or I won't agree to any of your *terms*," I ground out through my raw throat.

"These old things?" he asked as he kicked my mother. "You can have them. I don't want them anymore."

I was so consumed with hatred I couldn't see straight, but I stayed outwardly calm. The bastard was about to win. Unless I could pull some massive magic out of my ass, I was helpless to do a damned thing about it. I knew he had no intention of releasing my mother and brothers. That did not work for me. Staring at him, I tried to remember if I ever loved the man.

He continued to make more demands, but I could no longer hear him. It was fuzzy, but I think he might have held me once or twice as a child. What had happened for him to become such a monster—or was he just born a monster?

All I needed to do was pull up some magic. I watched his mouth continue to move and I turned my focus into myself.

Concentrating on his face, I drew on all the raw hatred I felt for him. It wasn't difficult, there was nothing in him to love. The magic refused me, no matter how hard I tried. My world had just gotten good after hundreds of years of sorrow and fear. He'd ruined my life by killing the ones I'd loved most—or so I'd thought. Was I seriously going to let him get away with it again?

There would never be a moment of peace for any of the people I cared about. We would all be running for our lives for eternity. He would get his money and reputation back and he would rebuild even stronger than he was before. Unacceptable.

It was one thing for me to have lived hand to mouth for centuries, it was another thing altogether for that to happen to Nicolai, Lenny and Maria. I loved them all—me, who didn't even rediscover what love meant until I had my child. I loved Nicolai and Seth and Elaina and Maria. I loved Lenny and Junior and Essie and Hank. I worshiped the ground Dwayne and Granny walked on and Daniel...I loved him more than life itself. And my mother and brothers, Sean, Timothy and Matthew—the four people I thought were gone forever—I'd loved them desperately for almost five hundred years.

My heart sped up and something beautiful and unfamiliar coursed through my blood.

Oh. My. God.

That was it. Magic wasn't based in hatred. It was rooted in love.

Why did the hardest questions always have the simplest answers?

"I accept your terms," I said cutting my father off mid sentence.

"I wasn't finished yet," he pouted. "There's more."

My Dragons were on edge and unsure what I was doing, but no one contradicted me.

"How long do I have to accomplish this?" I asked.

A heartless smile split my father's face and he feigned deep thought. "A week. I'll give you a week. If it's not to my satisfaction, I'll behead your sweet mother and brothers and send you the footage. How does that sound?"

"It sounds fine," I said looking for an opening to get at him. The fire wall was an issue…but maybe not.

"I hope to God you know what you're doing," Nicolai hissed inside my mind.

My eyes shot to Nicolai's and my mouth opened into a small O.

"Can you hear me?" he asked, wary yet hopeful.

"I can. Are you mind speaking with me?"

"Apparently. Do you have a plan here, Princess?"

"I do."

"Wanna share?"

"No, but you could help me out if you would cause a distraction on the right side of the room," I said getting more excited with each passing second.

"Big one or little one?" he asked.

"Big. Very big."

"*Are you going to cross the fire wall?*" he demanded tersely as he eyes narrowed dangerously at me.

"*In a roundabout way. Just please trust me and create a motherfucker of a diversion.*"

"*You've been hanging out with Maria too much,*" he said as he turned his head to hide his grin from my father who was still adding to his list of demands.

"*This is true. I love you, Asscanoe.*"

"*Back at you, Princess. On three?*"

I gave him a small nod. "*On three.*"

Chapter 25

"This is bullshit," Nicolai shouted as he strode purposefully across the large room, planted himself in the far right corner and glared at me menacingly. "I'm in charge here and I do not accept these ludicrous terms."

"Dima, I'd suggest you control your *mate*," my father hissed with deranged glee, most likely hoping we would kill each other and save him some time.

"Screw you," I shouted at Nicolai as the Dragons began to mutter in confusion. "You are a lowly common Dragon. I'm a Princess. You will bow down to me, you stupid man. You're pathetic and your Dragon is an embarrassment."

Smoke began to waft around the room as the Dragons tried to figure out which side they were supposed to be on. Only Lenny and Seth were calm and smiling.

"You want to see an embarrassment?" Nicolai roared. "I'll show your spoiled Princess ass *embarrassment!*"

I held my breath and couldn't believe he was going to do it. When I'd said big, he'd taken me at my word.

"I'll give you to the count of three to take back all you have said," Nicolai growled and bared his teeth.

I simply flipped him my middle finger.

My father sat down on his throne to watch the impending violence play out. He was safe behind his fire wall no matter what happened on our side. His smile was rabid and his position could not have been better.

"One," Nicolai ground out through clenched teeth as small fires broke out all around him. "Two…three."

And then he did it.

My glorious mate shifted into his big, beautiful, deadly Dragon and completely blew out the palace wall. Brick, glass and plaster crashed to the ground like a tornado had ripped through the building. It was magnificent and all kinds of perfect. It was the mother of all diversions.

As Nicolai's Dragon roared and sprayed fire I closed my eyes and transported directly behind the throne. I'd traversed the magic fire wall without walking through it. The pain was intense, but I'd made it through and come out in one piece. In the chaos, my movement went unnoticed. My ego wanted my father to see me before I ended him, but pride would be my downfall.

It didn't matter if he ever knew…it was enough that I would.

With strength honed through my years of having to fight for my life, I clamped my hands around his throat and squeezed—gouging my fingers deeply into the arteries to halt the blood flow. It wouldn't kill him, but it would make what I was going to do far easier. I knew this macabre fact because I'd done it before.

I prayed I would never have to do it again.

The chaos and noise in the room seemed to disappear. My heartbeat thundered in my ears and all I could see was the back of my father's head. All I could feel was the frantic pulse in his neck as he tried to pry my grip open. The movie of my family's brutal death replayed over and over like a broken reel that would never end. I saw a girl who resembled Nicolai and Seth being skinned alive and I visualized all of the horrors Lenny had endured.

Faces I didn't recognize joined the ones I did and with sickening clarity, I understood that by touching my father I could see his sins. Blood, terror, greed and power bathed my mind and the only thing I wanted to do was run. But I would never run again and neither would anyone that I loved.

The scream that left my body was horrifying—completely animalistic and straight from the darkest part of my soul. Using my feet to brace myself and the love I'd found to guide me, I did what I did best.

I killed him.

I jerked my father's head back over the jagged, ornate wooden carvings of his precious throne and twisted it with a violent white hot rage. With an ease that ashamed me, I tore his head from his shoulders. I let the bloody mess carelessly fall to the ground with a thud at my feet. The top half of him fell forward on his throne and slowly began to turn to ash. The King's decapitated body emitted small puffs of acrid black smoke as he disintegrated before my eyes and the wall of fire splashed to the ground and dispersed with his last breath.

I was finally free.

I felt nothing. No joy at his death—no sadness. There was no regret. I searched my soul for guilt and I found none. He'd been nothing to me for so long that his death—even at my own hands—was nothing as well.

Maybe the adrenaline hadn't worn off. Maybe one day I would feel remorse, but somehow I didn't think so.

An enormous velvety Dragon nose gently pushed at my stiff body and Nicolai huffed. "You're done now, my love. It's time to go home."

I laid my head on his powerful body and ran my hands over his smooth jet-black scales. This day would not have come without him and the others. My goal would have never been accomplished on my own.

"We did it," I whispered as tears filled my eyes. "He's gone."

"You did it," Nicolai said as black and silver smoke wafted down and wrapped a warm cocoon around my exhausted body.

"No. *We* did it," I stated firmly as I finally glanced out at what was left of our people.

They had gone to their knees for me. It was humbling...and it was all wrong.

"No," I called out. "Stand. We bow no more."

But they didn't listen. They began to chant my name along with Nicolai's. I would tackle the prostrating problem later. Right now there were four people I needed to touch.

Easing down to the floor I took the nearly lifeless body of my mother gently into my arms. Lenny ran forward as did Elaina, Seth and Maria.

"Hi, Mamma," I whispered into her tangled and matted hair.

Even through the years of degradation and filth, her delicate floral scent still remained. I breathed her in and my soul calmed. She was the most beautiful thing I'd ever seen. My brothers were being lovingly attended to. I would go to them next.

"I'm going to take care of you now. You will never have to live like an animal again," I promised her as tears rolled down my cheeks and splashed on her parched and cracking lips.

"Dima," she said so softly, I wasn't sure she'd spoken. "My daughter." Her smile was weak and her heartbeat even weaker.

I glanced up as I heard a ruckus in the back of the room and saw the Cows. All eight of them were primed and ready—top half, dressed and bottom half, naked. I couldn't believe I was capable of laughter after what I'd just done, but I was. Fate was kind and God was good. Only after Cade, who thankfully was still alive, explained what had gone down did the gals pull up their pants.

"Well, I guess they *are* girls," Nicolai said with a grimace and chuckle. He was back in his human form. He sat down beside me and wrapped his strong arms around both my mother and me. "And I think I need some eye bleach."

"I told you," I said as I tried to bite back my laugh. The Cows did not deserve our laughter. They'd been instrumental in our victory...but it was damn hard when they entered pants-less en masse.

My mother had fallen asleep in my arms with a contented smile on her lips and I carefully brushed her hair from her gaunt face.

"Nicolai, we have to take my family somewhere to heal. There's no way they can shift and fly. Should we drive? I'm worried about them being able to hold on if they fly on our backs."

My brothers were in as bad shape as my mother if not worse. Maria cradled her father Sean in her arms and rocked him like a baby. Her tears flowed and her smile was blinding.

"My name is Maria," she whispered as the broken man in her arms reached up and touched her beautiful face. "I'm your daughter."

The guttural sound that came from my brother's lips went straight to my heart and pierced it with deadly accuracy. The thought of not knowing about Daniel or losing him was far more than I could ever endure. My anger welled up again as I thought of all the lost years that my brother could have protected and loved his daughter. I thought of the desolation I'd suffered and the fear I'd lived with for hundreds of years. How much I had mourned my family...

Little sparks burst out on my skin and I closed my eyes tight to rein in my fury.

"It doesn't matter anymore," Lenny said quietly as he knelt down beside me. "It's over and we can't get the time back." He caressed my sleeping mother's face lovingly. "Do not let him win in death as he won in life."

"You knew he had them?" I asked.

"I suspected, but like you I had to give up hope after a time." He let his face fall to his hands and he sobbed.

I touched my grandfather gently. He leaned into me and pressed his forehead to mine. My mother rested quietly between us.

"You've got your hoard back," I whispered.

"No, my dear granddaughter. I already had my hoard."

"You did?" I asked, confused.

"I did." He nodded and kissed my cheek. "You, Daniel and Maria are my hoard. There is nothing more precious to me in the world. Now my hoard is bigger. And that blessing, my child, is because of you."

Emotion clogged my throat and I realized my hoard had grown as well. My hoard was now quite large and continued to increase. Luck had played no role in my life thus far so I had to believe this was fate—and that she was smiling down on me with love.

"You knew this would happen?" I asked, still confused.

"Seth had a vision and shared it with me when Nicolai rescued me all those years ago," Lenny said.

"What was it? Was it specific?"

"Not to him, but it was to me."

I waited as my grandfather gathered himself. "Are you sure you want to hear it?"

"Um...I don't know. Do I?" Today had been long, I wasn't sure if I could take anymore revelations.

"You do. After today, you are ready to hear it," Lenny said as he held out his arms for my mother.

He lifted her as carefully as if she was spun glass and pressed his shaking lips to her forehead. She was his daughter and his love for her moved me back to tears.

"The prophecy goes like this," Seth said as he stood behind the quietly weeping Lenny. "I saw that one day Lenny would get his hoard back. It wasn't clear to me exactly what the hoard was, but I knew it was meant to be."

"Is there more?"

"Tell her," Lenny said as Seth hesitated.

"Yes, tell her," Nicolai said. "I want to hear this too."

"I told him he had to wait for the true Dragon Queen," Seth said and then paused.

My gut clenched as I waited. I was pretty sure I didn't want to hear the rest of it.

"And?" Nicolai prompted his brother. "Out with it."

Unfortunately, everyone was interested now, including the Cows and the Vamps. The mood was somber as they gathered our dead, but they were all clear something rather large was about to go down.

Seth cleared his throat and winked at me. "I knew the moment I saw you Dima. I'd been searching for you for decades," he said.

"Knew what?" Nicolai was impatient now—nothing new...

"The true Dragon Queen will wear the mark of the Royal Dragon line. She will link the nations and by her side will stand the most powerful Dragon of them all. Together they will lead us to prosperity and peace." Seth finished with a smile as all the Dragons and even the Cows and their Vamps went to their knees and bowed their heads.

Oh. Shit. No.

"You must have deciphered that one incorrectly," I insisted as I jumped to my feet in agitation.

I didn't want to rule anyone. Ever. Monarchies were antiquated bullshit. Look at what my father had done with it. My God, I had a preschooler and a mate—which was somewhat the same thing as far as care went. I didn't have time to rule a nation of violent freaks that were hated by every other Were species alive. This was *not* in my future plans. I needed a damned vacation, not a list of responsibilities and a crown.

Frantically, I glanced around the room and wanted to scream. They were nuts to want me. I was grossly under qualified. I'd been away from my people for centuries. And then I saw Pat—face on the floor and hand in the air.

"Do you have a question Pat?" I asked cautiously. I never knew what was going to come out of the Cows' mouths.

"I do," she said but it came out all muffled because she was still face planted. "Can I rise, Your Majesty?"

I rolled my eyes and wanted to punch something, but the sooner we got the questions over with the sooner I could explain why this was not going to work for me—or them.

"Yes," I said reluctantly as I watched Nicolai grin at me like an idiot.

"I'd just like to put something out there as a possibility," Pat said. "We had a little pow-wow outside after we ripped the air sharts and offed the guards."

Oh my God, this was going to be bad…

"Since we don't actually have a population anymore and we're all mated to dead guys that don't have little swimmers and can't reproduce, we were just thinking maybe we could become part of the Dragons," she said as she gave me an awkward bow and then promptly face planted back to the floor next to her sisters.

"Sweet Jesus," Nicolai muttered under his breath as he successfully bit back his laughter—barely.

"Okay, everybody get up. This is making me very uncomfortable having to think while all of your asses are in the air," I said as I began to pace.

Pat had a fine point. They had earned their way into our weyr. Without them, this day might not have happened or we could have lost more of our army than we had. Maybe I could make this one call and then whoever was actually going to take the reins of this shitshow would honor it.

"I say yes," I announced to the slightly alarmed, but bemused Dragons. "The Cows have shown their loyalty to us and risked their lives for ours. If that doesn't earn them a place in our weyr, I don't know what does."

It took a minute or two of covertly exchanged glances and some quiet conversation, but once the cheering started I couldn't even hear myself think. The Cows were crying tears of joy and the Vampyres flew around the room like mosquitos on speed. Even the Dragons were pleased.

It felt good to do the right thing for my people.

Oh.

Shit…

Epilogue

Several months later…

"Mommy, me going to go watch cartoons wif my gwandma," Daniel announced as he raced from the kitchen in our new and *way too big* home.

I'd agreed to the monstrosity only after Nicolai argued that we needed the room for my family to convalesce under our watchful eyes. I knew he'd just wanted the damn mansion, but his reasoning was sound as far as my mother and brothers went, so I let him win.

I checked the clock on the wall and smoothed down my new sexy-not-slutty dress. I'd passed on all the dresses in the box that Dwayne had sent over—too much boob wasn't the best option for an outdoor picnic with friends and family. Everyone was due to arrive in fifteen minutes and I was so excited it was almost embarrassing.

Glancing out of the bay window, I grinned as Maria entertained her uncles and father with a story that I was certain was full of profanity. Sean didn't mind his daughter's foul mouth one bit, saying she came by it naturally as her mother cursed like a sailor.

It would take many years for my brothers and mother to heal—both mentally and physically, but with each day they made strides. The sheer will to live that had sustained them during their imprisonment and torture was a testament to how strong they were.

Turned out Maria had spent as many years gathering up degrees as I had and ironically, she was a doctor. She'd moved into the guesthouse on the estate and had taken on the medical care of the family. Of course Dragons were very different than humans, but Maria had adapted her skills to the chemistry of our kind. However, the truth of the matter was that it was simply going to take time. Their bodies could only regenerate themselves in small increments due to the abuse they'd received.

Lenny, Elaina and Seth had moved near us as well, along with the Dragons that were left and our honorary members...the Cows. Life was never boring and I'd never been happier.

"If we sneak into the pantry we could have a quickie," Nicolai whispered in my ear, startling me out of my reflections.

"Um...while the thought is truly tempting, Mr. Horny Dragon, fifteen minutes is not enough time for a *quickie* with you," I said with a giggle as I pressed my lips to his.

He tasted like heaven and my inner Dragon actually considered his lewd offer. Thankfully my saner side won out. Getting busted in the pantry by guests was not my idea of a good time. I sighed and marveled that as huge as the house was, Nicolai's presence was even larger. My Dragon was big and beautiful and *mine*.

"This is true," he boasted with a sly grin. "I'm kind of a three hour guy."

I rolled my eyes and punched him in the arm. "Do you think we have enough food?"

I'd bought out the grocery store's meat department and everyone was bringing a dish, but I was still worried. I'd never hosted a party in my life. I was a little ill thinking of everything that could go wrong.

"We have enough," Nicolai said with a chuckle and a shake of his head. "We have enough food to feed the entire state and then some. Stop worrying."

"I'm not," I lied. "It's just that the Wolves *eat*."

"And the Dragons don't?" he asked with a bemused expression.

"Shit," I muttered as I yanked open the refrigerator and ransacked it for other things to serve.

"Dima," Nicolai said as he closed the fridge, lifted me up and plopped my butt on the granite countertop. "Relax. These are friends coming tonight. We could feed them peanut butter and jelly and it would be fine."

"No it wouldn't," I shot back appalled, imagining offering Junior or Hank a PB&J.

"Okay, you're right. It wouldn't," he agreed with a laugh. "But as I've already pointed out, we could feed an army. We've got this handled. I promise."

"Swear?" I asked as I leaned into him and wrapped my arms around his warm body.

"I swear."

***

"So you think you're gonna like livin' in Hung, Georgia?" Granny asked Elaina as they sat on the porch and enjoyed the moonshine Granny had brought.

My mother sat quietly with them and smiled. She and Elaina had resumed their close friendship with childlike wonder. It was beautiful and gave both of them a new strength and purpose. Granny had now joined their club as well.

"I do believe I will, Bobby Sue," Elaina said with a smile as she clinked her glass with Granny.

"Well we sure enjoy havin' you fire breathers here. Shakes it up and keeps it interesting," she said with a cackle.

Interesting was correct and a slight understatement. It had taken weeks of negotiation with the Council and the Shifters of Hung to get everyone on board with having a weyr live in tandem with other species.

I'd spent a solid ten days in Chicago with Nicolai, Essie and Hank working a deal with the National Council to let Dragons have a seat on the board. It was drawn out and tedious, but worth it in the end. Seth was going to be the representative of our people to the Council.

After about a month of being hounded by my people from all over the world, I'd caved and agreed to be the Dragon Queen. The first thing I did was forbid bowing and made it very clear that I would never wear a crown. Some of the old school Dragons were displeased with my lack of decorum, but eventually came around.

Even the Dragons that had blindly followed my father were slowly beginning to accept my rule. Elaina had been correct. Dragons were steeped in tradition and needed the monarchy to survive.

I'd been challenged a number of times by those still loyal to the very dead King and had taken my challengers down with ease. This was a sad necessity with our kind. Some would never get past the might makes right way of living.

Nicolai was never happy when I took on an angry Dragon, but he was wildly impressed every time I kicked their ass. Which in turn led to mind altering sex—violence was hot to a Dragon.

We could dress up and play nice, but at the end of the day we were the race that needed to blow off some steam with a little friendly bloodshed.

"The party rocks," Essie said as she grabbed me and hugged me hard. "I have a proposition for you, Dragon."

"Should I be terrified?" I inquired with a smirk.

Essie was everything I'd ever dreamt a best friend could be—loyal, fierce and always ready to get into trouble. Sandy was awesome as well and I'd grown close to some of our Dragons. My life had changed so dramatically in the last few months it made my head spin.

"No you should *not*." Essie laughed and then pulled me to a quiet spot over by the swing set. "I'd like you to be a bridesmaid in my wedding. What do you say?"

I was stunned speechless. She wanted *me* to be part of the most important day of her life? I grabbed her arm because I thought my knees might give out. I could fry a Dragon with out blinking, but this was something different.

"Dude, you totally don't have to," Essie said as she held me up. "I just thought…"

"Yes!" I shouted as both of us winced at my volume. "I mean yes. I would be honored."

"Good," she said with a grin. "However, just a heads up…Dwayne is picking out the dresses. Be prepared to be exposing some boob."

I rolled my eyes and scanned the yard until I found the Vampyre in question. Dwayne was holding court and doing his Cher impressions for a group of confused Dragons and his daughters the Cows. Dwayne was still livid that his girls had eloped with their Vampyre lovers, but planning Essie's wedding had taken away some of the sting.

The Vampyres were on all fours being ridden like horses by the four year old Shifter posse. Daniel had both the Vamps and the Cows wrapped around his chubby little fingers. The visual I was looking at was all kinds of strange and all kinds of wonderful.

Daniel was going to nursery school with other Shifters his age. His happiness at having friends made me feel guilty about how sheltered his life had been, but Nicolai would hear none of it. He insisted repeatedly that the reason Daniel was alive was because I'd kept him hidden.

He was able to go to school now because I'd been such a good mother. The first day was a little rough as Daniel accidentally burnt the snack room to the ground in a blast of excited fire, but no one was hurt and the teachers assured me that things like that happened all the time. I didn't quite believe them, but was grateful that my boy was allowed to come back.

I checked on my brothers. They were sitting quietly, enjoying the fun. Seth sat with them and pointed out who was who. They still didn't speak much, but I knew from their smiles they were enjoying themselves.

At night I often slipped into my mother's and brothers' rooms and sang them the same lullabies that my mother had sung to us as children. It still broke my heart to see them as weak as they were, but having them back was a blessing I couldn't even describe.

Maria sat close to Sean with her head on his shoulder. She was rarely far from her father and that seemed to suit them both fine.

"I still can't get over it," Junior said as he walked over and trapped me in a bear hug.

"Can't get over what?" I asked.

"That," he said as he pointed to where Lenny was talking with a beautiful couple who didn't seem quite comfortable in their skin.

Junior, in all of his clumsy MENSA brilliance, had correctly guessed that my father had somehow used Lenny's magic to trap the wolves in their shifted forms. He deduced that the only way to reverse it was for Lenny to undo the spell.

Lenny had been more than game and the end result was the beautiful couple who were still trying to get used to standing on two legs instead of four. Not only had he reversed the spell on Essie's parents, but for the rest of the feral pack as well.

Granny had no words to be able to adequately thank Lenny, every time she tried she sobbed like a baby. Instead of using words, Granny decided that actions would speak louder. From what I'd heard Lenny had been receiving daily gifts of moonshine, fried chicken and apple pie.

Essie just hugged Lenny until he couldn't breathe whenever she saw him. It was a win-win-win-win.

"How's it going with Sandy?" I asked Junior as I pulled him to the kitchen to help me bring out the food.

"I reckon I'm about two and three-fourths dates away from gettin' in her pants," he informed me cockily.

"Really?" I asked with a laugh.

"Yep," he said. "That chick digs me."

"Actually," Sandy said as she popped her head into the kitchen as Junior flattened himself against the refrigerator and screamed like a little girl. "You just added twenty-two and a half *more* dates onto your docket before you get anywhere near my pants, Little Mister."

She narrowed her eyes at Junior who dropped his head into his hands and moaned and then she winked at me, grinned and left.

Junior was going to win. It was just going to take a little while…

"Sheee-ot," Junior whispered. "That's the fifth time this week she's busted me talkin' about gettin' into her pants."

"And what have you learned from this episode?" I asked him with raised brows and my stern mom look.

"I've learned I have to check the area next time I'm gonna talk about gettin' lucky with my girl," he said with a grin. "I ain't no idiot."

"Debatable," I muttered and I loaded him down with a huge platter. "Take this out to the table and don't get in any trouble."

"Yes ma'am," he said as he walked out of the kitchen whistling. "Get your little Dragon ass out here. There's a party goin' on and it's not in the kitchen."

"I'm coming," I promised as I gathered up the remaining food and made my way back outside.

I swung the porch door open and stopped dead in my tracks. My eyes filled with tears and I almost dropped the enormous tray of food I was carrying. Thankfully Essie was there to save the day—or dinner, as it were.

In my front yard all of my friends and family were huddled in a large group. In the front was Nicolai—grinning like a little kid and holding a birthday cake with more candles on it than I'd ever seen in my life. It defied logic and I was sure he was going to set his hair on fire.

"I love you, baby," Nicolai shouted as Daniel jumped around like a little monkey at his feet. "Happy Birthday. I couldn't fit five hundred candles on the damn cake so Daniel and I just shoved in as many as we could would fit."

The cheers were loud and my tears ran like a faucet from my eyes. I didn't have the heart to tell him my birthday was actually next week, so I kept it to myself and decided from here on out that today's date was my new birthday. Forever.

Through my tears I gazed at the crazy bunch as they sang Happy Birthday and I carefully approached the blazing birthday cake. I needed about ten people to help me blow out the absurd amount of candles—but in the end we succeeded.

"Did you make a wish?" Nicolai asked as his handed off the cake to his mother and took me in his arms.

"I did."

"You going to tell me what it is?" he asked with a sexy lopsided grin. "Maybe I could make it come true."

"You already have," I whispered as I kissed my man. "You already have."

It was the best birthday party I'd ever had…actually it was the first birthday party I'd ever had and it was perfect.

Happy Birthday to me.

Five hundred was going to be a very good year. I blew out the candles, but as I'd told Nicolai, I'd already gotten my wish. I had the family, the man, the child, the friends and the house in Hung, Georgia, but most of all I had love—real love.

Life was pretty damned perfect.

The End… for now

If you enjoyed this book, please consider leaving a positive review or rating on the site where you purchased it. Reader reviews help my books continue to be valued by resellers and help new readers make decisions about reading them. You are the reason I write these stories and I sincerely appreciate each of you!

Many thanks for your support,

~ Robyn Peterman

Want to hear about my new releases?

Visit my website at robynpeterman.com and sign up for my newsletter to be notified about release dates.

Want More Dragons and Witches?

I created a MAGIC & MAYHEM Kindle World. I'm so excited I could squeeeeeeeeee!

What is a Kindle World, you may ask? Well, let me explain...

It's basically fan fiction written by some amazing authors that I stalked and blackmailed! KIDDING! I was lucky and blessed to have some brilliant authors say yes! They have written brand new stories using my world and some of my characters.

And let me tell you...the results are hilarious!

For those of you who prefer a more mature and succinct answer... Kindle Worlds is an Amazon exclusive program. The titles written for the world can NOT be purchased at other ebook retailers or anywhere besides the Amazon US site, but they can be read on any tablet, computer, or smartphone using the free Kindle App.

There will be three launches a year filled with smexy, witchy, shifty, magical fun!

But wait, you may ask...Can I write in the Magic and Mayhem world too? Yes, you can!!!

Here is the link to the rules for writing in a world. Read 'em and write!

https://kindleworlds.amazon.com/how

Visit robynpeterman.com/kindle-world to see all the releases. Check out each and every one. You will laugh your way to a magical HEA!

xoxo Robyn

Except: How To Train A Witch

Book Description

She's the Jezibaba, not the Jezibooboo. Sleeping with Professor Hottie is out of the question… or is it?

After three hundred years of keeping the magical peace in the world, Jezibaba is a hundred years past being ready to hang up her witch's hat. The Council of Witches still can't be trusted but she will happily step aside to leave their treachery to her successors to punish.

Two new witches—two Baba Yaga—have been chosen as potentials to take her place. Yet before she can thank Morgana The Red for helping her survive long enough to retire her wand, Jezibaba uncovers one major snafu in the cauldron's prediction… the Chosen Ones are still children.

One way or the other, she's going to protect the girls, kill their would-be killers, and then she's going to torture each member of the Council until she discovers the traitor funding the attempts on their lives. What she is not going to do is sleep with a sexy dragon just because he wants to help. She and Professor Hottie have way more in common than the magical world is ready to know.

Chapter 1

Making a quiet, sedate entrance had never been her style, but getting struck by lightning would definitely be a mood buster. Winds of change were blowing all around.

The edges of her red dress fluttered around her legs as the seven of them materialized on the lawn of the Witchery U campus. Jezibaba looked up at the rumbling sky and read the darkening clouds before sighing at the violent storm she felt brewing. She told herself the lack of welcoming sunshine didn't matter. It wasn't necessarily a bad omen.

But then it wasn't just the weather she was questioning.

Looking across the manicured campus lawn, she watched a bunch of teenagers playing some sort of game. The boys pelted each other with balls thrown from skinny stick baskets. The girls cheered and yelled at the boys. She rolled her eyes at the nonsense of it, even though they appeared to be having a good time.

Thank the Goddess those years were several centuries behind her. She cringed just thinking about all the emotional drama the very young delighted in putting themselves through.

Yes, it was good to be older. It was even better to be an older witch whose power had yet to stop growing. Not that she wanted to keep the title of the great and powerful Jezibaba forever. Wasn't that why she was here? She had to find a way to keep her two replacements alive long enough to secede her.

"Gentlemen, I need to find the proper motivation for this task. Tell me again why our presence here is necessary. I'm not used to jobs where I don't have to kill someone."

Jezibaba rolled her eyes when she heard a shuffling of seven gray robes sweeping the grass behind her as they silently communicated with each other. They were probably drawing mental straws about who would give her the bad news.

All were male witches, or warlocks as her testosterone laden posse preferred to be called. They were powerful seers, great conjurers, and fairly good at fetching coffee. Outside of that though, they were merely a bunch of devout magicals stuck in their heads. In her opinion, the whole lot was afraid to use their damn balls.

No wonder the Jezibaba was always a female witch. A female's irrational anger fueled a what-the-hell bravery few males could ever match. Feeling it now, she pushed her long mass of curly red hair over both her shoulders as she turned to favor them with a knowing and superior smirk. Maybe glaring was a tad mean, but it felt so damn good to vent her frustration.

"Look, I'm not going to turn you guys into toads just for answering my question. I'm not in the mood to torture you today. It's just that I'm having trouble believing we have to be directly involved with the lives of two children. For Goddess's sake, Nathaniel—will you stop shuffling in your robe and *speak to me*. Why in Morgana's name are we here? Nothing seems amiss."

Her most trusted warlock finally cleared his throat. She had been with Nathaniel for two of her three centuries in service to the Council of Witches. The warlock looked older than dirt, but he was still her junior by nearly a hundred and fifty years. She trusted the man for many reasons, but she liked him because he was the only one of her warlocks who wasn't scared completely shitless of her.

And okay—maybe she liked the way Nathaniel talked to her. The man spoke like they were all still living in medieval times. Goddess knew, sometimes she wished they were, except for the whole lack of plumbing thing, of course.

"M'lady, the last divination of the Council of Witches revealed that the magical world would be switching to a multiple Baba Yaga system instead of continuing the current Jezibaba system of one witch protectoress. Two candidates have been deemed worthy prospects already. We're just here to check on them. Their identity is being kept as quiet as possible by Council order."

Jezibaba snorted over the last comment because she knew better. Her gaze went back to the cheering, squealing, annoying teenagers again.

"If the Council of Witches could be trusted to keep their silence on the matter, none of us would be here to check on the chosen ones. Personally, I trust your instincts about them being in danger far more than I trust the meager integrity of the Council. You all know how I feel about those backstabbing, sanctimonious, magic-wielding ass monkeys."

Ignoring the in-drawn breaths over her irreverent cursing, Jezibaba checked her nail polish before glancing at the teenagers again. She was not good at dealing with magical children of any age. The young tended to abuse their powers and that always made her angry. Her patience about such things was nil.

Nothing Nathaniel had said meant she had to oversee the brats personally. She would gladly find them guardians which was being far kinder than the previous Jezibaba had been to her. She'd almost been killed dozens of time before she hit her mid-twenties. In fact, she'd been a woman of twenty-six before she'd even begun her training.

"So the prophecy was correct then, I am to be the last of my kind unless I become a babysitter. Is that what you're telling me, Nathaniel?"

Her chief warlock stiffened behind her and his instant alertness to her tone made her smile.

"I'm not telling you to do anything, Jezibaba. I would never presume to do that. I am merely informing you of the same details we discussed yesterday when we were planning this trip. You alone will have to determine if the children need additional protection."

"I guess I'd pushed that annoying discussion from my mind."

She wanted to laugh when Nathaniel's eyes narrowed beneath his black hood.

"Don't get your loin cloth in a twist over my honesty. I'm here, aren't I?" she declared, lifting a hand to point to the teenagers.

Real intimidation was a power rush for her... and the closest thing to an orgasm she'd had in months. Men who could handle her real nature—and her power—didn't grow on trees, not even those in the sacred grove of Morgana The Red. She knew that for a fact because over the years, she'd bedded every mythical creature the Goddess had made, but had never found one she could care about more than a few months.

In the last decade, she'd shrunk to an all time low, seeking out those like herself who at least respected her magic. Unfortunately, she'd found nothing but self-absorbed warlocks who couldn't get a witch off properly without magical help. Her feminine ego had nearly hit rock bottom before she'd figured out that she was better off alone.

Maybe her libido was more unhappy over her abstinence than she'd realized because it suddenly conjured a man who gave her body hope. She lifted an eyebrow as she watched a professor exit one of the buildings and head towards another. Professor Hottie certainly filled out his clothes well for an intellectual type. Muscles rippled under the loose white shirt he wore beneath his forest green academic robe. His slacks molded the rest of his shape in a way that immediately jumpstarted a fantasy or two about what remained tantalizingly out of sight.

But something about him triggered a memory… or an instinct… or some sort of something. It was one of those feelings a smart witch would never ignore.

Dreading the truth but having to know, Jezibaba waved a hand over her eyes and swore at what her magical sight revealed. Knowing now what he truly was only made her appreciate her innate caution more. Professor Hottie, with all those rippling muscles, was a fire-breathing dragon, which meant he was totally off limits to her.

Sighing in resignation, Jezibaba gave up watching his sexy, masculine walk and started trudging towards the field of teens who were still screaming at each other. They had never ceased as far she could tell. Might as well get the introductions over with so she could put the frustrating day behind her as quickly as possible.

"Forgive me, m'lady… but you're going the wrong way."

Jezibaba swung a questioning gaze back to an equally confused Nathaniel, her eyebrows shooting up and making her whole facial expression match.

"What do you mean the wrong way?"

Nathaniel cleared his throat, adjusted his druidic style hood, and pointed a long boney finger at the building the now off-limits Professor Hottie had exited a few moments before.

Jezibaba fisted hands on her hips. "You can't be serious, Nathaniel. That's elementary level. Are you telling me the chosen ones are not even riding their brooms yet?"

Nathaniel nodded. "Believe me, mistress. I'm not confident in the matter either, but I consulted the Fates to check the Council's determinations."

"The Fates! Goddess, I hate those nosey old biddies." Jezibaba stalked back to the front with the rest of her warlock posse.

"Yes... well, the feeling is mutual between you, m'lady... they seem to hate you as well."

Since killing Nathaniel was out of the question, Jezibaba genuinely glared at the messenger instead. "The Fates have a burr up their butts because I refuse to die on their command. If they don't like me surviving their many predictions, they can take it up with Morgana. She's the one who made me Jezibaba. I didn't have any choice in that either. It was decided generations before I was born."

"Regardless of your tragic history, I must unfortunately report that the two chosen ones are merely ten years old. I sought the counsel of the Fates in order to confirm their ages. The Fates laughed when I asked for more information. They said we'd have no trouble finding them if we went looking. Both descend from proper lineages. There's no other reason to question this, unless you can think of some reason the other warlocks and I haven't."

Jezibaba sighed in frustration. "No. I guess I can't think of any reason the chosen ones can't be ten if they're freaking ten. Very well, Nathaniel. What are their names?"

"Hildy and Carol."

"Rather ordinary names for the chosen ones," Jezibaba said, making a face.

"Indeed, m'lady. I thought the same. Your birth given name is much nicer," Nathaniel stated.

"Oh, you're sucking up now? Good show, Nathaniel. That's why you're still my favorite."

With a long suffering sigh, Jezibaba started towards the "right" building, her fashionable red dress billowing in the breeze. The first thing she'd done when she'd inherited the position was change the damn dress code. She was the Jezibaba—the most powerful witch ever born—not some drab mythological hag from a children's story.

She refused to wear her ceremonial black robe for anything but Council proceedings. She wanted to garner attention not pity from those who saw her. The red dress was far more striking and commanded a lot more attention when she needed to get people focused on doing her will. Nathaniel carried both her emergency witch hat and her ceremonial robe within his own grim looking clothes. That was as traditional as she was freaking willing to be.

Before she could put out a hand, the youngest of the warlock posse scrambled around her to open the door. She had barely nodded at his deference when Professor Hottie zoomed through the opening ahead of her, cutting her entry off on his mad dash inside. Her indignant huff over his rudeness caught his attention. Instead of apologizing though, he turned to her and smiled.

"Sorry, beautiful. You have very nice legs, but I'm extremely late for class," he explained, his admiring gaze dropping to them as he spoke.

Jezibaba stepped through the door enough to allow Nathaniel to enter behind her.

"How would you like to teach class as a giant dragon toad today?" she asked faux politely.

Even knowing the fire-breather was on her forbidden list, Professor Hottie's husky chuckle over her threat still made her woo-hoo vibrate. She raised a hand to make good on her threat—and to show her woo-hoo who was boss—but lowered it when two children rushed out of a nearby classroom and grabbed one long, incredible fit man's leg each.

The Council of Witches would fine her and reduce her salary if she reduced innocent kids to tadpoles for no good reason. Goddess knew, she couldn't afford any garnishments. Retirement was on the horizon for her and she was hording every cent she made. Her daily ritual of checking her investments allowed her to sleep more peacefully at night.

"Professor Smoke, did you see them run out here?" Hildy demanded.

"See who, Hildy?" he asked gently, running a hand over her hair.

"The kittens. They were three of the tiniest, cutest kittens ever. They danced and let me pet them before they disappeared."

"Because *I* scared them away," Carol bragged, laughing as she looked up in her favorite teacher's face. "But I swear I didn't hurt them, Professor Smoke. I just let them blink out the way they wanted. I even waved goodbye and they said they'd see me again."

"*Us* again—they said they would see *us* again," Hildy corrected.

"No. *Me*," Carol insisted. "They said *me*. You just can't believe animals might like me better than you for once. Admit it, Hildy."

"How would you like to look like the big lying toad you are, Carol?" Hildy demanded. She turned loose and raised her hands.

Jezibaba fought back a grin when Professor Hottie's larger ones closed around the little witch's hands while he shook his head in warning.

"Hildy, do you want to lose your recess privileges and your best friend?"

Jezibaba covered her mouth as Carol turned loose of his leg, crossed her arms, and smirked when Hildy narrowed her eyes.

"They said *me*, Hildy. Live with it."

To keep from openly laughing—and from being pissed at the Fates for being right about these two miscreants—Jezibaba decided she needed to intervene. She let loose a shrill whistle which split the air, effectively ending the debate. All eyes turned to her with proper respect at last as she slowly removed her fingers from her teeth.

Professor Hottie had the audacity to wink at her attention-getting ploy. She gave him a warning finger wag for his grin which she took as flirting because his gaze kept returning to her legs. The girls were both still frozen in place, staring at her in outright fear now, which suited her just fine. But she ignored them to glance over her shoulder and smirk at the cloaked warlock staring at them in equal shock.

"The future's so damn bright, I need to wear shades... or maybe have ten tankards of troll ale so I can deal with this," Jezibaba declared merrily, sweeping her hand at the frightened girls as she looked back at them. She snorted at their continued stares. "I swear if you two were older, I'd throw you both in the magic pokey and hire smelly tutors for you. I bet you'd learn to appreciate each other then."

Both girls drew in sharp breaths over the cursing... and the threat.

Jezibaba smiled brilliantly at their quaking knees, her power swelling to fill the area with a fine golden mist. Stressful situations caused the occasional power leak, but it was not enough to worry her. No one seemed to mind walking around in gold glitter when it happened and she'd always liked sparkly things anyway.

"M'lady—it's impossible not to notice that the one named Hildy apparently shares your fondness for turning people into amphibians," Nathaniel pointed out, leaning in close enough to her to whisper. "However, Carol's superior attitude is oddly reminiscent of your demeanor when we first met. They are both tiny mirrors of your greatness."

"They're children, Nathaniel. Just children," Jezibaba declared, but she could also feel their power tugging on hers as they stared. "Neither can be called yet and I won't allow it to happen anyway. The Council is probably just worried because I've served longer than any Jezibaba before me. I realize three hundred and sixty-six seems old to some of them, but I don't look a day over a human fifty. And these children are not—I repeat *not*—to be called until they are of a proper age to choose the path for themselves."

Professor Hottie held her gaze as he leaned down to talk to his charges. "Girls, head to class now. Tell Ms Turner to start reading the spells, but no casting until I get there."

When they didn't move, Jezibaba met his inquisitive gaze and shrugged to show him she was not holding them with any kind of restraining spell.

Grinning at her reaction, he lifted the girls by the backs of their shirts and turned them away from her. Once released from his hold, they shot off into the room like bolts of lightning flying off his fingertips.

Jezibaba watched Professor Hottie turn and walk slowly toward her. His guard was up now, wondering who and what she really was. But she could tell his worry was mostly for the children and rightly so. They would need a champion or two... or seventy... before they were old enough and strong enough to take over her work.

When Professor Hottie stopped, her heart fluttered in response to the dragon's protective stance. Goddess, it would have been nice to have had someone like him guarding her while she was growing up. It might even be nice to have someone like that having her back now.

One of the advantages of being older was that she knew better than to take her attraction to the dragon shifter seriously. She wouldn't call it being wiser exactly. More like street smart and maybe she was simply not stupid enough to fall too hard for a nice ass anymore. Most nice asses had a matching one sitting on their shoulders. She'd learned that the hard way, as she had every other hard lesson.

Bottom line for her flutters? Her insides needed to stop that shit. No way was she letting a dragon into her pants just because he cared for her future replacements.

No witch with any sense would stoop so low. Even if dragons hadn't been on her don't-fuck list, they had a tendency to mark females they slept with so no other dragon would go there. She was not getting a dragon fire created v-jay-jay tattoo guaranteed to wilt the dick of any future lover she took.

Her attention left her thoughts and returned to him when she realized he was scanning her face and not her legs anymore.

"You're the Jezibaba. I'm sorry I didn't recognize you. I'm Professor Damien Smoke."

A sharp retort about his oversight was on her tongue. It hovered there letting her taste the pleasure it would give her to say it and see his eyes flash in anger. But the nastiness just wouldn't come out. Damn her weakness for sexy men.

"Quite understandable given the circumstances, Professor. Your primary focus wasn't on me," she answered calmly.

"No, but we both know my attention could be on you if you wanted it to be," Damien replied smoothly, grinning when her eyebrows shot up again. "Sorry. I can't seem to behave any better than the girls today. It's just that you're every bit as mesmerizing in person as I imagined you being. Of course you were alluring even before when I thought you were just... never mind that. Perhaps I better shut up now."

Pretending not to care was a trick to pull off, but she'd had a lot of practice doing so in her life. "No worries, Professor. Power. Glamour. It momentarily draws attention. You'll forget me a few minutes after the warlocks and I leave. In my experience, most unnatural enchantments never last longer than that, though I promise you, I do nothing to draw it on purpose. It is innate."

Professor Hottie looked thoughtful for a moment, opened his mouth to speak, but then appeared to change his mind. When her stomach dropped in disappointment, Jezibaba narrowed her eyes.

"I came here on business. Point me to your headmaster," she ordered, wanting to move things along. Action would no doubt lessen the distraction Professor Hottie presented.

Chuckling, Professor Hottie reached out and lifted one of her hands before she could stop him. Magic buzzed along her palm and down to her fingertips. He kissed the back of her hand reverently as was due someone in her position, and then shocked her by placing her palm flat on his well-endowed chest. The contact was just as nice as she'd expected it might be.

"The unfortunate headmaster of Witchery U stands before you—guilty as charged. I'm the one you seek, but you can call me Damien."

Jezibaba slid her hand away, remembering the heat of his muscles even after the contact was broken. Damn dragon. Damn sexy, panty-melting dragon. He'd made her touch him on purpose. Why was he being so charming? He was hiding something—trying to distract her further. That had to be the case. Well, it wouldn't work. She'd dealt with sneaky dragons before.

In fact, there wasn't much she hadn't dealt with in her tenure as the current witch protectoress. Professor Hottie might be teaching the future versions of her—and lucky them for it—but she had been taught at the school of hard knock spells, troll curses, and angry gods with vendettas.

"I've come about two of your students, Professor. Apparently, they've been chosen as my potential replacements," she stated stiffly. "We're not taking them today of course."

She turned around to the grumbling warlocks behind her who had quietly filed inside the building behind Nathaniel. "No, we are absolutely not taking them. They're children. Did you hear me? *Children*."

264

She turned back to the sexy dragon and smiled as neutrally as possible. "We just wanted to make you aware of their futures, Professor Smoke. Perhaps recommend you take a few extra precautions with their safety."

"You're talking about Hildy and Carol," Damien stated.

"Yes," Jezibaba confirmed. "I am speaking of Hildy and Carol."

He nodded as he thought about it. "I knew those two were powerful. We always look out for those with that level of magic at their beckoning—mostly because they be a danger to everyone—but they're only ten. Real power doesn't manifest at such a young age. I find it hard to believe they've been singled out already."

Jezibaba nodded and frowned. "Indeed. You echo my concerns, Professor Smoke. This early tapping of my prospective replacements is a strange situation. I'm sure in a couple of decades their power will make it obvious they should be considered contenders. Though it's not unheard of to be singled out early. In fact, I was chosen before I was born. When I got my menses, I fully expected the warlocks to come get me, but they never... *what now?*"

Jezibaba stopped her story and shook her head at the rumbling and groaning going on behind her. Her gaze met the sexy dragon's. "I could write a damn book about the fragile sensibilities of warlocks. They don't like to think about the fact I'm female in all regards."

Professor Hottie's responding grin made her day. It was nice to finally have someone recognize the political agony she bore for the sake of doing her job.

"So you were chosen shortly after your passage into womanhood?" he prompted.

She snorted at his words. "More like I was expecting someone to come collect me. Passage into womanhood? You're obviously much better with nice words than I am. Not surprising, given your profession, I suppose."

"On the contrary, you might be more surprised by my past than you ever imagined. I wasn't always a teacher. Perhaps we can have dinner sometime and share our stories. I would like that very much. But for now, let me tell Ms Turner to finish the lesson. We can go to my office and talk about what measures need to be taken for the children's safety. Have their parents been told about the prophecy?"

"No," Jezibaba said firmly. "And we have no intentions of telling them until it is unavoidable. There is enough drama happening. The Council of Witches and the Fates have chosen my successors, but I will choose their protectors. There is discord in both of the children's families and no one is going to take their normal life from them a moment sooner than necessary if I can prevent it from happening. That is my firm decision about the matter."

Her eyes blazed with determination and only softened when Professor Hottie bowed to her.

"I agree with you and it will be my pleasure to see your will about this manifest," he promised. "Now excuse me for a moment and I will join you in my office."

Charmed despite her misgivings, she fought off her urge to sigh in frustration. "Why did you have to be a damn dragon?" she whispered under her breath.

For a second time that day, she couldn't stop herself from staring at Professor Damien Smoke's perfect ass as he disappeared into the classroom.

Chapter 2

Always on guard, Nathaniel stared out of the room's single window, while she stared at Professor Hottie. She was finding it very challenging to have a conversation about something other than the two of them running off alone.

No matter how much her inner witch chanted "no dragon, no dragon". All she really wanted was to curl up in his lap and wriggle until his control snapped and he threw her across his shiny, neat desk, and... *damn it.*

Jezibaba sat up straighter in the chair, but it was hard shaking off her fantasy. It had been a long time since simple lust had taken her mind off her business so completely. Now she'd missed what Professor Hottie had said while she was imagining him naked on top of her.

Her frustrated groan garnered both Nathaniel's and Professor Hottie's full attention. Hellcat's fury. Her sexual deprivation didn't matter. Protecting her successors did.

"Are children their age allowed their familiars yet?"

Professor Hottie frowned at her question. Even that was hot. Dragon hot... but still... hot. She ran both hands through her hair and reminded herself of her purpose. Professor Hottie glanced behind him to study Nathaniel standing like a sentinel. The warlock's attention seemed fixed on the manicured campus lawn, but she knew he was listening to every word that was said.

"Speak your mind freely, Professor Smoke. I trust Nathaniel with my life and do so every day. All day. He came with the job and yes... I had no say in the matter. However, he's the only one of the warlock posse I bring into serious discussions like this. Now speak. I'm getting edgy and impatient."

"Yes. I can tell. You get all glittery when you get tense."

Jezibaba snorted when Professor Hottie's gaze fell to her ample cleavage before rising back to her eyes. It sent her off into another fantasy. She pulled her mind back with a hiss. "I'm still waiting, Professor..."

"At the risk of offending you, I don't think you heard what I said just now. The girls have been attacked twice already. One attack was a swarm of insects which they took care of themselves without even understanding the danger."

"And the second attack?"

"It happened just a few hours ago and I had to incinerate a vampire assassin disguised as a giant bat. The girls thought I had killed a real bat. When you arrived, I was taking his ashes to the high school science lab to see if they could find out who sent him."

"But we just found out about the girls two days ago..." Jezibaba stopped her defense. It was useless. There was only one real explanation for the attacks. "Someone on the Council must be trying to kill them. Whoever it is wants to end the cycle. Without a witch protectoress, the Council of Witches's combined power would rule the magical world. I can't let that happen, Professor Smoke. No Council will protect the magical community as me and my predecessors have done—not to mention what could happen to all the humans in our lives."

She leaned back in her chair. Nathaniel's gaze turned to her. He was thoughtful for a moment and then nodded

268

in agreement with her rant. She swore internally. Damn. There went her easing into retirement plans while she pretended to babysit.

She nodded back that she accepted his judgment in the matter. The truth did not make her happy—not at all. Now she had no choice but to get involved.

Professor Smoke put an elbow on his desk and leaned forward. "After the insects, I called up my horde and got some of my old guards to come watch over the girls. Dragon warriors are pretending to be janitors, teachers, assistants, and the younger ones are college placed student aides. What they don't have to pretend is how deadly they are, especially since they'd be immune to shifters and vamps. Whoever is after the girls is in for a big surprise the next time they try something."

Jezibaba stood because she needed to pace. It helped her think. Nathaniel's eyebrows rose when she put her hands behind her back. He knew it meant she didn't trust her hands not to conjure up something to match her darkening mood. The idea of the children being targets went way beyond them being her replacements. They must be truly powerful... which meant they had to be protected until they came into full use of their magic.

She stopped and glared across the room. "Is this why you wanted to take the children and lock them away? You knew they were in trouble, Nathaniel?"

Nathaniel shook his head. "No. Only suspected, M'lady. Being in danger was merely conjecture on my part without any evidence to back it up."

"*Conjecture?* You're the most proficient seer who's ever lived," Jezibaba declared sharply. "And we've already had this ageist discussion. You and I might be waning in some ways, but trust your magic, old friend. Use every ounce up until it's really gone. Don't let self-doubt rob you of a single second."

She frowned and shook her head when Nathaniel turned back to the window without answering. She hadn't meant to lecture him in front of an audience. It had just slipped out.

Worry made her tongue sharp and her brain irrational. That hadn't changed for her in over three hundred years. She'd just learned to work around it. But even her Goddess had given up trying to tame her bossiness.

She would have to do something to apologize to Nathaniel later. Making personal amends when she was wrong was more of a challenge than killing a thousand evil magicals.

Mind returning to the task at hand, she felt Professor Hottie's gaze on her again and turned to meet it. "With death threats happening, I can't avoid being involved in all plans for their safety. I want the girls to have their familiars. It is my intention to talk you into this, Professor Smoke. How hard is it going to be?"

His lips twisted into a sexy grimace as he considered it. She'd love nothing more than to bite that lip he was punishing with his very sharp-looking teeth. She'd crawl into his lap, plant her ass over his rising… shitballs. What was wrong with her freaking mind today? Lust never did this to her—never.

"The other children are not going to like the situation," Damien warned.

Jezibaba shrugged. "Tell them Hildy and Carol earned their familiars because of their progress. We'll let one or two other exemplary students have them as well. That should lay rumors to rest and give them all a goal worth striving for. This is only a year or two earlier than it is usually done. I will take care of the bestowance."

Professor Hottie's beaming smile had her hand coming to her stomach to calm the flutters it evoked in her. She had a feeling she could chant "no dragon" all day long and it would never lessen the power that flash of white teeth would have over her.

"Jezibaba—I think you'd make a damn good teacher," he said sincerely.

At the praise, she favored him with a beaming smile herself. He leaned forward on his desk, his own smile fading. She knew it was to hide what was happening in his lap and she enjoyed the feeling of getting a little even with him. The wickedness conveyed in her twinkling gaze affected every male she encountered to some degree, but she was thrilled to know Professor Hottie—the off-limits dragon—wasn't immune to her.

"I'm so glad you think that, Professor Smoke. Because there's a second part to my plan."

***

Damien couldn't keep the smile from his face as he introduced her. All eyes were glued to the mesmerizing witch at his side and he hadn't had to chastise a single student to get their complete attention focused up front.

"Class, this is the Jezibaba. I'm sure you've heard your parents talking about her. She's started a new education project here at Witchery U and will be one of your teachers for the rest of this academic year. One of her many specialties is magical protection, so you'll be learning all sorts of ways to protect yourselves in her classes."

A student raised their hand. Damien sighed and nodded. "Yes, Rory?"

Rory squirmed in his chair, but finally mustered up his courage. "My dad said the Jezibaba turns people into toads when she gets mad at them. Is she allowed to turn us into toads if we're bad, Professor Smoke?"

"What's so scary about that, Rory? Hildy does that too when she gets mad at us," Carol blurted out. "It just doesn't last long because she's a magical wimp."

"I am not a wimp," Hildy declared. "I just don't want to hurt people. All I try to do is stop them from making me angrier."

Jezibaba narrowed her eyes at Carol who shrunk down in her seat under her stare. She turned a smile to the original questioner.

"That's a very good question, Rory. I suggest you don't make me angry enough to test the theory and get a personal answer. My spells last quite a bit longer than Hildy's—like hundreds of years longer."

Rory's eyes widened as he nodded. "Yes, ma'am. Jezibaba, ma'am."

Damien fought back a smile when Jezibaba's twinkling, amused gaze met his. She shrugged her elegant shoulders.

"I hope my honesty with your students doesn't offend you, Professor. I used to incarcerate magic abusers. But the jails got full and there was all that overhead to feed the prisoners. There's so much more room in nature. I find a few days catching flies and croaking as a toad work just as well as a few years spent behind bars," she explained.

He covered his mouth so the students wouldn't catch him smiling. He wiped it away before removing his hand, but it was difficult. "Your restraint in my classroom will be appreciated, Jezibaba. We don't have that many flies around campus," Damien said gravely.

Jezibaba turned and faced all the frightened stares. "Fear, such as you are feeling about me, is a healthy response. My power is great and yours is not. All strangers with magic require approaching with caution. I'm going to show you some tricks about how to protect yourselves, but today's not a day for those lessons. Today, four of you whose power has manifested greatly already will receive a first line personal protector. We are assigning familiars a bit earlier than usual."

Her gaze zeroed back to her questioner. She motioned with a hand. "Come forward, Rory. You're on my list."

Rory's eyes widened in alarm and his classmates drew in a breath as they turned to stare at him. Jezibaba enjoyed knowing he wanted to pee his pants, but that wasn't going to serve her purposes. She didn't want to spare the time the boy would need to change clothes.

"I promise not to turn you into a toad today. Witches Honor," Jezibaba said sharply. "Now come here. When a challenge is presented, a confident witch or warlock should never hesitate. In your hesitation, your adversary will have ample time to finish a spell. Disrupt their thinking in any manner possible as you challenge. Can you walk a little faster, boy? I'm aging as you dawdle."

Damien watched as Rory picked up his pace, but only barely. Finally, the kid stopped about two feet in front of her.

Jezibaba paced around him, turning her head. "Lift your chin," she ordered, and Rory complied. "Ah, you have a nice long neck. Are you afraid of snakes, Rory?"

"No ma'am—I mean—no Jezibaba ma'am."

"Good," she declared and pulled a two foot gold and black snake out of one of her sleeves.

When it hissed at her, she hissed back and spoke to it in a tongue Damien had never heard leave a woman's mouth. The witch was obviously well versed in reptilian languages. He found himself wondering if she spoke dragon.

Smiling she walked to Rory. "Hold out your arm, boy."

When he did, she placed the snake's head on his hand. The snake wound slowly around his arm, crawling until it had wrapped itself lightly around the boy's neck. The snake hissed, its tongue flicking against Rory's cheek making him giggle. He looked beyond delighted, which delighted her in return.

"After you trust him, get him to bite you. Then you two can share thoughts with each other. His name is Saigon. This is his normal form, but he has others. It costs him greatly to use his magic to shift to them, so he won't change forms until there is dire need. You must care for Saigon as you would yourself, Rory. He will protect you with his very life. Be worthy of the sacrifice or no other familiars will have anything to do with you in the future."

"Yes, ma'am—I mean, I will—Jezibaba ma'am. I like him. He's really cool."

"I know. Now take him back with you to your seat. He must stay with you at all times. You can wear him like a scarf, but sometimes he likes to sleep inside your clothes where it's warm. He'll most likely leave you at night to hunt, but he'll always return by morning."

Damien grinned when Rory looked up at Jezibaba in adoration, even as she turned him and gave him a shove to get him walking. He felt his giant dragon's heart squeeze alarmingly within his chest. The woman was a legendary badass. It made her huge efforts to shield these innocents from her true nature all the more impressive.

"Hildy. Come forward," she called, tucking her hands behind her back.

Braver now because of Rory, Hildy slid from her seat and walked to where she stood. Damien fought back a chuckle when the girl swallowed hard as Jezibaba looked down in her eyes.

"It is very difficult to choose a familiar for someone with your affinity for all Morgana's creatures, but we'll do the best we can. I believe I heard you asking Professor Smoke about some special kittens."

Hildy nodded. "Yes. They come, but they don't stay long. I see them all the time."

"I bet they are asking permission to be your familiars—all three. It is very rare to get a group like that. Only special witches get those sorts of followings," Jezibaba said sharply. "Have you asked them to stay with you?"

Damien snapped to attention when Jezibaba's gaze darkened. It went across the room to Carol shifting in her seat and frowning. He went on alert when she chastised the girl.

"The kittens are Hildy's. And they will see you again because you are Hildy's best friend. So there was no lying in their statements. Get that unworthy thought out of your head before it turns to a darkness you can't control. Am I being clear, Carol?"

Carol hung her head and nodded.

Jezibaba's gaze lightened as it came back to Hildy. "Now I wish your future could be different, but it cannot. Natural healers bear a great burden, but they also have a capacity to appreciate joy in a way most creatures don't. So you might as well have amusing familiars to keep your heart light and a smile on your face. Call them to you, child. Call them like you usually do."

Damien heard Carol snort, but she sunk into the seat when Jezibaba glared at her for the noise she made. He turned back as Hildy made a face.

"Here, kitty, kitty, kitty."

Jezibaba snorted. "Do they actually come for that weak calling? No. Try again, Hildy. Forget all of us. Call them as if we were not present in the room. Do it, girl."

Hildy frowned and stooped to the floor. She patted it three times, putting her concentration into her palm hitting the cool tile.

"Here. Kitty. Kitty. Kitty."

Three kittens appeared out of thin air, materializing within reach of her hands. She laughed as she petted them.

"Jezibaba said you can stay with me and be my familiars. I would like that. Please stay."

Damien's eyebrows rose when the kittens froze in place and turned their heads to stare at Jezibaba. He smelled large amounts of fear radiating off all three of them. She was glaring at the kittens, one eyebrow raised in question.

"Did you think I didn't know you keep sneaking out of your confinement? Your vile personal habits best not ever be a part of this child's life—and I mean ever—or you will all three spend the other seven of your lives living as toads instead of cats. Now promise to serve Hildy during this life you now lead. In exchange, I will lift the remainder of your punishment and restore your powers."

Damien stood transfixed as the kittens trotted over to the Jezibaba, wound themselves around her ankles one at a time, and then trotted back to Hildy and did the same to her.

"Good. It is done then," Jezibaba declared. "Hildy, you don't have to pat the ground anymore. They'll come for any call you make. Kittens are a little more distracting than a snake or a grown cat though during school hours. I would suggest you let them blink out and come to you only when you want them around."

Hildy's head bobbed fiercely. "Yes, Jezibaba. Thank you. They're wonderful. I will take the best of care of them."

"I know you will. You are welcome, child. Now say goodbye to them and return to your seat."

Hildy finger waved and said bye. She nearly skipped to her seat when the kittens disappeared. Her smile was radiant. It was the happiest Damien had ever seen her be.

Jezibaba called up a girl named Faith and gave her an older cat with one green eye and one blue. The cat trotted back to the seat with the girl and crawled under the desk to curl into a ball.

Then Jezibaba fisted her hands on her hips. "Carol— get up here. Don't dawdle. I need to be somewhere else shortly."

Looking anything but happy to be summoned so sternly, Carol trudged up to stand in front of Jezibaba lifting her chin and glaring back. Damien covered his mouth, this time to hide a grimace at the girl's show of disrespect. He was amazed when Jezibaba favored the girl with a wicked, beaming smile. To him, it was far more frightening, and Carol seemed to know it, but the kid was holding her own.

"Professor Smoke, please open the window. I need to call Carol's familiar to her," Jezibaba ordered.

She turned and smiled down at the girl as she gave a long suffering sigh.

"You like using your power against people. It makes you feel strong and I think you revel too much in that feeling. By the laws of the Goddess, I could lock you away for a hundred years even at your young age, but you'd just grow into a bitter martyr for evil. I can't allow that to happen to you because you're far too powerful a witch to not be serving the magical community."

Jezibaba wrestled her gaze away and walked in a circle around the child, chanting to constrain the girl from reacting when her familiar arrived. There was absolute silence in the room, but she could feel Hildy's worried gaze on them both. Jezibaba couldn't afford to comfort the other of her prospects, so she didn't bother to even glance her way. What was most important was that this mirror of her know she always meant exactly what she said.

"Carol, I'm assigning you a special guardian who will teach you right and wrong. He will judge your abuses, and if he finds you guilty, your familiar will mirror your spell back to you. Empathy is a very effective teaching tool. I can guarantee you will learn your lessons... just like I did under his tutelage. After you have sufficiently progressed in a few years, then you will be free to choose your own familiar. In the meantime, you will use *mine*."

Carol looked to the window in fear.

Jezibaba leaned down. "What kind of beast do you think my familiar is, child?" she whispered in her most stern voice, raising goosebumps on the girl's arms. "He is a powerful creature of many forms. Let's see what he chooses to show you first, shall we?"

Jezibaba stood tall and held out her arms. She put all the power she had into her voice, mostly for dramatic effect in this instance, but she knew her familiar would understand her reasons.

"Great Emeritus, come to me. As I will, so mote it be."

Damien winced as an ear shattering "Caw" filled the room as a giant black raven flew in the window and landed on Jezibaba's arm.

"I have a new pupil I would like you to consider," she said to the raven.

Damien saw the raven look down at Carol who stared up at him in great fear. The raven turned to Jezibaba and nodded his head, cawing again.

Then the bird lifted from her arm and transformed into a large black dog with hellhound teeth and red eyes. He landed lightly on the floor and paced around the girl, looking like he was going to eat her. Instead, the creature leaned in and licked the side of Carol's face with a large tongue.

"Oh, good. Emeritus has agreed to take you on," Jezibaba declared, clapping her hands once in great pleasure. "Now pet him. Go on. He's waiting for a sign of your agreement."

Carol looked at Jezibaba and back to the dog thing. "Do I have to pet him?"

"You were so brave earlier, Carol. Are you now afraid?" Jezibaba challenged.

"No," Carol protested, looking back at the waiting animal. She reached out a trembling hand and ran it down the dog's neck, shivering herself when it shivered under her touch. Whimpering, it turned to look at the Jezibaba.

"Yes, I know. I told you she was strong," Jezibaba said, speaking to the hellhound.

Damien watched the hellhound turn to look at Jezibaba, transforming once more, this time into a large white owl who jumped onto the edge of his lecturing podium.

Jezibaba bowed her head to the animal and went down to one knee. "Thank you, Great Emeritus. I do

278

realize what I am asking, old friend. If Morgana favors me in my plans, this is the last pupil I will ask you to train."

Damien swallowed tightly at the sight they made. The Jezibaba never bowed to anyone—she didn't have to. The owl bobbed his head to her, then lifted into the air, becoming the giant black raven again before he flew back out of the window.

Jezibaba rose to her feet. She looked at Damien's shocked expression before moving to the girl's equally shocked one.

"A witch, no matter how powerful, is no match for a creature like Emeritus. He is a guardian of old and you should feel lucky he finds you worthy enough to serve, Child. You have been blessed this day in ways you will not understand until a hundred years from now. I hope you are good to him. Otherwise, Emeritus could bring about your death. He is a stronger believer in balance than I am."

Carol turned without prompting and returned to her seat. Damien saw her staring straight ahead. Jezibaba showed no remorse for terrifying the girl beyond anything he'd witnessed done to a student.

"Now I must go, but I will return soon. Professor—if you will show the warlocks to my room, they will see to it that my things are brought along. Until tomorrow…"

And just like that, she and Nathaniel were gone from the room. Damien looked around the class at the stunned faces. Their expressions probably mirrored his.

"Okay. Let's take a break. Pick a flying spell book from the bookshelves and we'll try it on one of the brooms later."

As the children scrambled, he walked to the window and closed it, sighing with relief that the school day was almost over, but also that Jezibaba said she was returning. She was the first female in the seventy-five years he'd been without a mate to stir in him an urge to seek a physical connection. Since he couldn't leave the school, it would be a lot easier to explore that strange urge she prompted if the powerful woman remained nearby.

And he certainly wasn't sure how he was going to explain to his pure dragon family he was falling for a witch, but he'd figure that one out once he knew if their connection held what their attraction promised.

Jezibaba or not, the witch was the first female he'd wanted in too long of a damn time. The magic of a dragon's desire for his female was far stronger than any spell a witch could ever weave.

He'd been alone far too long. He would not risk turning away such a gift, even if the female had come into his life through the wicked Goddess, Morgana The Red.

Visit **www.robynpeterman.com/kindle-world** for information about how to purchase this title and others.

Want A Whole Witch Series?

Book Description

Released from the magic pokey and paroled with limited power is enough to make any witch grumpy. However, if you throw in a recently resurrected cat, a lime-green Kia and a sexy egotistical werewolf, it's enough to make a gal fly off the edge.

Not to mention a mission…with no freaking directions.

So here I sit in Asscrack, West Virginia trying to figure out how to complete my mysterious mission before All Hallows Eve when I'll get turned into a mortal. The animals in the area are convinced I'm the Shifter Whisperer (whatever the hell that is) and the hotter-than-asphalt-in-August werewolf thinks I'm his mate. Now apparently I'm slated to save a bunch of hairy freaks of nature?

If they think I'm the right witch for the job, they've swallowed some bad brew.

Book Lists (In Correct Reading Order)

HOT DAMNED SERIES
Fashionably Dead
Fashionably Dead Down Under
Hell on Heels
Fashionably Dead in Diapers
Fashionably Dead Christmas
Fashionably Hotter Than Hell

SHIFT HAPPENS SERIES
Ready to Were
Some Were in Time

MAGIC AND MAYHEM SERIES
Switching Hour
Witch Glitch
A Witch In Time

HANDCUFFS AND HAPPILY EVER AFTERS SERIES
How Hard Can it Be?
Size Matters
Cop a Feel

About Robyn Peterman

Robyn Peterman writes because the people inside her head won't leave her alone until she gives them life on paper.

Her addictions include laughing really hard with friends, shoes (the expensive kind), Target, Coke Zero Cherry with extra ice in a Styrofoam cup, bejeweled reading glasses, her kids, her super hot hubby and collecting stray animals.

A former professional actress with Broadway, film and TV credits, she now lives in the South with her family and too many animals to count.

Writing gives her peace and makes her whole, plus having a job where you can work in your underpants works really well for her. You can leave Robyn a message via the Contact Page and she'll get back to you as soon as her bizarre life permits! She loves to hear from her fans!

Visit **www.robynpeterman.com** for more information.

Made in the USA
San Bernardino, CA
12 July 2018